CAROLYN
ARNOLD

MURDER AT THE LAKE

DETECTIVE MADISON KNIGHT BOOK 13

A Devastating Crime Thriller and Police Procedural

Published by Hibbert & Stiles Publishing Inc.
hspubinc.com

ISBN: 978-1-998095-01-8
eBook ISBN: 978-1-998095-00-1
Paperback 5 x 8 ISBN: 978-1-998095-02-5
Hardcover ISBN: 978-1-998095-03-2
Large Print Edition: 978-1-998095-04-9
Audiobook ISBN: 978-1-998095-05-6

ALSO BY CAROLYN ARNOLD

Detective Madison Knight

Fatal Testimony (prequel)
Ties That Bind
Justified
Sacrifice
Found Innocent
Just Cause
Deadly Impulse
In the Line of Duty
Power Struggle
Shades of Justice
What We Bury
Girl on the Run
Her Dark Grave
Murder at the Lake
Her Buried Past

Brandon Fisher

Eleven
Silent Graves
The Defenseless
Blue Baby
Violated
Remnants
On the Count of Three
Past Deeds
One More Kill

Detective Amanda Steele

The Little Grave
Stolen Daughters
The Silent Witness
Black Orchid Girls
Her Frozen Cry
Last Seen Alive
Her Final Breath
Taken Girls
Her Last Words
Missing Before Daylight
The Wildfire Girl
Her Deadly Rose
Hidden Angels
Three Girls Gone
Dead Woman Walking

Sandra Vos

Save Her Life
Every Last One
Nowhere to Hide

Sara and Sean Cozy Mystery

Bowled Over Americano
Wedding Bells Brew Murder

Matthew Connor Adventure

City of Gold
The Secret of the Lost Pharaoh
The Legend of Gasparilla and His Treasure

Standalone

Assassination of a Dignitary
Midlife Psychic

MURDER AT THE LAKE

In memory of Rebecca Ross Hendrix,
who dedicated her life to serving others
as a member of the law enforcement
community.

PROLOGUE

24 years ago

Life didn't get any better than this. Emily was on top of the world and didn't want this moment to end. The summer night was warm on her skin, but a gentle breeze coming off the lake cooled her down. Stars sparkled like diamonds in a cloudless sky of black velvet, and the full moon appeared oversized. Everything felt magical and inspiring. What she could do if she had her paints and a canvas…

But tonight was about letting loose and forgetting that in less than a week she'd be off to college. Then her parents would expect her to grow up. Boring, if her parents' lives were anything to go by. They were zombies, slogging themselves off to their nine-to-five jobs every morning while living for the weekends and holidays. Emily wanted more out of life.

She dropped, giggling, onto a fallen tree trunk and curled her toes in the warm sand. There were a lot of grads here tonight, and many faces she'd never seen before. The tunes pumping out of Jimmy's boombox vibrated through her. Every song was perfect. The weed was premium, but the booze was cheap.

Brooke, one of her best friends, fell beside her, laughing so hard she was crying. She bumped Emily's shoulder with hers and lifted the doobie she had in her hand toward Emily. She gladly relieved her of it and took a hit even though her head was already spinning.

She breathed it in, letting it overtake her. Surrendering. She didn't need to think tonight.

"Woo-hoo!" Melissa, her other bestie, started dancing in front of them. Her arms were flailing over her head, and she shook her hips. "I love this song! Come on, you guys. Dance!" She wriggled her hands to summon Emily and Brooke off their butts.

Emily popped up first, smiling like a moron. She would have been wiser to get to her feet more slowly. Her vision blurred, and her head spun, but she didn't care. She rolled into it. If this was her last night of being young and free, she was going to soak up every second.

She laughed, the sound striking her ears and causing her to double over. If only she could stay right here in this bubble forever. But her damn bladder was betraying her.

Emily slipped away from her friends, who were already busy grinding up against a couple of guys, and headed toward the tree line. If she hurried, she could get back before the next song started.

She hustled along the beach, prancing in her mind, but her movements would probably look a lot less poetic to a sober observer as she rolled her ankle over some uneven ground. That might hurt tomorrow, but it didn't right now.

She started toward a worn-down path that led into the woods. It was mostly flattened grass and sand, but there were also small stones that bit into the bottoms of her bare feet. Even high and drunk, those hurt. She slowed her steps and turned around to see if here was secluded enough to take care of her business.

Next thing she knew, she jammed her toe into something and stumbled forward. Her arms pinwheeled, and she managed to collect her balance without falling. Surprisingly she hadn't pissed herself either.

A tree root jutted out from the ground and mocked her. She retaliated by letting loose with a string of expletives. Her big toe was throbbing, and she lifted her leg, standing there like a flamingo as she inspected the damage in the moonlight. Her toe was bleeding, and the nail had broken to half its normal length. *Ouch!*

But she couldn't stand here forever. Her bladder was screaming at her to get a move on.

"Just get this over with," she told herself, while hobbling a bit farther into the woods. She ducked behind a tree and squatted.

She could still hear the song from Jimmy's boombox thumping, the bass being carried in the night's humid air as if she were seated right next to it. She sang along for a few verses but stopped at the sound of cracking branches and twigs. Someone was coming.

Hurrying to finish up her business, she'd only just gotten herself together and stood when he rounded the tree.

"Oh, it's just you," she told him, relieved that if it was anyone, it was him.

"Yeah. Just me." He leered at her and smirked as he moved toward her. He grabbed her breasts, and she stepped back and swatted at him.

"It's not happening."

But he wasn't listening. He was coming closer, and his eyes held a brooding intensity.

"I told you no." Her heart was racing. The fact he kept advancing in silence was really starting to freak her out. She mirrored his steps, retreating backward, but ended up stumbling and falling to the ground.

Her head struck something hard, and a thunderous *thwack* had her vision flashing white and an instant, all-consuming headache moving in. "Help," she tried to yell, but it didn't reach the volume of a whisper.

Above her, the moon was now a hazy orb, and a large looming figure was coming toward her. He was fiddling around with the fly of his pants.

No, no... this isn't happening! She tried to speak again, but she couldn't get the words to leave her mouth. Her eyelids became heavy and lowered as she fought to stay conscious.

He lowered himself over her and pinned her arms above her head, gripping both of her wrists with one of his hands.

She tried to squirm away, but her body wasn't responding. Any screams for him to stop ricocheted in her head. Nothing left her lips. Her limbs were paralyzed, leaving her powerless to fend him off. Warm tears splashed down her cheeks.

She drifted in and out of consciousness as he violated her, unable to rouse a call for help.

When he finished, he relinquished his hold on her wrists but put his hands on her neck and squeezed.

She couldn't even slap him away. As her brain screamed for oxygen, the spinning in her head began to slow. *This is how I die!*

Before closing her eyes for the last time, she watched a shooting star cut across the night sky.

CHAPTER 1

Twenty-four years later
Braybury, USA
10 AM, a Wednesday in December

The stiff was on the floor of his home office, a hole blown in the side of his head and his desk chair toppled next to him. A purported suicide, but there was something off about it. To start, the gun that was in his left hand. How had he managed to shoot himself and retain a hold on the weapon?

Detective Carson Snow of the Braybury Police Department was a veteran officer who was far closer to retirement than his rookie days. He'd seen a lot of death in his twenty-something year career, and what he saw before him sent mixed signals.

The victim was Dylan Graham, forty-one, divorced and living alone. He was discovered by his maid when she came in to clean that morning at nine AM. She was a mess and giving her statement to Carson's partner, Jeremy

Friedman. He was nearly a decade younger and still eager to please the higher-ups. Carson had stopped trying to please everyone years ago because it wasn't possible.

"Detective Snow, you and Friedman can see this now." A crime scene investigator, one that Carson respected, handed him a sealed evidence bag.

"Thanks." Inside was the suicide note that had been found on the desk. *Suicide…* Carson rolled that around in his head again. Right away, Carson's mental reconstruction hit a snag. The gun would have recoiled, especially since he'd need to have fired one-handed. He wouldn't have the stabilizing factor of using both hands, but even if he had, death would have had his hand releasing its grip. The gun would have fallen to the floor and been found beneath the victim.

The investigator stood there while Carson held it for himself and Jeremy to read.

> *I'm sorry for past sins but take these with me now. To the grave.*

"Man of many words," Jeremy mumbled.

"It's certainly short and sweet." Carson was still holding on to his suspicions about the manner of death regardless of the note.

"Uh-huh. And don't suicide victims typically apologize to those they're leaving behind?"

And there was that... Carson flipped the words around in his head. "It reads like he's apologizing to himself or an audience of one."

"Okay," Jeremy said, skeptical, "but he didn't address it to anyone."

"Detectives, I found something else you'll want to see." The investigator gestured for them to join her in front of an open desk drawer. She held some printed sheets but bobbed her head toward the drawer, where there were more. "I'll leave you to it." She then moved to another section of the room.

Carson took the papers from her and collected the rest with gloved hands and shuffled through them. They were news articles that had been printed from the internet, and all of them reported on the rape and murder of a teenage girl, Emily Kane, from twenty-four years ago. His gaze snatched some of the headlines, and he gathered enough to know her attacker, a man by the name of Richie Klein, had served twenty-four years and was released from prison yesterday. After Carson was finished, he handed them off to Jeremy.

Jeremy held up one piece focused on Klein. "Maybe this guy was wrongly imprisoned, and our DB was the real rapist and killer. Hence, the whole 'I'm sorry for my sins' bit?"

It was far too early to leap to their dead body being tied to a twenty-four-year-old case. And it was certainly too soon to leap to a reason why this guy killed himself. If that was even what happened.

Carson looked back at the drawer and withdrew a hardcover journal. He cracked it open. "There's only one entry in this thing, dated a few days ago. To paraphrase, Graham says he should have come forward and said something long before now. He implies that an innocent man went to prison and says it was Troy Matthews who raped and killed Emily Kane."

"And who is Troy Matthews?"

"Don't know yet, but Emily is the girl from the articles." Carson chewed on that. He already had his doubts about the way the scene presented itself, but the little treasure trove in this drawer clinched it for him.

Dylan Graham hadn't committed suicide. He was murdered. And, as it stood right now, Troy Matthews was their prime suspect.

CHAPTER 2

Present Day
3:45 PM, Stiles
Home of Madison Knight and Troy Matthews

Madison Knight didn't even recognize her own reflection in the mirror. She wore makeup, having been applied at the hands of a skilled cosmetician who did house calls. She was lucky any other day to slap on foundation. Her hair, that was usually tousled like the crown of a cockatoo, was professionally styled. Each strand lying in harmony with the others. A tiara sat on top of her head, the cubic zirconias winking in the light as if they were real diamonds and not imposters. More of these jewels nestled against her collarbone and dangled from her earlobes. It had been a surprise her piercings hadn't closed up, as neglected as they were.

The most shocking thing was her body draped in a white gown. She wasn't a fan of formal, and she was far from a blushing virgin. If she'd had her way, she'd have walked down the aisle in a cream pantsuit. The only reason she conceded to the traditional garb was due to the petitioning from her mother, sister, and her best friend, Cynthia Baxter. Or one could call it a guilt trip. They had all said, "Can't you be a girl for one day in your life?"

So here she was all decked out, smelling of floral perfume, wearing jewelry and a gown, a garter belt, and lacy underthings. She had drawn the line at a thong, though, and went bikini.

"Just when I thought this day would never come." Her mother came up behind her and put an arm around her.

Jeez, thanks!

Mothers were expected to get sentimental on their daughter's wedding day. Cheek to cheek, looking at their reflection in a mirror and tearing up. Not Donna Knight. She was checking *marriage* off the list she'd had in mind for Madison's life from the time she was born.

"Oh, Mom, be nice." Chelsea, Madison's younger sister by six years, stepped in to her defense. Chelsea was the "golden child," wife for over eleven years and mother to three girls. If their mother was counting on grandchildren from Madison, she'd be disappointed.

"I'm not being mean. I was just saying." Her words said one thing, her tone another. Donna presumed to know what was best for everyone. She was right while everyone else was wrong.

"Just let it go. Please," Chelsea beseeched, adding a smile to her request, which had their mother holding up her hands.

Madison faced those in the room. Present were her mother, sister, her six-year-old niece, who was the flower girl, and Cynthia. Her friend looked the least comfortable, as she was due to give birth to her first baby in a few weeks. She complained of being bloated and said her belly was the size of an inflated beachball. Those were her friend's words, and Madison wouldn't dare to agree. She'd faced off with Russian Mafia hit men, but she wasn't prepared to face the wrath of her pregnant friend.

They were all gathered in the primary bedroom of Madison's new home, which was acting as a bridal suite today. She and her fiancé, Troy Matthews, were already living together and had been for over a year. But this house was new to them. Though it wasn't to Madison. In fact, she had a history with the home, and it held special meaning for her. It had belonged to her mother's parents, and Madison always had a special bond with her grandma Rose. Their relationship wasn't formal, didn't stand on pomp and ceremony. Her grandmother welcomed Madison to call her by her first name, and their bond was tight. It was why Madison put in an offer without a second thought when the house hit the market a few months ago. From her first walk-through, the feeling of her grandmother's presence cemented the deal. Madison was meant to share her life with Troy in this house. She imagined Grandma Rose was smiling down at her from heaven today.

Cynthia sucked in a deep breath through her teeth and grinned. "Well, are you ready? You do look incredible."

Not that looking good was the barometer for determining readiness, but Madison graciously accepted the compliment and kissed her friend's cheek.

"Just one toast, and we'll head down." Chelsea poured champagne into three flutes and filled two with sparkling nonalcoholic cider. One of these was for Cynthia, the other for Madison's niece.

After everyone had their drinks in hand, they raised their glasses following Chelsea's lead.

She toasted, "To Madison and Troy finding a life of happiness and love."

Everyone echoed the sentiment and added, "Here, here." Glasses were clinked and generous sips taken.

Madison lowered her glass, and with the motion, it was as if the import of today was finally sinking in. This was actually happening. She was getting married. While she'd been engaged in the past, she never got this close to going through with it. Her previous fiancé had been a cheat, and it took Madison a solid decade to give love another chance. But that heartache had brought her to where she was now. With Troy. And the universe had blessed her.

Troy was so much more than Toby Sovereign had ever been. Troy understood her and held to the same values. He appreciated that honesty, loyalty, and integrity were the foundations of any lasting relationship and a code to live by. But he'd experienced Madison's pain for himself when his first wife and supposed best friend betrayed him by having an affair. Instead of letting it ruin his view on love, though, it gave him the understanding and patience Madison required from him. He offered a supportive shoulder, despite her inclination to handle everything on her own.

Chelsea gathered Madison's glass and set it down with hers. She tapped a finger to Madison's tiara. "All right, are you ready to roll?"

Madison's heart picked up speed. Her impulse was to run and hide. And she hated running. The thought of Troy waiting for her had her nodding. She tapped her clammy palms against her gown and took some calm, even breaths. "Okay, let's do this."

Her sister smiled at her, her eyes disclosing she had read Madison's fears. But she wasn't good at hiding her feelings, which was both a blessing and a curse.

The group made their way to the main level with Madison's mother leading the way. The ceremony was being held in the living room.

Her mother would go in first, and Troy would walk her to her seat at the front.

The bridal party stopped midway down the steps, and her mother continued.

Oh, this is getting real!

When Madison and the rest of them landed in the entry, the French doors were once again closed, and the curtains they had installed would keep Troy from seeing Madison too early. This was just one change that was made to facilitate the wedding.

Their regular furniture was stored in the basement, and a rental company had brought in chairs and handled the setup of those. Another business took care of the decorating. Madison's and Troy's jobs with the Stiles Police Department didn't leave them much spare time, so they delegated what they could. It hadn't been a small feat to convince her to book two weeks off from work for their honeymoon. He sold her on a week at a five-star resort in Cancun, Mexico, followed by a week of nesting at home to celebrate a quiet Christmas. It would be them and Hershey, her chocolate Lab.

Speaking of… Hershey wagged his tail at the sight of Madison and wriggled his body toward her, but Terry, her job partner, had him on a leash and gently encouraged him to stay back. But what she would give for just a brush of his velvet ears.

"It's okay," she told Terry.

"Maddy, your dress," Chelsea cautioned.

Hershey was so excited that he was starting to whimper. Between that and the bow tie he had around his neck for his upcoming performance as ring bearer, Madison smiled. "Hey ya, fella." She reached out, keeping some distance between herself and the dog, but she would have loved to inundate the guy with cuddles. A pantsuit would have been more conducive to that, which she'd point out, but why waste her breath? His ears were so soft, and they chipped away at her stress.

Terry wasn't the only one in the entry. There were four other men. One of whom was Madison's father. He did a double take when he saw her. His eyes watered, and it had her tearing up.

"You are beautiful, sweetheart." He braced his hands on her upper arms and leaned in and kissed her cheek.

When her father pulled back, Terry stepped up in his place. They were more than work friends. He was like the brother she never had, but she was likely to lose him soon. He'd passed the sergeant's exam and desired to settle behind a desk, where there was less risk of some psycho killing him. For the wedding, his role was master of ceremonies. He was also responsible for cuing up the music and opening the doors along with Lou Stanford, Cynthia's husband.

"You, wearing a dress?" Terry teased with a wink. "You actually look like a—"

"If you say *girl*, I might..." Madison narrowed her eyes and formed a fist. She drew her arm back as if she were going to hit his shoulder. He juked out of the way. It was a long-running schtick between them. Though she usually made contact, and he'd make a show of pretending to be wounded. Just further proof they were more like brother and sister than simply colleagues and friends.

The two of them started laughing, but it rang somewhat hollow. It wasn't far from mind that everything between them was about to change.

Terry hugged her, firm yet not too tightly, to not crush her dress.

Lou was the next to step up. He smiled and dipped his head. It was Madison who opened her arms for a hug. He was her best friend's husband, and a good friend and family by extension.

Marc Copeland and Nick Benson, who were standing up for Troy, waited there in their tuxedos, hands clasped together in front of them like they were bouncers at a bar. They had known Troy for over a decade and reported to him in the Special Weapons and Tactics division. Like him, both were muscular and over six feet. Marc was especially built like a tank, and his primary task on the SWAT force was breacher. Nick was a shield operator.

They hugged her and kissed a cheek, having grown close to her over the time she'd been with Troy.

"You ready?" Terry asked her.

She eyed the front door, then looked at him. "If I wait any longer, I might take my cold feet and run out of here." An empty threat. As nervous as she was to take the step of marriage, she hadn't been this sure about anything in her life.

"You? Run? By choice? That would be a first."

This time she did hit Terry's shoulder. He pretended it hurt. But he deserved the potshot. Terry showed her up by running miles on his treadmill every morning. What sick bastard *chose* to do that? Meanwhile, she found ways to avoid the activity. If a suspect ran, she set Terry free. Thinking of that, her new partner better be a runner too because she wasn't taking it up anytime soon.

Tears stung her eyes as she nodded to everyone, and the wedding party got into position.

Chelsea and Marc stood side by side in front of the doors. Cynthia and Nick were behind them.

Terry hit the music, and he and Lou each got a door.

As Madison watched the couples disappear, her nerves had her heart pounding. Not long from now, she'd be saying "I do." A cold sweat blanketed her arms.

Her father smiled at her as he held out his arm, and she slipped hers through.

Brie, her niece, was in front of them and turned around. "Now?"

"Yes." Madison smiled at her. They'd had a rehearsal last night, but Brie's nerves must have been getting to her too.

"Okay." Brie grinned and disappeared through the French doors into the living room.

Seconds later, the music was changed to the "Bridal Chorus," and Madison's mouth went dry, her head faint.

"You're up," Terry whispered to her.

No turning back, Knight. Deep, slow, steady breaths... Deliberate, conscious breathing, just like her therapist would recommend.

Madison and her father paused in the doorway. Brie had done a great job of sprinkling rose petals onto the long runner ahead of them. The room also looked incredible, with ribbons and bows on the chairs and the large urns full of flowers. She made these observations quickly before her gaze went to Troy at the other end of the room. Locked on him, her chest heaved, her lungs froze mid-inhale, and her legs weakened as if made of jelly.

Maybe if she focused on the sea of familiar friendly faces of those nearest and dearest to her and Troy, she'd regain her strength. They were standing with their eyes on Madison.

Terry's wife, Annabelle, and their infant daughter, Danny; Chelsea's husband and her two other daughters; Officer Higgins aka Chief, Madison's training officer and someone she highly respected; Joni Weir and her girls, Troy's goddaughters; Cole Richards, the area's medical examiner, and his wife; Jennifer Adams, Samantha Reid, and Mark Andrews from the crime lab, who worked with and reported to Cynthia; Andrea Fletcher, who was Troy's sister and the Stiles PD police chief, and her husband, Robert. Absent from Troy's side were his parents, who had died years before he and Madison had started dating.

As Madison approached the front of the room, she couldn't avoid Troy any longer. Seeing him made her breath catch again. His broad shoulders filled out a tux to perfection. His blond hair was trimmed short, and his green eyes were electric and piercing.

Her father put her hand in Troy's and kissed her cheek before taking a seat by her mother.

Troy was smiling, an expression he rarely showcased, and her heart was at risk of beating out of her chest. He was so much more than the spectacle before her. His character and personality completed the package, and he was all hers.

This man wants to marry me, accepting all my strengths and faults. How did I get so lucky?

She smiled at him as they turned to face David Murphy, who was acting as their wedding officiant. He also worked with Troy in SWAT. His specialty was explosives.

David offered her an encouraging smile and said, "Troy and Madison want to welcome you to their home and their wed—"

A commotion of raised voices from the entry interrupted David. One man distinctly called out, "Braybury PD!"

Madison spun around as two police officers crashed into the living room and headed right toward her. Terry and Lou were standing there, arms raised in frustration and surrender.

Her father stepped into the aisle to play interference and block them from reaching the front of the room. "You need to leave now. You have no business being here."

"You need to get out of our way, sir, or I will be forced to arrest you," one of the officers said as he and a colleague skirted past her father.

"Excuse me, but what the hell is happening here?" Andrea Fletcher closed the distance to the officers. "I'm Police Chief Fletcher, and I demand an answer."

A man in a suit stepped through the opening of the French doors. He sauntered toward Andrea and stopped mere inches in front of her. He was looking past her to Troy when he said, "Troy Matthews, you're going to go with these fine officers."

"Who are you?" Andrea spat.

The man held up a gold badge. "Detective Snow, Braybury PD."

Braybury was a large city a couple of hours away from Stiles. Madison turned to Troy when he put a hand on her lower back. "What's going on?" she asked him.

He shook his head. "I have no idea."

The officers each grabbed one of Troy's arms and attempted to pull them behind his back. Troy resisted their efforts.

"Let go of me," Troy said. "You have no right to—"

"Oh, we have every right." Snow was right in Troy's face. "You're under arrest for the murder of Dylan Graham."

"What?" Madison spat, her voice high-pitched and panicked. Her shocked mind couldn't make any sense of what had been said. *Who the hell is Dylan Graham? Why would Troy kill him?*

"Please just let us do our jobs, ma'am," one of the uniforms said.

Madison detested being addressed as *ma'am*. She formed a fist at her side, but Cynthia stepped up and tapped her hand. It was a poor time to try to calm her down. Her fiancé was about to be hauled off like he was some criminal. On their wedding day, no less. No number of deep breaths was going to calm her down. Hitting this guy might. Though the pleasure would be temporary and likely land her in a jail cell too.

Andrea stood next to her brother. "I don't know what you think you're doing, but you have no right to storm in here and do this. This jurisdiction belongs to the Stiles PD, and as I told you, I'm the police chief. There's a way of doing things, and this isn't how it's done. You intend to cross the boundary lines, then you give the governing PD the courtesy of a phone call. My brother isn't a criminal. He's a reputable officer of the law."

"Your brother," the detective pushed back. "That fact right there is why we didn't clear this past you. You're too close."

Andrea glared at him and crossed her arms. "Who did you put this past?"

"Listen, lady, if you have problems with people in your department, that's on you to figure out. I've got a murder, and all the evidence is pointing at him." He nudged his head toward Troy and signaled for the officers to apprehend him.

Andrea clenched her jaw, and her cheeks were bright red with anger. She gestured for Troy to go along and told him, "We'll get to the bottom of this."

Madison retreated inward, observing all that was going on. But this couldn't be real. She must be dreaming, and she'd surrender to that if it wasn't for Cynthia, who kept touching her. But her caresses went from offering comfort to flurried and persistent finger jabs. Then Cynthia squeezed Madison's hand and cried out in pain.

"I think... *I think* I'm in...lab... Ouch!" Cynthia's legs buckled, and Madison rushed to hold her upright. Lou pushed through wedding guests and Braybury officers to get to his wife. In the commotion, Troy was disappearing down the aisle, being carted away in cuffs. She had to go after him. Once Lou got to Cynthia, Madison made a move in that endeavor.

Andrea popped in front of Madison and shook her head. "You stay with your friend. I've got Troy."

Madison nodded, but in her head, she was screaming, *What the hell just happened?*

CHAPTER 3

Troy shifted again, uncomfortable in the plastic chair they had in the interview room at the Braybury police station. The commute to the city was a two-hour drive, and a look at his watch told him it was six thirty. He may have only been in this room for thirty minutes, but it felt much longer. It could be the fact it followed being stuffed into the back of a police car. As a career cop, he deserved better treatment and consideration.

But they think I killed a man…

The detective's words continuously played out like an irritating earworm. "You're under arrest for the murder of Dylan Graham."

And why Dylan Graham, of all people? It was a name from his past and one he never expected to hear again. It belonged to what should be his long, dead, *and* buried past. Now ironically, Dylan himself was dead. Murdered supposedly. Allegedly at Troy's hands.

But what had led the Braybury detectives to suspect him? Where were his means, motive, and opportunity?

The door opened, and Troy sat straighter. *About time!* He could clear up whatever misunderstanding there was and get back to Madison.

He expected Detective Snow or his partner, Detective Friedman, who he met outside his house, but it was Andrea. She was with a man in a suit who looked and smelled like a lawyer. The stranger was under six feet tall and in his late fifties with gray hair, deep grooves in his forehead, and a cleft chin. Heavy cologne hit Troy's nose before the formal introduction.

"Troy, this is Vincent Park. Your lawyer," Andrea told him, all business. No warm hugs or placating remarks were offered, and Troy appreciated the absence of both. There wasn't room for emotions.

Your lawyer... That didn't sound like his life. He was on the side of the good guys, for frick's sake.

"Nice to meet you, Mr. Matthews." Park held out his hand, but Troy left it untouched.

There was nothing *nice* about this meeting. None of them should even be here. He should be at his wedding reception, already married to Madison. And, thinking of her, she must be just as angry and upset as him. She'd also be confused because he'd never mentioned Dylan

Graham to her, but for good reason. He was honestly disappointed she wasn't here. "Where's Madison? How is she?" He directed these questions to his sister, disregarding the lawyer.

"She's shocked, but she's with Cynthia. I told her to stay there while I came here for you. Cynthia started having contractions and was taken to the hospital."

"She's in labor?"

"Seems so."

This day had more twists and turns than a good mystery novel. Madison didn't *need* anyone, but he still wished he was there to offer her comfort. Even if part of her troubles were due to him, or at least in a roundabout way.

"Did you say anything since you were picked up?" Park was making himself comfortable, taking off his winter coat and draping it on the back of the chair across from Troy. Next, the lawyer sat down, set his briefcase on the table, snapped the clasps, and pulled out a legal notepad and a pen. He clicked it and was poised to start writing.

Troy angled his head. Did this attorney think he was stupid or had lost all mental function? "I assume you know that I'm a detective with the Stiles PD. I'm not about to say anything without a lawyer present."

"Good, I'm glad to hear it. From this point forward, you only speak when I'm present. And you keep your responses brief and to the point.

You never volunteer information or flourish your responses." The lawyer laid that out as if he were addressing a child and watched Troy as if curious whether he comprehended his words.

"I know how this works," Troy said. Surely it wasn't necessary to point out that he was usually the one doing the questioning. "But I'd like to know what they think they have against me. This is utterly ridiculous." He looked at Andrea and expected her to nod in agreement, but her face remained expressionless. "Tell me what I'm missing." He didn't care if they came from his sister or the lawyer, but he wanted some straightforward answers.

Park continued to hold his pen over the page of his notepad, a writing implement that probably set him back a few hundred dollars. "I assure you that the matter is quite serious, and the evidence they have against you is, as we say, damning."

The lawyer's statement settled as a heavy weight on his chest. "What evidence?" Never had two words taken more effort to push out.

"Before we get into all of that, when did you last speak with Dylan Graham?" Park squinted, regarding Troy as if he were a specimen in a laboratory.

"Why?" He wished the lawyer would just get on with sharing the facts of the case. Or at least what the Braybury detectives perceived as evidence against him.

Park clasped his hands in front of him. "According to Graham's phone records, he called you five days ago."

"On Monday? Okay," he dragged out. "I'm missing what that has to do with his murder."

"Troy, if you spoke with him, that's fine, just be honest," Andrea pleaded, and it wasn't a tact she typically employed. The approach had him recoiling, as did her implication he could be dishonest.

"Have you ever known me not to be honest?" he leveled at her.

Andrea's lips pressed into a straight line, and she crossed her arms. It was the posture of an older sister who was his police chief, he, her underling. "It's just best to get out in front of things."

"Jeez, Andrea!" He sprang to his feet. "You make it sound like I've done something wrong here." But that's exactly what everyone thought, maybe even his own sister. Suddenly the bow tie around his neck was suffocating, and he pried the knot undone. And why was it suddenly so hot in here?

Andrea and Park remained quiet for a few beats. The attorney was the first to speak.

"Does the name Emily Kane mean anything to you?" he asked, overlooking Troy's outburst.

He hadn't heard that name in a very long time. Truth be told, it was one he had pushed from his mind and desired to eradicate the memory of altogether. She was the reason he had cut Dylan Graham out of his life. He was a reminder of Emily and what had happened that summer night.

"Mr. Matthews," Park prompted.

Troy shed his tuxedo jacket and put it on the back of the chair he'd been sitting in. "Emily was a girl I went to high school with."

"Your friend Richie Klein served twenty-four years for her rape and murder. Is that right?" Park asked.

Troy gestured emphatically. "You tell me. You brought him up. It's obvious you did your homework, read the old news articles."

"Troy, please, just answer his questions," Andrea said. "We're on your side here."

He shook his head and couldn't bring himself to look at his sister.

Park didn't give any visual indication that Troy's snide response had affected him, but there was an unmistakable shift in energy. It had darkened. Park proceeded calmly. "The police now think they may have locked away the wrong guy."

"I tried to say that at the trial." Troy had testified to Richie's character in court, at the age of seventeen, just as Dylan Graham had and Troy's late friend, Barry Weir. Of his three closest friends from that time, Troy had only remained in touch with Barry. He had become a cop too, but he had fallen in the line of duty fifteen months ago, leaving behind a wife and three girls. But he and Barry had made an unspoken pact that they would never talk about Emily Kane. Life would be easier forgetting she ever existed.

"Troy." Andrea paused, her cheeks flushing red, and she wet her lips. "What Mr. Park is trying to say is they also think you raped and killed Emily Kane."

CHAPTER 4

Madison was pacing a hole in the floor of the hospital's waiting room, but she couldn't sit still any more than she could quiet her thoughts. And there were so many. They were accompanied by confusion and shock, anger and disappointment. Though the ruined wedding paled in scale next to Troy's arrest for murder. For murder… She tried that on again, but it didn't settle. The man she loved wasn't a killer. And if that wasn't enough to process, Cynthia had gone into labor.

"You should sit, Maddy." Her mother had insisted on coming along, but her sister hadn't volunteered to join them. Lou was in with Cynthia, and that left Madison alone with her mother.

"I'm fine." She didn't understand why her mother wanted to control everything all the time. It was like a sickness.

"You're not fine, you're fretting, and it isn't going to change a thing."

Madison stopped walking, took a deep, centering breath. Her mother probably meant well, but dispensing shallow advice wasn't helpful. She would have no idea what Madison was going through. Not really. If she did, she'd know Madison needed to sulk a bit and spend time wishing for things to be different. If only that made them so. Grief rolled over her to think of all the hard work and planning that had gone into today for it to blow up in her face. Was it an omen that she wasn't meant to get married or just a dose of bad luck?

She had ditched the tiara and the rest of the jewels and swapped the gown for jeans and a sweater before coming here. She wasn't about to linger in a waiting room wearing her dress. It was already jaded enough by what had happened. She didn't need to risk any bad luck transferring to Cynthia.

Her chest squeezed in on itself, and hot tears filled her eyes and threatened to fall.

"Sorry I took so long getting here."

Madison turned to the sound of Terry's voice. He was walking toward her, and just the sight of him injected her with relief. He'd be a buffer between her and her mother. "I'm just happy you're here."

"I would have been sooner, but I had to get Annabelle and Danny home. By the way, Chelsea saw everyone out and locked up. Far as I know, your sister's gone home now. Oh, she took Hershey too, as was the plan."

Madison had given her sister a copy of the key after she and Troy had moved in. But how it seemed *the plan* mocked her now. Her sister was to care for Hershey while she and Troy were in Mexico. Their honeymoon was just one more thing that was ruined today. "Did you hear that, Mom?" Though it wasn't necessary to ask. Her mother had the ears of a bat and was an unapologetic eavesdropper.

"What's that?"

Madison resisted rolling her eyes or lashing out at her mother. Her response was another characteristic certainty. Listen, then deny. "You can go to Chelsea's now." Her mother and father lived in Florida but were staying with Chelsea while in town for the wedding. When her mother didn't make a move to leave, Madison added, "I'll be fine, Mom. Terry's here now." She hustled over and gave her the key to her Mazda as added encouragement.

Her mother took the key and regarded it in her palm as if were an alien entity.

"Mom, you can leave," Madison prompted, her voice firmer than she'd intended. She attempted to soften the delivery by adding a smile.

Finally. Her mother started to move. She gathered her purse to her chest and stood. "Call me when Cynthia has her baby, and I'll come back."

"You got it."

Her mother left without a hug or kiss, not uncommon for them. While their relationship had found more solid footing in the last year, displays of affection remained at a minimum. Troy had tried to tell Madison she was a lot like her mother, in that they were both guarded, but she was having none of it.

Terry turned to her. "Have you heard any more about what's going on? Either with Cynthia or Troy?"

Madison shook her head. "Nothing here. And I've tried Andrea several times but ended up needing to leave a voicemail." She didn't mention it had been a *few* messages, with each one growing more concerned and forceful. Her phone rang, and she pulled it out of her pocket. "It's Andrea. Her ears must have been burning." She answered, "Andy, what's going on?"

"I only have a few seconds, but I wanted to let you know that I got Troy a lawyer. Vincent Park. Supposedly he's one of the best defense attorneys around."

Madison was familiar with the name, but they hadn't crossed paths before. And she certainly wouldn't have expected their first meeting to be due to him representing her fiancé. She did trust that Andrea would have only hired the best for her baby brother though. "What are the Braybury detectives saying? Where do they get off arresting him for murder?" She spoke the latter bit at a lower volume as some people walked past.

"It's not good, Maddy. Troy is possibly facing two murder charges and one count of rape."

"Two and—" She snapped her mouth shut as her loud response had drawn attention from those in the room. Among them were parents with a young girl who was obviously unwell with a bad cold or pneumonia. "How is this even happening? What could they possibly have against him? Who is this Dylan Graham person? And the other person he's allegedly..." She spared anyone overhearing *murder* a second time.

"It's best you don't worry about this."

"Don't worry? You do know who you're talking to?"

"It will get sorted out. When I know, you will."

"And I'm just supposed to what? Stand around, waiting?" Sitting idly by had never been a strong skill of hers.

"That's exactly what you need to do. Or sit."

Now she thinks she's funny.

"Just stay put. And I mean that. If you start poking around, you could make things worse."

That confirmed that her future sister-in-law knew her well. Madison would move a mountain if it stood in the way of justice.

"Promise me," Andrea demanded.

"Sure. But where are you? Are you still with him?" She hoped that Andrea didn't pick up on the fact she hadn't actually promised anything.

"I'm at the Braybury police station, yes, and trying to get more information. I'll reach out again once I have more to share." With that, Andrea hung up.

Madison was left holding her phone. She slowly lowered it from her ear, her body trembling as it mourned the ebbing adrenaline.

"It's not good?" Terry asked tentatively.

She shook her head, on the verge of breaking down.

"Come here." Terry opened his arms, and she moved in for the hug.

Every minute was like sitting on a ticking bomb waiting for word that Terry was leaving her behind. As if that wasn't enough, one of the other men she cared most about was being taken from her too. Yet she was supposed to just sit still and do nothing? No way.

She tried to let Terry's embrace wash away her worries, but her mind replayed her conversation with Andrea. She never answered Madison's question about Dylan Graham. Who the hell was he?

CHAPTER 5

"Why do they think I killed and *raped* her?" The accusation that Troy was such a violent offender churned the acid in his gut and gave him instant heartburn. He kneaded his knuckles against his chest.

Andrea hurried over and placed a hand on his shoulder. "Are you okay?"

He pulled back at her question, fast, as if he'd been burned. "You're kidding, right?"

His sister's eyes flooded with tears. "You just looked like… Is your heart all right?" She nudged her head to her where he was still massaging his chest.

He lowered his hand. "Just a bit of heartburn."

Andrea left the room. Troy recognized the trait. She often retreated to regain her composure. His reaction to her expressed concern had stung her, but what did she expect? This certainly wasn't his finest hour. Surely, she'd see that.

"Here." The lawyer pulled out a sleeve of antiacids from the inside pocket of his suit jacket and extended it to Troy.

Leave it to a lawyer to have heartburn medication within hand's reach. Troy dismissed the offer.

"Up to you, but..." Park made a show of slowly returning the chewables to where he'd plucked them from.

A few minutes later, Andrea slipped back into the room but stood near the door.

"Back to Emily Kane," Park said. "Do you remember the night she was—"

"Is this even necessary?" Troy rushed out, cutting off the lawyer's question.

Park glanced at Andrea, as if looking for her to step in.

"Please, just tell us what you remember," she told Troy.

He didn't want to revisit that point in his past ever again. Let alone recall the horror of it in front of his sister. She'd been away at college and was spared the fallout of Emily's murder at the time.

Silence gnawed on the room, growing and expanding like a malignant cancer.

He detested the idea of going down memory lane, but he wasn't sure he had another option. "Fine. It was the last weekend of the summer, and there was this huge party at the beach."

"Who was there?" Park inserted, leaned forward, his left hand arched over the page, ready to put Troy's words into writing.

"Seniors from Stiles High, maybe others from surrounding areas. It's not like there was a guest list, and it was a public beach. There was music, dancing, and alcohol."

Park stopped his scribbling long enough to ask, "Drugs?"

"Uh-huh, I think some people were smoking weed." He had been drunk off his feet, but he had never touched drugs. The same couldn't be said for his friends. Images from that night started creeping in. He told the memories to go away, but they were proving more powerful than him. *Loud music, dancing, faces…*

"Did you see Emily that night?"

Emily… Dancing with her friends around the bonfire, her arms flowing loosely above her head, her hips swaying, her blond hair fanning out when she shook her head wildly to the beat of the music.

"Mr. Matthews?"

"Yeah, I saw her there. She was with her friends."

"From the account, she went off alone to the woods, where she was sexually assaulted and then murdered."

Troy leaned back and flailed a hand. There wasn't anything he could add to that.

"And it was your friend Richie Klein who raped and murdered her?"

Troy bristled, detesting the package. Murder, as horrid as it was, was nothing compared to the vileness of rape. "I never believed he did. No." He was aware his answer contradicted the findings of a jury. They had found Richie guilty of murder in the second degree, and he was sentenced to twenty-four years without eligibility for parole. It was light for the charge, since second degree typically meant life in prison. A concession had been made due to his age and the fact he was under the influence of marijuana and alcohol at the time of the crime.

Park tapped the tip of his pen against the page, little black dots forming in its wake. "He was found guilty and sent to prison."

"I know that," Troy hissed.

"Yet you just said he didn't do it. Is that because you think it, want to believe it, or *know* he didn't?"

The implication wasn't hard to miss, and Troy was offended. "I didn't do it, if that's what you're implying, and if you're asking for a confession, since when do defense attorneys care about the innocence of their clients?"

"Troy, please," Andrea said.

"No, get me another lawyer, Andy. Someone who will just do his job."

Park flinched and grimaced. He straightened his tie, the tell of a man gathering his thoughts, peacocking himself to imply confidence. "I am doing my job, Mr. Matthews, and I am on your side."

"You're doing a piss-poor job of showing it."

"You think those detectives aren't going to ask you these questions? I'm telling you they will, and you better have your story together. And your emotions in check. That's why I'm trying to get you to think about that night, remember it, so you're prepared. I don't care whether you're innocent or guilty, and I don't need or want to know either. You just need to be prepared," he reiterated.

Troy studied the attorney's facial expression. Steadfast eye contact and a relaxed jaw and mouth. Add to that, the lawyer's words were clear-cut, honest, and authentic. Troy may have misjudged this man's abilities as a defense attorney. "All right, then," Troy eventually said.

"What can you tell me about Richie Klein?" Park hovered his pen over the legal pad again. "Obviously, there's something about him that makes you feel he was wrongly convicted."

Troy identified that in the place of judgment was a desire for straightforward communication. "Richie could be a hothead. But he never would have forced himself on a girl, or strangled her, for that matter." His mind flashed to the past when he'd alluded to the same thing on the stand. Had he pulled out these words now because they were familiar? More to the point, did Troy even believe them? He had been a kid then. What if his faith in Richie had been misplaced? Twelve strangers had deliberated over the facts and found him guilty.

And there was that other girl… The thought struck, dredging up another memory he had long ago forgotten. Richie had been accused of raping one of their classmates in ninth grade. Troy couldn't remember her name now, but he recalled the prosecution had resurrected the allegation at the murder trial. It had been a direct attempt to combat the stellar character testimony that Troy, Dylan, and Barry had provided. Apparently, it had worked.

"Were you there when this happened to Emily Kane?" Park said, the implication was hanging out there and not easily missed.

"No."

"Then if you weren't present, how can you know for certain whether or not Richie Klein did this to her?"

Troy crossed his arms and huffed. "I just know," he mumbled. Though why he was stubbornly clinging to his earlier expressed conviction was beyond him. But recanting his statement now wouldn't look good. It would make him appear more guilty than just keeping quiet. But the silence wasn't comfortable either. It had been born from his unsupported *I just know*. His sister was refusing eye contact and left him to speculate if she was losing her faith in him. But if she was questioning his character and his innocence, send him away now. Such betrayal, coming from his own flesh and blood, would be worse than prison. "You're asking all these questions about Emily, but you haven't told me why the Braybury detectives think I killed her. Enlighten me."

Park looked at Andrea. "Do you want to tell him, or should I?"

Andrea pressed his lips together, parted them just slightly, then pressed them again. The mannerism was a sign she was weighing a response. She then nodded at the lawyer and said to Troy, "Dylan apparently kept a journal. The detectives suspect this was to get out his feelings about what happened all those years ago to Emily Kane. A way for him to process what a friend had done."

"Okay. None of that sounds very strong. They *suspect…?*"

"More to the point, your name is in Dylan's journal, Troy. In his handwriting. There he named you as Emily's rapist and killer." His sister's chin quivered, and a rogue tear fell, which she palmed from her cheek.

Troy sat back, his shoulders dropping, as if all the air had left his body. *This isn't happening…*

A few beats later, Andrea added, "And that call we mentioned, the one that shows Dylan contacted you five days ago? The detectives suspect he called to tell you he was going to turn you in."

And there was that word again. *Suspect.* But this accusation was more damning. He rubbed his forehead and met his sister's eye. "They think I killed Dylan to stop that from happening."

CHAPTER 6

Madison wished for someone to pinch her and wake her from this nightmare. But she'd have no such luck. This was her reality. And she was left to juggle her thoughts alone. Terry was off getting them coffees from the hospital cafeteria. To think it had begun at four o'clock that afternoon, a time that was supposed to mark one of the happiest moments of her life. Now it was seven thirty, three and a half hours since Troy's arrest. All hell had broken loose and didn't show any signs of letting up. The uncertainty alone was enough to fray her very last nerve. Despite being told by her therapist that control was an illusion, she clung to it and derived comfort from it regardless. The fact she hinged stability on smoke and mirrors was her choice, her comfort zone. At least, it usually worked for her. This time not so much.

Terry returned and handed her a cup. "Here you go."

Madison took the coffee with thanks. It smelled strong and slightly burnt, reminding her of the brew from the police station. That sludge would clog an engine.

"I tried to find you a Hershey's bar. I know you consider them a meal." He smiled at her.

"We've been through this. Chocolate is made from cocoa, which is a plant, aka a vegetable." Not that she could think of eating anything, as her stomach was clenched into a tight ball from stress.

"Well, let's agree to disagree on whether it ticks off dietary requirements, but here you go." He produced a Hershey's chocolate bar from his coat pocket.

"You just said you couldn't find any."

"You need to start listening better. I said *I tried to find you* one. Nowhere in there did I say I was unsuccessful."

She narrowed her eyes. "Smart-ass."

"Hey, if you're going to be like that"—he pulled back, taking the chocolate from her reach—"I'll eat it. Mmm-mmm."

She laughed despite the ache in her chest. When Terry became a sergeant, it was going to be her loss.

"Here you go." Terry handed her the bar and sat beside her. "Any word from the Stanford crew yet?"

"Nope." She peeled back the wrapper, surprised she was even giving food a try with her stomach in the upset state it was in. But *this* was chocolate. It was supposed to cure all that ailed, smooth over hard times and help one get through. She took a big bite. *It doesn't hurt…*

Doors opened off the waiting room, and Cynthia and Lou came out. They looked around the seating area, and Lou pointed toward them. Madison and Terry were already on their feet.

Madison folded the wrapper over the bar and burrowed it into her coat pocket. She hurried to Cynthia. "What's going on?"

"Braxton Hicks," Cynthia said. "Doctors say it's nothing to worry about."

One wouldn't guess that by looking at her friend's crestfallen face. Though, she came here expecting to have a baby and got a practice run instead.

Terry was bobbing his head. "Oh, they are completely normal. Annabelle had them too."

Lou wrapped an arm around Cynthia. "The doc says it was brought on by stress."

No one was looking at her, but she felt the impact. Though, it wasn't like what had transpired was her fault. The blame rested on the Braybury PD.

"Lou." Cynthia stepped out from under her husband's hold and touched Madison's arm. "Be careful what you say. Think about how it must make Madison feel."

"Oh, sorry." Lou smiled at her. "I didn't mean to imply that was your fault."

Madison wished this awkward exchange wasn't even happening. Voicing her assumptions made her feel worse, giving them validity. Maybe this wasn't all about Troy's arrest either. The stress of being a maid of honor so close to her due date might have been too much. Madison desperately wanted to shift the attention from her. "But you're okay now?"

"Yeah. Tired though."

"Glad you'll be fine, Cyn." Madison smiled at her friend, and Cynthia pulled her in for a tight hug.

Cynthia stepped back, put a hand on her stomach. "This beachball is enormous. I can't wait for little bug to be with us." She smiled at Lou, but her expression turned serious when she looked at Madison. "What's going on with Troy? You should be with him and not here with us."

Madison held up a hand to slow her friend's thoughts. *Crap, I* am *my mother… I need to let her feel and express herself how she wants…* She lowered her arm.

"None of this makes any sense," Cynthia said, not deterred by Madison's actions. "Who is the man he was accused of killing?"

"Dylan Graham." *Otherwise known as the enigma.* "I've never heard Troy mention him before." It still festered that Andrea hadn't told her anything about the guy. Even in response to a direct question. That seemed intentional, but why?

Terry cleared his throat. "I might have looked him up."

Madison leveled her gaze at him. "Might have? And you're just telling me this now?"

"Trust me, I was getting around to it." Terry stepped back.

But could anyone blame her for being touchy on the subject? Surely, he must have seen how she'd stewed for the last three and a half hours. Then again, how could he have known she didn't know who Dylan Graham was? She didn't remember coming out and telling him as much. Still, she clamped her mouth shut, trying to exercise some patience. But Terry didn't approach life like she did. He was more the tortoise and she the hare from the child's tale. Yet she refused to accept that moving slower was faster in the end. It was just aggravating. "Don't let me stop you now."

"Graham was found shot in his home three days ago in Braybury," Terry said. "Beyond that, the news isn't saying much."

Three days ago would have been Wednesday. "And what's being said through official channels?"

"As you know, it's Braybury PD handling this, so I'm not getting much. But your— Well, the police chief is with him. I'm sure things are under control."

Terry's near slip had Madison's heart pinching. She imagined he was going to say *your sister-in-law*. "Under control? Now that's funny. She didn't even know they were going to crash our wedding to arrest Troy." Suddenly all the anger she was feeling about the situation and the obtrusion directed itself at Andrea.

"I heard her ask that detective who he cleared it past," Terry admitted.

"Me too, and he didn't give her an answer," Madison countered.

"I know you won't want to hear this," Terry began, "but regardless of who it was, it doesn't change the result."

She stiffened. "It certainly does. Someone within the Stiles PD knew that the BPD was going to apprehend Troy on our wedding day. That person didn't even have the decency to call Andrea, or any of us, Terry."

No one said a word in the wake of her anger. Surely, they had to share her view.

Cynthia and Lou excused themselves, commenting on how it had been a long night and they were headed home. They told Madison to call if she heard anything more about what was going on with Troy.

Madison remained standing there for a few moments as she watched their retreating forms.

"Want a ride home?" Terry eventually broke the silence that had wedged between them.

"Actually, to my sister's, and I'll get my car back."

"You got it."

They walked out of the hospital, and she tried to make sense of how Troy got roped into any of this. "Surely this Graham guy had an enemy who wanted him dead. There's no way Troy killed him. I've never even heard him mention this guy's name before." She was certain she sounded like a record on repeat, but her mind was obsessing.

Terry didn't respond but unlocked his van and got inside. She hopped onto the passenger seat and did up her belt.

"You hear me?" she prompted.

Terry turned the vehicle on and let it idle and warm up. He then faced her, keeping one hand on the wheel, as if steeling himself. "I'm not sure what to say to that, but there is something you should know. I googled Dylan Graham, and his name came up on a blog in reference to an old case. Twenty-four years old, to be precise. A seventeen-year-old girl named Emily Kane was raped and murdered here in Stiles. And this is hard to say, but Troy's name was also mentioned."

She stared at him, blinking slowly, not wanting to accept that any of what Terry said had any connection to her fiancé. Andrea had mentioned a second murder charge and a rape.

Did it have anything to do with Emily Kane? The name didn't mean anything to her, but Madison had grown up in a small town outside of Stiles. She was also a few years younger than Troy, so she never would have crossed paths with him or Emily anyhow. "Troy would have been a teenager then too."

"Troy and Dylan were likely schoolmates. Same for Emily."

"You said this was a blog, though, right? So that's basically an online diary where anyone can spill their opinions like diarrhea."

Terry didn't comment.

"But this post had Troy's name mentioned in reference to the rape and murder of a teenager?"

"I'm sorry."

Even though she needed more context, Madison's heart felt like it was breaking.

Do I know the man I was about to marry at all?

CHAPTER 7

It was just one short phone call. A connection between old friends. Troy never should have answered when he saw Dylan's name on the caller ID.

The doors to the interview room opened, and the Braybury detectives came inside. Friedman was the younger of the two. Snow was in his fifties with a settled physique and silver hair. He had a manila folder tucked under his left arm.

"Time's up, Ms. Fletcher," Detective Snow said.

"That's *Chief* Fletcher." Andrea peacocked her stance and took her time leaving. She stopped and spoke to Troy first. "Listen to Mr. Park, and do whatever he advises you."

Troy nodded, and Park pushed his legal pad and briefcase to Troy's side of the table and dragged the chair he'd been in over and sat down.

Detective Snow sat in the remaining chair while Friedman stood behind him. "By now you should have a very clear picture of why you're here, Mr. Matthews," Snow said.

"It would have been beneficial if you afforded me a bit more time to confer with my client," Park said. "We haven't had a chance to cover everything."

"What have you been doing in here all this time then?" Snow volleyed back.

Park scowled. The fact his lawyer hadn't gotten around to telling him everything was Troy's fault. He'd been preoccupied trying to process and make sense of what he had been told. It was like his mind could only handle these updates in tiny pieces.

When neither Troy nor Park spoke, Snow went on, putting his focus on Troy. "You were friends with Dylan Graham. That right?"

Park nodded for Troy to answer.

"I used to be. A long time ago." Troy didn't typically have a problem with respecting authority. Without a hierarchy, there would be chaos and confusion. But this was his first time being governed by a defense attorney. It made him feel like a child who needed permission for his next steps.

"We have proof you and Dylan Graham were in recent contact." Snow produced a piece of paper from the folder he'd brought into the room and gently tossed it across the table.

Park retrieved it and leaned in toward Troy. “It’s a call log. What about it?”

“If you look at the duration, the call between your client and the victim lasted three minutes,” Snow said.

It hadn’t felt that long. Troy resisted the urge to react and play into the detective’s hands.

Seconds passed, then Snow said, “Why did Mr. Graham call you?”

“I don’t remember.” Coming out with the truth might be best, but to what end? The Braybury detectives already had their minds made up about him. He imagined they’d just twist whatever he said. It was best he didn’t volunteer a thing until he had a better handle on all the supposed evidence against him. A decision that was sure to please his attorney.

Snow scoffed. “We’re talking about a measly five days ago. Is a bad memory how you plan on playing this?”

Troy didn’t bite.

“Fine,” Snow pushed out. “Have it your way. But we will figure it out, Mr. Matthews.”

Detective Snow was fishing for a response, a reaction, but Troy refused to give him one. Did the detective honestly believe he’d have success with this bully approach? Troy wasn’t a fool. The less he said, the better. Besides, there was no way he could *figure it out*. They had all a telephone service provider could give them. Proof that a call had taken place.

Snow leaned back in his chair. "Why not just tell us what you and Mr. Graham discussed?"

"Detective Snow," Park stepped in, "Mr. Matthews has the right to his privacy. Unless you can prove this brief conversation between old friends pertains to his murder, that door is closed. Let's move on."

Snow narrowed his eyes on Troy. "I'll tell you what we think."

Before that *we*, Troy had almost forgotten Detective Friedman was lingering in the corner of the room.

Park shook his head and smiled. "Come on. It doesn't matter one iota what you think. It's what you can prove."

"All right. How's this for evidence?" Snow opened the folder again and shoved a picture of a Smith & Wesson M&P 9 across the table. "This was the gun used to shoot Dylan Graham. The real kicker"—he made a point of looking at Park—"is it's registered to your client here." Then he turned his full attention to Troy. "Mr. Matthews, can you explain why your gun was at the scene of a man's murder?"

Troy looked at Park. They'd never covered this, but the attorney didn't seem surprised. He must have known about the gun. Andrea too. But Troy had been so busy fighting everything they did say, this juicy tidbit was never shared. Sweat gathered at the base of Troy's back. He had an S&W M&P 9, but it was locked up in his gun box at the house. At least it had been the last time he saw it, which was… *To hell if I can remember.*

Snow smiled. "Don't tell us it was stolen."

Troy racked his brain. He'd last seen the gun in the old house, but it would have been taken from his bedroom closet there to the new house. A mindless transfer from one place to another.

"Will we find your prints on it?" Snow asked.

"Kind of a stupid question, don't you think?" Troy spat. "If it's my gun, yeah, there's a good chance of that."

Park put his hand on Troy's forearm but directed his words to the detective. "There can be an innocent explanation for my client's gun being there."

Snow splayed his arms open and glanced at Friedman. "We're all ears."

Park shook his head, just subtly. Troy followed his lawyer's suggestion and stayed quiet. But he wished he hadn't goaded the detective in the first place with the suggestion they had prepared a response.

"Don't have anything to say, then? No *innocent* explanations?" Snow attributed finger quotes to the word *innocent*, and this bozo wondered why Troy didn't want to talk to him.

"Tell me, does this method of interrogation normally work for you?" Troy asked.

"Yeah, it does. As it should," Snow said. "But that's fine if you're not talkative right now. I've got all night. So do you. It's not like you'll be going home to your lovely bride to-be any time soon."

Troy clenched his hands into fists, wanting to lash out at this guy and beat some sense into him.

Snow gathered the pictures into his folder. "Whenever you're ready to talk, we'll return. But I'd get comfortable. We have more than enough to lock you up, Mr. Matthews."

Troy remained silent while his mind ruminated on everything he'd just been told. His gun at the scene. A damning journal that leveled an accusation. Dylan's phone call. But why was Emily Kane being dredged up after all this time?

CHAPTER 8

Madison had somehow convinced Terry that she'd be fine home alone. Her mother and sister too. That blasted word had returned to haunt her. Fine. It was deceiving and she wished to eradicate it from her vocabulary. That was, if her life didn't keep serving up reasons to use it.

She unlocked the front door, and the smell of flowers hit her nose along with a cacophony of colognes and other fragrances. Just a number of hours ago, those she and Troy loved the most had been gathered here to watch them exchange vows. It would be easy to dismiss it as a fantasy if not for the hard evidence in front of her.

The French doors stood open, and the living room looked as she'd left it, with the rows of chairs draped with ribbon and bows, tall urns of flowers, and rose petals on the runner. A ball of grief knotted in her chest and bubbled out in a gasp and was joined by tears laying tracks down her cheeks. She palmed them away, angry at this display of emotion even in her solitude. Now wasn't the time for a pity party. Troy needed her strength and support.

She put her keys into her coat pocket, hung it on a hook by the front door, and slipped out of her shoes. Normally they'd sit on a boot tray by the door, but it wasn't exactly good aesthetics for a wedding venue, and Chelsea had insisted on making it disappear. Madison would have to ask where she'd tucked it away and bring it back out. After all, the winter weather brought snow, slush, sand, and salt. But it was *fine* wherever it was for now.

Her mind kept churning over Troy's name being mentioned in reference to the rape and murder of a teen girl twenty-four years ago. But what could that possibly have to do with Dylan Graham's murder this past week? She'd need more information to even start speculating.

She practically ran to the office at the back of the house. It was on the main level and the smallest of three bedrooms, making it the most suitable for a desk and computer. Her grandmother had used this space as her sewing room, and in her time, it had been overflowing with bolts of fabric. The memory of that struck Madison often when she stepped through the doorway. It was no different now. The images in her mind were so intense, they resurrected her grandmother's lavender scent. The nostalgia cradled her in the arms of comfort and infused her with strength.

"Thank you, Grandma." Madison spoke to the air. *To Rose's ghost?*

Madison sat down and brought up her browser and googled *twenty-four years ago, Dylan Graham, Emily Kane, murdered teen, Troy Matthews.* That was a lot of parameters, but it gave her confidence she'd find the blog post Terry had mentioned. She should have just asked him for the link, and she would if she didn't have any luck on her own.

The results filled in. The first was a news article titled "Trial Starts for Rape and Murder of Emily Kane." Troy and Dylan were crossed out as not being in the post. The next article down was entitled "Justice for Emily Kane." Again, their names weren't there.

She clicked on the top piece, gathering up tidbits. The journalist had summed up points of the crime. Emily Kane, a seventeen-year-old, had been the victim of rape and murder. Richie Klein, also seventeen at the time, was standing trial for the crime. It had taken place at a summer beach party, and despite fifty-plus kids being there, no eyewitnesses came forward. As for the evidence against Klein, those details were not made public. According to the reporter, the jury heard testimony from the accused's friends "who will remain unnamed as protected under the juvenile act."

There was this swirling in her gut. Had one of them been Troy?

Next, Madison found the blog post Terry must have read. There, her earlier hunch was confirmed. Terry's use of *schoolmates* must have been to dampen the blow. Troy had been *friends* with Richie Klein *and* present at the party that night.

Her doorbell rang, and she flinched.

Just a little jumpy, Knight!

She got up to answer the door, angry as hell. Not at her unexpected visitor but at Troy. His not confiding in her about this time in his life felt like a betrayal, a deceit. It wasn't like it was some insignificant event in his life. He took the stand in a murder trial as a young adult. One would think that was worth bringing up at some point during their nearly two-year relationship. That was, unless he had something to hide.

CHAPTER 9

Madison opened the door to find Andrea standing on the front step. Tiny snowflakes swirled around her, dancing through the air, glistening under the streetlights and the front light next to the door. And where's that boot tray when you need it? The thought, silly and insignificant, flashed through her mind, providing temporary respite from her dark thoughts. She looked around Andrea, hoping, anticipating, that Troy would be with her.

"It's just me," Andrea said, as she must have picked up on Madison's wish.

Madison stepped back to let Andrea inside, neither woman saying a word for a few beats.

Andrea unwound her scarf and took off her coat and boots. She'd take that as an indication Andrea was settling in for a duration and intended to lay everything out for her.

"How's he doing?" Madison could barely get the question to leave her lips, uncertain, in part, if she wanted the answer.

"Good, considering. As I told you before when we spoke, he's got a good lawyer."

The fact Troy even needed a lawyer was hard for Madison to wrap her head around. "If he's so good, why isn't Troy with you? This is ludicrous. Troy murdering someone doesn't even make sense."

"You know that, and so do I."

They parked on stools at the kitchen peninsula. The room had been completely updated by the previous owners, who got their hands on it through her grandmother's estate sale. They installed marble quartz countertops with wisps of gray, white cabinets, and chrome hardware. It was a far cry from the seventies-style oak cabinetry and dark brass handles that had been there when Madison was younger.

Andrea sat hunched, her shoulders rolled forward, as if she were a marionette that had its strings cut.

"When is he coming home?" Madison's insides were knotted with rage over the situation, with Troy, from feeling so powerless.

"That I don't know entirely."

"Andrea, how can you not—"

She held up a hand. "Remember, I'm on your side and Troy's."

Madison softened. "I know this. It's just all so surreal."

"I get that." Andrea rubbed her right temple. "So Troy's going to be held until his arraignment on Monday morning."

"Monday," Madison gasped, ready to lash out at the situation, but it wasn't fair to lay this burden on Andrea's shoulders. As she simmered, she turned over the fact in her mind that she and Troy were supposed to be leaving for their honeymoon tomorrow. From the sound of it, she'd need to call and cancel. Just another casualty of the delayed nuptials. All because some Braybury detectives saw fit to tromp out of their jurisdiction to arrest Troy. "What's the charge?"

"Murder one." Andrea laid that out so calmly, Madison envied her control. This was her baby brother facing these charges.

Murder one... It wouldn't matter how many times Madison kicked that thought around in relation to Troy, it would never settle. She'd just entered some other reality, but it couldn't be ignored that Troy did have a connection to Dylan Graham. "Before you got here, I did a bit of googling."

Andrea remained silent, and shadows passed over her face. It was obvious she didn't agree with Madison doing so but didn't rebuke her.

Madison went on. "I found out about Emily Kane and that Troy was friends with the man he's been accused of killing."

"Dylan Graham."

Hearing the name coming at her had Madison's temper flaring again. "Troy never spoke his name once. Or told me about all this. I know it was a long time ago, but still… It makes me so angry." She stopped there, flexing her fists in her lap, her heart beating rapidly.

"You know how Troy is, Maddy."

"That he's crap at dealing with intense emotions. Yeah, I know." When he lost his friend Barry, his grief had him pushing her away. Then there was another time something really upset him, and he'd walked out on her for an entire night. That happened once.

"I'm sure you can understand why he'd want to forget that time. It wouldn't exactly bring up pleasant memories, and to him the matter was closed."

Madison could concede to that, but in a serious relationship, didn't you share your past with each other? Or was she expecting too much from Troy? She wasn't that good about sharing her feelings either and often bottled up her emotions.

"I'm not sure how much digging you did, so I'll fill you in," Andrea said. "Troy was at the party that night with three of his friends. One was Dylan, another Barry Weir, who you knew."

The past tense wasn't missed, and even a year and a half after his death, it didn't hurt any less.

"The third friend, Richie Klein, was the one found guilty of rape and murder in the second degree and sentenced to twenty-four years without possibility of early parole."

She hadn't gotten that far in her research. His age at the time of the crime must have been given consideration. Madison's strong suit wasn't math, but twenty-four years ago would mean that Klein was due for release this year. "When does Klein get out?"

"He was a free man as of last Tuesday."

"And when was Dylan Graham killed?" She was grasping for a connection.

"He was found Wednesday morning. I haven't been given the time of death."

"So it could have been sometime on Tuesday. Either way, it's very possible Klein got out of prison and killed Dylan. He could have motive. Maybe he holds Dylan responsible somehow. Oh, or he was falsely accused and knew that Dylan killed Emily. Did the cops even bother to look at him?" This made sense in her head. After all, Troy wasn't a criminal.

"They arrested Troy because they have evidence against him." Andrea's lips quivered, as did her voice.

"How is that possible when there's no way he killed this man?" Again, her mind assaulted her with the fact this couldn't be happening. She recognized she was stuck in a state of denial. Though it served her right for thinking the ground wouldn't fall out beneath them. They had been happy, and she had dared to give herself over to positive thinking. "I don't understand."

"There was a phone call from Dylan to Troy on Monday. The Braybury detectives believe Dylan was threatening Troy that he was going to come forward with the truth."

"Threatening. Come forward. The truth?" Add confusion to all the emotions whirling inside her, and she couldn't stitch her words into a full sentence.

"There was a journal. Graham wrote Troy was the one who actually raped and killed Emily Kane. He was going to come forward with that."

"What?" Madison burst out and popped to her feet. "Based on what? Did this Dylan even note any proof? I'll tell you he couldn't have. And the police arrested Troy because of some phone call and a journal? They can't even prove what the conversation was about between Troy and Dylan. What is Troy saying about the call?"

Andrea pressed her lips. "He's not saying anything."

Madison stiffened, anger pulsing through her with a life of its own. Why would Troy choose to keep quiet? This would all go away if he spoke the truth. The fact he wasn't talking suggested again that Troy had something to hide. But what? "So they have a journal and some story they sold themselves about a phone call. There must be more than that." She leveled her gaze at Andrea.

Andrea's cheeks flushed, and she nodded. "Dylan Graham was shot with Troy's Smith & Wesson."

The statement had Madison's entire body going weak, but that should be easy to dismiss. She'd just go to the gun box in their closet, find his gun, and the charges against him would go away.

Madison bounded up the staircase. Andrea's steps thumped behind her.

She took the box down from the top shelf and cussed, remembering she needed a key to open it. Going to the nightstand where she kept a copy, she collected it and stuck it into the slot and opened the lid.

The box was empty.

CHAPTER 10

Madison was parked back at the kitchen peninsula, the empty gun box in front of her on the counter. It was inside a plastic evidence bag that she had grabbed from the trunk of her car. She'd have it sent to the crime lab to process for prints.

"Here you go." Andrea handed her a huge glass of red wine from across the counter.

Madison took a few gulps. "I don't get this. It's impossible."

"Obviously someone got to it."

"I just don't see how. The box was locked. Where did they get the key?" She'd find it easier to imagine them taking the gun box with the gun or picking the lock. But it was locked behind them. They must have used her copy of the key. And then—what?—put it back? She took more gulps of wine, draining the glass at a quick rate. Meanwhile, Andrea was delicately sipping hers and watching Madison without judgment.

"Somehow, they knew where you kept it. They must have broken in just for that."

"Which means this was all premeditated," Madison said. "This person wants Troy to take the fall."

"You don't remember anything standing out, do you? The feeling that someone had broken into your home?"

Madison shook her head. "Not at all. Troy never mentioned anything like that either. Though, he'd need to actually talk to me to tell me that." She chewed on her bottom lip. "But that must have been what happened. Troy is your brother, my fiancé. We know him, and he's not a killer."

Andrea tapped the back of Madison's hand. "The truth will come out."

Madison nodded, but she wasn't going to sit back and wait. From her experience, the truth usually required painful drilling to expose. "Tell me everything you know about Graham's murder."

"Huh. Not much to tell yet." Andrea drank some of her wine and set her glass on the counter.

It was a lead Madison should follow. The amount she'd guzzled was already messing with her head, but she appreciated the light fuzzy edges where she could burrow in denial.

"The Braybury PD are being very tight-lipped with me. I'm quite sure they're holding back."

If it was anyone else but Troy standing accused, she could extend understanding. A murder investigation demanded confidentiality and discernment.

"All I know for certain is Dylan Graham was found by his maid Wednesday morning. No word about TOD, as I mentioned already."

"What about people who had an issue with him? Strained relationships?"

"Graham was divorced. His ex lives in Stiles. That's all I know about his personal life, aside from the fact both his parents are alive. Though I doubt they killed their son."

Madison drained the rest of her wine and only then set her glass on the counter. "The Braybury detectives aren't even bothering to do their jobs. They think they have the killer and are happy to stop there. The lazy sons of bitches." Her earlobes were sizzling hot with rage. She could never live with herself if she did such a piss-poor job.

"I know you're trying to just dismiss this, Madison, but they do have Troy's gun. It was found at the murder scene."

"And that's all it takes to convict a man?"

"I don't know what you want me to say here, but the Braybury PD isn't fooling around." Andrea shot back the rest of her wine.

CHAPTER 11

Everyone else in the department was long gone, even his partner, Jeremy Friedman. Carson Snow was at his desk, staring out the window on the other end of the bullpen. The stars were twinkling as if nothing in the world were amiss. If only that were true. Usually, Carson let the cases he worked roll off his back. He was good at keeping detached and objective, and it had earned him respect within the department and from his superiors. None of that was coming easy this time around.

Troy Matthews wasn't with the Braybury PD, but he donned the badge and fought for justice, nonetheless. Just like Carson. The difference between them was Matthews was facing a murder charge. And Carson owed it to the victim to do a good, thorough job regardless of whether the accused was a brother in blue. He couldn't allow himself to be blinded by personal feelings or the fact that he could be in the same jam himself one day. No, he'd follow the evidence. If it solidified a case against Matthews, then so be it. He wasn't about to be accused of playing favorites or turning a blind eye to the evidence. Though, speaking of which, one aspect from the scene niggled at him. It might be nothing, but it could be everything.

He hadn't shared this with Matthews's attorney or sister, but Carson could justify holding back. After all, this was a murder investigation. Add to that the close tie between the accused and the neighboring city's police chief. If he disclosed everything, she'd be relentless in pressuring him to follow through. Which Carson would, of course, but he didn't need the additional stress. He also didn't want to risk having his vision tainted or pigeon-holed. He would consider the whole picture, but he wasn't sure it would take Matthews out of his sight.

But he was holding on to the one thing weighing on him. It was a photocopy of the suicide note, and while his eyes scanned the page, he didn't need to read a word. He'd committed the letter to memory after already reading it a hundred times over. Not that it took that repetition to assimilate it. A grand total of fourteen words: *I'm sorry for past sins but take these with me now. To the grave.*

But while the note was short, it wasn't straightforward. Neither was its presence at a murder scene. There had to be some clue in that, but to hell if he knew what. Maybe if he could figure out what constituted Graham's "past sins," he'd be on his way, but good luck there. At fifty-six, Carson toted around a multitude of regrets, of *sins*, that he wished he could erase. A reminder of his biggest mistake was looking at him from an eight-by-ten silver frame on his desk.

Ashley, his seventeen-year-old daughter, wanted nothing to do with him anymore. She blamed him for her mother's affair, but he hadn't been there for his ex-wife. His dedication to his badge had been his mistress, and the job had taken his marriage as a casualty. At least they had parted on good terms. His ex was the reason he had Ashley's photo in the first place. She'd forwarded it, along with encouragement not to give up on the girl. Carson had tried to reach Ashley several times, but his calls always went to voicemail.

Just seventeen... The same age Emily Kane had been when she was raped and murdered. Carson couldn't imagine something so horrendous befalling Ashley. Emily's poor parents, and the hell they would have endured. How had they even moved on with their lives? Had a conviction helped ease their grief? It still didn't bring their daughter back to them. And now there was an accusation against another person. What would that mean for the Kane family? Surely it would strip them of any closure they'd grasped on to. Life really was so fragile and unpredictable.

"Oh, sweetheart, please give your old man a chance," he whispered to the photo, pleading with his daughter's image as if she could really hear him and grant his request. It was too late now, as it was after eleven at night, but he'd call her tomorrow, see if by chance the universe saw fit to grant his wish. For now, this investigation deserved his focus.

Were the past sins mentioned in the suicide note tied to the passage in his journal? Did it refer to guilt from keeping silent as to the real culprit behind Emily Kane's violent end?

His words had pointed directly at Troy Matthews. Meanwhile, Dylan Graham had sat back and watched his other friend Richie Klein be carted off to prison. That may very well be true, but what gnawed at Carson was the presence of a suicide note in the first place. Other elements of the scene suggested murder.

Was it a poor attempt to make a murder appear as suicide? But surely Matthews, with his history in law enforcement, wouldn't have messed up like this. Staging murder to look like suicide would have been easy for him to pull off. And he certainly wouldn't have left his gun at the scene. Yet one more thing eating away at Carson.

First thing in the morning, he'd make sure the lab processed the note and journal. He wanted them compared to other samples of Graham's handwriting to see if they were a match.

Despite these little anomalies, Carson wasn't holding his breath that it would be enough to release Troy Matthews from suspicion.

CHAPTER 12

Last night was one of the longest in his life. Between other people in the drunk tank—cop slang for the holding cell—mocking him as "Mr. Fancy Pants" and a few hookers and men hitting on him, Troy had hardly caught any sleep. When he dared to close his eyes, he saw Madison walking down the aisle in her wedding dress. How close they had come. And to think there were times he'd doubted if their relationship would progress that far. Not because he didn't believe in their future, but his first marriage had him swearing off the old institution. It was impressive he hadn't let his ex-wife's betrayal shatter his faith in people altogether. But he didn't see the point in living if that was his philosophy. Madison, on the other hand, had let her heartbreak make her far less trusting. He just hoped this latest turn of events wouldn't topple her belief in him. Would she see his arrest as a sign they shouldn't be together?

A uniformed officer came to the cell door and called out, "Troy Matthews."

Detective Snow stepped out from behind the officer.

Troy wasted no time pushing off the bench to get the hell out of there. "You're here to tell me I'm free to go?" He would latch on to the bubble of hope that rose up inside, but the sour expression on the detective's face told him the answer before his words.

"I'm just allowing you a visitor, Mr. Matthews," Snow told him as he stepped out of the cell and the officer locked the door again.

It wasn't a ticket home, but Troy was on the other side of the bars.

Snow took him down the hall and gestured for him to go inside a room. Troy hesitated, not sure how many more surprises he could handle, but he stepped into the doorway. It was a soft interview room, one that cops used to question suspects who didn't necessarily know they were suspects. There was a couch, a couple of chairs, a coffee table, some potted plants, and a credenza with a coffeemaker, cups, sugar, sweetener, and creamer.

Madison was on the couch, a carry-on bag at her feet. She looked up immediately when his shadow crossed the threshold.

Seeing the luggage burrowed the ache in his chest deeper. They were to be leaving for their honeymoon today. Was she here to say she was going without him? That she was leaving him? It must have been his tired mind messing with him. He knew her better than that. Madison was a fighter and loyal to those she cared about. Though she also tended to cut and run if she thought it would save her pain.

He was torn by his dual and competing reactions to her. Part of him wanted to retreat, embarrassed for her to see him like this. The other part wanted to run to her and sweep her into his arms.

Detective Snow left and closed the door behind him.

Madison stood, and the two of them bridged the distance. They stopped about a foot apart, peering into each other's eyes. He read hers, and they spoke of conflict, while her facial expression was soft.

He closed the remaining space between them and folded her into his arms. She hugged him back, melting against him, and laid her head on his chest.

"I'm so sorry," he said. "I should have called you last night, insisted that the detective let me." Did he get into the fact he was embarrassed, too angry, and lost for words? He knew Andrea would fill Madison in on where things stood.

Madison drew back and put a finger to his lips. "No apologies," she said, and then kissed him.

His heart swelled. *God, I love this woman!* He never should have doubted she'd remain by his side.

"We'll figure all this out together. Okay?" She leaned forward, and he lowered his forehead to meet hers.

"I'm so sorry for all this. Our wedding was ruined."

She stepped back and shook her head. "None of this is your fault. Well, unless you did kill the guy." Her attempt at joviality had the corners of her mouth lifting in an attempted smile.

"Don't even joke about it. Please."

"Now I'm sorry. Too soon?" She winked at him and touched his arm as she returned to the couch. He sat beside her and took her hands in his. Now that she was here, he couldn't bring himself to have any space between them.

"I brought you a change of clothes." She indicated the bag on the floor. "I thought you might be feeling a little overdressed."

He was still in his tuxedo, now wrinkled, and his sore feet were in dress shoes. "I appreciate that more than you could know." He almost confessed where his mind had gone when he saw the carry-on, that she was going on their honeymoon without him. Guilt grabbed hold that he had doubted her loyalty for an instant. "Thank you, Maddy."

"For the clothes? Of course."

"For them, yes, but also for standing by me."

"You doubted I would?"

He hesitated, not wanting to insult her, and landed on the right thing to say. "I can imagine it's been a trying experience for you."

She touched his cheek. "Trying, yes, but I'm not going anywhere. How are you holding up?"

"I've been better, not going to lie. How are you?" His voice came close to cracking. He just hated that she was dragged into all of this because of him.

"Same here. Not gonna lie either." She attempted another smile, but the expression faltered.

"You never could lie." Her honesty was just one characteristic he loved and respected about her. "I guess we'll need to rebook our honeymoon."

"I called this morning and took care of it." She was solemn as she informed him of this. She was likely thinking, as he was, that the trip might never get rescheduled. Madison added, "The resort is giving us a credit to use in the future, and we're getting a full refund from the airline because we had cancellation insurance."

Now wasn't the time to point out they had bought that at his insistence. "Not bad, then."

"We'll figure out all that later. Right now, we need to focus on getting you out of here." She looked down at their intertwined hands, obviously hesitating to say what she had on her mind.

"Maddy, what is it?"

"Why did you never mention Dylan Graham before?" She slowly pried her eyes up to meet his.

He suspected she was tiptoeing into Emily Kane territory. He was under no illusion that she hadn't learned about her and the basis of the case against him. This soft approach told him how much she loved him. Normally, she attacked, then stood defensive. The fact she was considering his feelings in all this when she'd be confused, frustrated, and sideswiped endeared her even more to him. "I wanted to forget that part of my past. Barry was the only person from that time that I stayed in touch with through the years." Just thinking about his lost friend again, the grief rushed back as if it were fresh, the wound still tender.

"And Joni? Was she with Barry then?"

Joni was Barry's widow. Troy shook his head. "They were seeing each other, but Joni wasn't at the party." He was going to talk as if Madison was aware of the Emily Kane case. If she had questions, she'd ask. The fact she hadn't raised any at the mention of the party confirmed his suspicion that she had done some research.

"Would she have known Dylan Graham and Richie Klein?"

"She would have."

"And Richie did that, to that girl?"

Troy wasn't comfortable talking about this in such depth with her. With anyone, really. He just wanted the past done and buried, no offence to Emily Kane.

"Troy, answer me," Madison said with a touch of heat.

"He was sentenced to prison, so I guess he must have."

"That's not what I'm wanting to hear. *I guess*?"

He pulled his hands back, anger coiling in his chest like a cobra. "What do you want me to say? Must I tell you I didn't do that to her?" All his earlier thoughts about her loyalty and faith in him washed away. This felt like she was accusing him. If she trusted him, if she really knew him, she wouldn't need him to state his innocence in so many words.

"Would it be nice to hear? You bet." She was breathing heavily, her chest heaving. "But it's not necessary." She reached for his hands again, which he reluctantly let her take. "I believe in you, Troy, but in exchange, I also deserve respect and straightforward answers. I heard that Dylan Graham thinks you raped and murdered her, not Klein. Why would he think that? Again, I'm not questioning your innocence. I'm just trying to wrap my head around where he'd get such a ludicrous notion."

"I have no clue." And he really didn't. He'd tossed that thought around a lot during the night.

"The Braybury police say they have your Smith & Wesson in evidence lockup, Troy. They're saying it was used to kill Graham, that you shot him to silence him from exposing you. I checked your gun box at home, and it was empty. Locked and empty."

"*Locked?*"

"Yep. But I still have my copy of the key. I assume yours is on your keychain?"

Now he was left to wonder whether it was. "I'd assume so."

"Well, you should check. But really that's neither here nor there. Someone got a hold of the key and helped themselves to your gun. Do you have any idea when it went missing or who might be trying to set you up?"

"None." He raked a hand through his hair. "But like you said, I'm being set up. Surely, the detectives will see that."

"Unfortunately, I don't think they can see past their noses. They think they have their man." Madison blinked, fat tears beading on her eyelashes. She swiped them away and waved a hand. "We'll get to the truth, though. When did you last see your S&W? Before the move? After?"

Troy had been over that in his mind too. "Before the move."

"Then someone broke in and stole it in the old house."

"Or stole it from the new one. It's not like I've reached for it for a long time. Either way, I think it's safe to conclude whoever is framing me has planned this for a while."

She nodded but didn't say anything.

"Neither of us noticed anything that indicated someone broke into our home."

"That just proves their only interest was your gun. Otherwise, other things would be missing. They were careful and watched their steps. The scary part is, if this person came into our home, they could easily have killed you, Troy."

"And you."

She shook her head. "I don't think they have an issue with me. It's you they have a vendetta with, and while they didn't kill you, they seem determined to destroy your life in other ways."

"Like framing me for Dylan's murder."

"Uh-huh. They don't just want you dead, they want you to suffer. Who hates you that much?"

"Good question. I'm to pick only one?" He was going for jovial, but it landed with a thud. He was forty-one and had been a cop since he was twenty-two. During that time, he put a lot of people away. Any one of them could be out for revenge, but he had a feeling this was more personal. As Madison pointed out, they wanted him to suffer, and this case also had Emily's name all over it. So who from his past was returning after twenty-four years to frame him?

CHAPTER 13

Madison didn't know what she had expected to see or feel when she brought clothes to Troy. No matter how much she braced herself for seeing him, she never could have prepared for the intense sadness that washed over her at the sight of him. Bags underscored his green eyes, which were slightly muted in color and bloodshot from exhaustion. Not that he'd admit how rough things were on him. He always put her feelings ahead of his own. He wouldn't want her to witness that he was hurting and disempowered.

Tears fell as she drove back to Stiles, and she let them go unchecked. Her heart tugged her to turn the car around, but there was nothing she could do hanging around the Braybury PD. While she had no doubt that Troy was innocent and being framed, she held no sway over the Braybury detectives. They told her they weren't free to discuss the details of the case with her, and she couldn't see a way to change their minds. Such utter bullshit! She was a detective herself, though Troy's badge wasn't making any difference for him. They had him locked up in a holding cell with actual criminals.

The worst part for her was not knowing what she could do to help him. It was frustrating as hell having so much falling outside of her control. That made her vulnerable, something she loathed.

Though one step she could take was getting a security system set up on the house, including cameras. That would provide some assurance of their safety and privacy.

Safety... She didn't want to dwell on what would have happened if the intruder had intended to kill them. It would seem they had gotten in and out of their home with Troy's gun undetected. They had been fortunate then, but she wasn't taking chances they would be again.

She turned up the music to drown out her fears. The primary one was Troy being wrongly convicted and sent away for life. As much as she believed in the system, it wasn't infallible. Innocent people were put behind bars. Some were even executed. And no one lost any sleep. The prosecution drifted into peaceful slumber convinced justice had prevailed. All because they whitewashed their consciences by clinging to incriminating evidence that was sometimes left to perception and interpretation. The same was happening here. Troy had a connection to the victim, a plausible motive, and his gun was on scene. On the surface, it was all damning.

Madison ended up turning the radio off. Her thoughts had just become louder to compete with the music. Instead, she played voicemails that were left while she'd been in with Troy.

The first message was from Chelsea. Her sister said that Hershey was good to stay with them as planned unless Madison wanted him back. It was tempting to get him and pet those soft, velvety ears of his, but having him hanging around the house wouldn't be fair to him. He was already set up at Chelsea's house, and he'd be the focus of her nieces' attention.

Cynthia called to check on Madison's well-being, and Terry said he was there if she needed anything. The most recent was from Andrea.

"Detectives Snow and Friedman agreed to a meeting at one o'clock this afternoon," she said. "Just me though. I'll fill you in as soon as I have more, but please, please, please, just wait for me and keep out of this."

Madison looked at the time on the dash. *12:05 PM.* It was tempting to turn around, if not for Andrea's desperate pleading that Madison keep out of it. But Andrea was greatly mistaken if she thought Madison wasn't going to do anything. If her and Troy's roles were reversed, and she was in trouble, Troy would stop at nothing to free her. She owed as much to him.

But where to start...

While the evidence against Troy seemed indisputable, Madison was armed with something the Braybury detectives were not. She had knowledge of Troy's character to keep her on track. He'd never kill a man in cold blood, and he certainly wouldn't have raped and murdered that girl as a teenager.

And along the lines of Emily Kane, it was clear that Graham's murder was linked to hers. The journal entry pointed there. It stood to reason this person was from Troy's distant past. But why stir up the past after all these years? And why frame Troy?

Troy had testified at Klein's trial. So had Graham. He was dead, and Troy was being framed for his murder. Was that a coincidence? Barry was the third friend but beyond the reach of retaliation. Assuming any of this was about that. This left Richie Klein, who was released from prison that past Tuesday. How did he factor in, or did he? She still didn't know Graham's time of death, but could Klein be seeking revenge on his childhood friends because their testimonies hadn't saved him? Maybe his time behind bars had warped his thinking. It would be easy to imagine as he had been just a boy when he went away. Whether or not he was guilty of the crimes against Emily Kane, he could want payback.

To accept this theory, though, how did that explain Graham's journal? But one step at a time. It would help if she could talk to Richie Klein, but she didn't have a clue where to find him.

Madison called Terry.

"Hey, Maddy, how are you hanging in?" His voice came over the Mazda's speakers.

She hadn't even stopped to consider the effect his empathy would have on her. Fresh tears filled her eyes. "I'm… Well, this isn't about me as much as it is Troy."

"This affects you just as much. What's the latest?"

She filled him in about the arraignment Monday morning and the so-called evidence they had against Troy, including the journal and allegation that Troy also raped and murdered Emily Kane. She left out mention of taking Troy a change of clothes and that she'd left him the better part of two hours ago, not trusting herself to keep an even emotional keel. And she needed to project strength for what she wanted to ask Terry.

"For what it's worth, this is ridiculous. There's no way Troy would kill a man."

"It might be up to us to prove that."

Terry went silent, probably gnawing on the *us* part.

"You know what I mean," she said. "The evidence. It's up to that to prove his innocence."

"Uh-huh. I think you meant it the way you originally said it, Madison. But you're too close to this, not to mention the case belongs to the Braybury PD."

"This is Troy we're talking about."

"I get that, but I'm sure it will all get worked out."

So people kept saying, and she wished she had their faith. What she did have was hardheaded determination to make their words come true. "Then if I asked you for a favor, you'd tell me where to stick it?"

"I never said that."

"Then I need a favor."

Nothing. Not a sound. She was starting to wonder if the call had been dropped.

"Terry?"

"Whatever you need."

His willing response had her taking a couple of beats, especially after his caution a moment ago. When he said to call if she needed anything, she'd been certain there would be restrictions. She looked at the dash of her car, as if she were looking at Terry. Normally, her partner took extreme measures to keep the metaphorical boat level. Heaven forbid there was any rocking. "I need to know where to find Richie Klein. He was released from prison last Tuesday. He needs to be staying somewhere. Family, a friend, at a motel? I have no way of knowing. That's why I need your help."

"It's fine. I'll do what I can, as fast as I can."

She was prepared to defend her position, placate him, tell him no one needed to know he was helping her. His agreement let a sliver of light into the darkness that had otherwise engulfed her. "Thank you. I can't say that enough."

"You don't even need to say it. We're family."

She bobbed her head, as if he could see, too choked up to speak. Eventually, she muttered another thank-you and hung up.

Madison was overcome with gratitude mingled with grief. Their time as partners was running out.

She took the turn into her driveway. The sight of the house knotted sadness into her chest. She and Troy should be leaving on their honeymoon, not stuck in limbo wondering what tomorrow held.

She sat there with the car idling, unable to bring herself to go inside right away. It was as if by doing so she was surrendering and giving up. But there must be something she could do. And then it hit. She wasn't without resources. The murder seemed to revolve around Emily Kane, and she knew just the person who might be able to shed some light on her.

CHAPTER 14

It was twelve thirty when Madison pulled into Joni's driveway. Andrea would be meeting with the Braybury detectives in thirty minutes. If Madison hadn't figured out a way to make good use of her time, she'd have been going crazy thinking about Andrea being there while Madison sat on her hands.

Joni opened the front door and waved Madison inside. "Just set your shoes on the front mat. Hang your coat on any hook you want. Tea?"

"Coffee?" Madison countered, grateful that Joni was a close enough friend that she didn't overload her with questions on sight.

"You got it. Make yourself at home."

"Thank you."

"Don't mention it." Joni's voice traveled from the kitchen, in the back of the house.

Madison went to the front sitting room and stared out the picture window. Light flurries had started to fall. She wished to let the snowflakes distract her, pull her into a daydream where everything was right in her life. Instead, she was noting the contrast between the beautiful imagery and the current nightmare she and Troy were living.

In the background, Joni was working a K-cup machine. A distinct clunk of the pod being punctured. The ensuing hiss as the coffeemaker pushed hot water through the grounds. The dripping into the waiting cup.

"Maddy?" It was Allison, Joni and Barry's eldest daughter, and she was the spitting image of her mother. Allison hugged her.

"How are you doing, kiddo? Enjoying Christmas break?" At the age of sixteen, she might be too old to be called *kiddo*, but if it bothered her, she hadn't let on.

"It's just started, but I'm sure I will."

That's right... Madison had known that because she and Troy had considered this when planning their wedding date. That had slipped her mind with all that had taken place over the last couple of days. "Any big plans?"

"Not really, no. Christmas was more Dad's thing than any of ours."

This would be the second Christmas without her father. Madison might do best to keep her mouth shut, but disregarding any mention of him didn't seem right either. "He sure did like it, didn't he? I remember he'd always be handing out candy canes to people."

"Yeah. Even strangers sometimes." Allison rolled her eyes but smiled.

"Well, I'm sure you and your sisters will find something fun to do. Speaking of, where are they?"

"Around. Say, what's going on with Uncle Troy? Is he going to be okay? That detective who carted him off looked like a—" She bit her bottom lip, likely running her word choice through a mental filter.

Madison would save her the trouble. "He did, and he is." It was a safe bet that would cover any adjective the girl had in mind.

Joni walked into the room, holding two mugs, and gave one to Madison. "Thanks."

Joni shook her head. "No need to say that to family." She dropped onto a recliner near the window and leaned back to pop out the leg support. "Allison, could you give me and Maddy a chance to talk alone?"

Allison looked between them and then seemed to decide she'd do her mother the favor of honoring her request.

With her gone, Joni leveled her gaze at Madison. She didn't say a word and took a sip of her coffee. She must be curious about Madison's reason for being there, but she didn't pry.

Madison sat on the couch, which faced the window. She'd do Joni a favor and save her from asking, but she'd ease into it. "Troy's facing murder charges."

"I heard the detective say that. Isn't he a piece of work."

Madison nodded, not caring much for him either, but at least he'd allowed her to see Troy and bring him a change of clothes. Still, that didn't offset the fact he'd had Troy dragged from his wedding in cuffs. Or that he might be lazy and incompetent.

"But Troy wouldn't murder anyone, let alone Dylan."

Madison perked up at the nonchalant way she'd put Dylan's name out there. She had come here to get more information on Emily Kane and just may already be on her way. In a mere handful of seconds, Joni had confirmed remembering Dylan. Though she could be getting carried away putting any stake in this meaning anything. Joni had been dating Barry back then, so it made sense she'd know his friend Dylan. Still, she asked, "You knew Dylan Graham?"

Joni bobbed her head and sipped her coffee.

Madison drank some of hers. She felt it go all the way down her throat and land in her stomach. As much as coffee had sounded good in theory, her gut was in knots. "Did you also know Emily Kane?"

Joni's face shadowed, and she cradled her cup with two hands. "It's been a very long time since I've heard that name. Why are you asking about her?"

Hot tears came to Madison's eyes, so unexpected and unwanted.

"Oh, sweetie." Joni popped out of her chair, setting her mug on the table beside it, and sat next to Madison on the couch. She grabbed her hand. "Anything I can do?"

She nodded but couldn't bring herself to speak. She hated showing vulnerability, even to Joni. And just when Madison had thought she'd gotten better at accepting that aspect of herself. As her therapist put it, to be vulnerable was to be human. It didn't make her weak or less-than in any way. Troy's arrest was testing her therapist's belief. "I'm not sure if you can help, but I came here hoping so." She swiped her cheeks of the few tears that had fallen.

"Whatever it is. Does it have to do with Emily? Is that why you asked about her? Though I'm not sure what that has to do with Troy's arrest." Joni narrowed her eyes, her brows pressed down.

Madison took a few staggered breaths to calm herself, choosing to implement this lesson from her therapist. She'd also pull from her cop training and push from her mind that the questions she came here to ask could affect Troy's future. Rather, she'd view it as making inroads to uncover the truth in a murder investigation. "I'll get to that. Let's just say the Braybury police have evidence against Troy for Dylan Graham's murder."

"How could they?" Joni was shaking her head. "I mean, there's no way he would have killed him."

"I know it, you know it, but they are convinced they have their killer. I'm not supposed to poke my nose in, but how can I not get involved? This is Troy."

"Yeah, yeah, of course." Joni rubbed Madison's arm. "I'd be the same if... Well, if a loved one was in trouble with the police. And Troy is family. What is this evidence?" she asked timidly, as if she were afraid the answer would bite her.

Madison told her about the phone call, the journal, his S&W, and summed up with, "On the surface, it's all damning."

"Sadly, it is. I'd say he's been set up," Joni said. "But who would do such a thing?"

Madison pressed her lips and shrugged. She had considered Richie Klein, but at this point, her suspicion about him wasn't rooted in anything definitive, only her theory that he might now see his teen friends as his enemies. "I'm hoping I can figure it out."

"And it's because of this journal they think Troy was actually responsible for Emily's rape and murder? And Troy killed Graham to keep him quiet?"

"That's right."

"That's the most ridiculous thing I've ever heard. Now, Richie might not have done it though. You know who he is, I assume?"

"I do. Are you suggesting you had doubts about Richie's guilt?"

"Not sure. But there were a lot of people who had it out for Emily. She wasn't just part of the in-crowd. She was the in-crowd. Well, her and her two close girlfriends. The three of them called themselves the Holy Trinity and looked down on pretty much everyone else."

It didn't sound like Joni was a fan, and Madison didn't blame her, but the fact remained Emily did not deserve what had happened to her. Emily never had the chance to grow up or to shed the arrogance, but hopefully her two friends had. "What were the friends' names?"

"You really are trying to get my memory working. Melissa Hatfield, if I remember right, was one. That could be different by now. She could be married. The other is Brooke Morales. That is her married name, which I know for sure because we're friends on social media."

"You did good remembering that much." Madison was impressed. "You said a lot probably had it out for Emily. Anyone specific come to mind?"

"I've got a good memory, but nothing's sparking."

That might be because Joni had never truly suspected someone else of killing Emily. "Well, with Emily being so popular, I assume she had a lot of admirers and boyfriends."

"And groupies." Joni smiled, but the expression faded quickly. "She had guys lapping out of her hand."

Madison overlooked the cliché, sensing an underlying jealousy. "You had Barry though, right?"

At the mention of her late husband, Joni returned to her chair and curled her feet up under her. "I did. We hadn't been seeing each other for long when Emily was murdered."

"And you weren't at the party that night?" Madison hated that all the questioning struck her as if she were interrogating Joni, but her friend said she was willing to help. Doing this was offering Madison some comfort, as mining for answers was familiar ground.

"I see you've been talking to Troy about me?"

"Your name came up when we were talking. It's why I came here," Madison admitted. "I thought you might know something that could help. Why weren't you at the party?"

"I wanted to be. How badly I wanted to be," she added with a smile, her eyes taking on a wistful daydream look. "I was crazy about Barry, and he was excited about the party. But my parents had different plans for that week. They insisted on dragging me out of town for a *family vacation*." The pitch of her voice took the place of actual finger quotes. "Meanwhile, Dad was on the phone all weekend with business, and Mom was drinking vodka martinis by the pitcher."

Madison had met Joni's parents when Barry died, and given that it sounded like they had gone through a rough patch, they had traversed it successfully.

"I found out Emily was killed when I got back," Joni said. "Barry came over to tell me in person. I could hardly believe it. What I haven't told you yet was Emily and I were best friends in elementary school. We just went our separate ways come high school. Suddenly I wasn't cool enough for her. But she did have a gentle and caring side that she'd show me. She dreamed of being an artist from the time she was little. Her parents wanted her to become a doctor, told her there was no money in the arts. But even in eighth grade, she was really good. Of course, I am speaking the opinion of a child."

"That's understandable." Madison had a friendship like that herself that hadn't survived the transition to secondary school. It was probably more common than a person realized. "So in your personal opinion, do you think Richie did it?" Joni had deflected earlier by saying there could have been many others, so Madison thought she'd ask again.

"Who am I to say? A jury of twelve found him guilty."

"But I'm not asking about them. I'm asking for *your* opinion."

Joni took a drink of her coffee. A few seconds ticked by. "I don't know. I really don't. Richie was a jokester and could be a bit of a chauvinist. Barry told me he picked that up from his father. I wasn't a fan of his for that reason. But to rape *and* kill Emily? I don't know if he was capable of something quite that evil."

"Quite *that* evil?" Madison angled her head, her cop instincts telling her there was more Joni hadn't said.

"Well, back in ninth grade, a rumor went around that Richie assaulted some girl. A rumor," Joni stressed. "It must have just been that, as nothing ever came of it."

Madison wasn't so confident. Rumors usually contained some nugget of truth. And going from assault to rape and murder wasn't an enormous leap. He could have been emboldened from getting away with his first crime. It could be as she'd theorized before, and he was taking revenge against friends he felt didn't fight strong enough for his innocence. Still, she asked, "And you're sure no other names pop into your head?"

Joni shook her head. "I have no clue."

Madison tamped down her frustration and took another drink of her coffee. The brew curdled in her gut, and she set the cup on the coffee table. Just because Joni didn't think Richie was capable didn't mean he was innocent. There was that rumor. "Do you remember that girl's name, the one that Richie was accused of assaulting?"

"Really? You know how long ago that was? I like to think I've got a good memory, but I had no reason to hold on to her name. I never believed the allegation. Barry always liked Richie, even with his rough edges, and he was sort of the leader of the group. Richie, not Barry."

It was surprising a young Troy would tolerate a chauvinist, let alone be submissive to one. "Who stepped up when Richie was sent away?"

"The boys went their separate ways, well, except for Troy and Barry. Dylan disappeared not long after the trial. I heard he went to college out of state. He obviously came back at some point because, well, he was killed in Braybury. I just keep thinking the police actually arrested Troy for murder. It's on a replay spool in my head. It's unbelievable."

"I know the feeling."

"It's shock. Like after Barry died. As sick as this sounds, I kept picturing him lying there not breathing. It was unimaginable, until one day it seemed to sink in. He was gone."

She'd done the same when her grandmother had died. It must have been a natural part of grieving and acceptance. "He was such a good man."

"That he was. Such a loving husband and father."

"And friend," Madison added with a smile. While it might take time for Troy's arrest to sink in, she didn't want to accept it. Unlike a loss to death, it wasn't over for him yet. If it took finding the real killer herself, so be it. *Just how to do that...*

"Now, I keep going over all you told me," Joni began, "and I keep thinking about how this person could have gotten their hands on Troy's S&W. Could it have been when you moved? You did hire a moving company, I assume, and you would have noticed if someone broke into your house."

She and Troy had considered someone breaking into their home, but not what Joni had just suggested. Madison jumped to her feet. "I've got to go."

CHAPTER 15

Sunday afternoons were good for lazing around and watching football. At least that was what Carson's partner, Jeremy Friedman, would tell him. Personally, Carson wasn't much of a sports fan and preferred to spend his time doing something physical, hiking being one of his foremost pleasurable ways of passing free time. Not that this job allowed for much. And there would be no football or hiking today.

Carson entered a meeting room with Jeremy, where Andrea Fletcher was already seated at the conference table.

Andrea crossed her legs when they sat across from her and eyed them, clearly sizing them up. And he didn't blame her. They did drag her younger brother in on murder charges. Even though there was cause, he didn't expect this to be a friendly meeting.

Carson himself would need to set aside his minuscule doubts, or she might read them easily. He'd made his concerns with this case known to his sergeant, but the man was having nothing to do with it. He should have expected as much. Sergeant Joseph Durham was a rank climber and eager to make a name for himself. He'd swooped into the position, taking over when Carson thought he would be considered for the job. The slight shouldn't have come as a surprise either, as Durham was the brother-in-law of the Braybury police chief, but it still stung. Carson felt he was far more qualified, and he would have been a fair, objective boss. Durham was more concerned with how things might look if they relinquished Matthews this soon after his arrest. He expressed fear over the department being seen as affording leniencies to Troy Matthews simply because he was a cop. Then and there, Carson's mediocre respect for the man had diminished altogether. Following the evidence to justice was a commitment one made to the badge. Unfortunately, if Carson ever wanted to see his retirement package, he was forced to play along for now.

Jeremy had pulled his chair out from the table, swung it around, and straddled it backward like he was some sort of cowboy. *The ridiculous cockiness of youth,* Carson thought. Between Jeremy and a green sergeant, an early retirement held allure.

Andrea drew her gaze from Jeremy to him, and he pressed his lips and dipped his head in greeting.

"Tell me everything you have, Detectives." Andrea had her chair out from the table and clasped her slender, manicured fingers over her crossed knee.

"We can't tell you *everything*."

Carson abruptly turned to Jeremy, and he stopped talking. *Praise the Lord!* Normally any reprimands went unheeded. "Ms. Fletcher—"

"*Chief* Fletcher, though I believe we had that conversation." She kept glancing at Jeremy, likely fixated on his declaration they weren't ready to share all they knew.

"*Chief* Fletcher," Snow began, "you are familiar with the evidence we have against your brother, and we're not at liberty to discuss any more." He wished to come clean about the suicide note, but he was told in plain language not to cause trouble for the department. They wanted the case closed quickly.

"Well, now I'm confused. If you don't plan on being open with me, why agree to this meeting?" She cocked her head to the right, her lips in a tight line.

"I should have clarified. We are prepared to discuss aspects aside from the evidence." He was to stick to the basics, like time and cause of death. The sergeant had stressed *under no circumstances* were they to mention the suicide note.

Andrea's jaw stiffened, and she gestured for him to speak.

Carson didn't mistake her silence for concession or surrender. She was angry and biding her time. It was the fire in her eyes that gave her away. They belonged to a tiger roaming the jungle that was ever cognizant and aware. Carson was well familiar with her type, and they kept everyone around them on guard. Her gaze also had a way of penetrating Carson's mind. As long as she couldn't read his thoughts.

He resisted the urge to clear his throat, even though he desperately needed to do so. "Dylan Graham's time of death was Tuesday night between four and six PM. He was found by his maid the next morning, Wednesday, at nine AM. She was cleared, before you ask." He prattled off the details, adhering to the script his sergeant wanted him to follow. *Such an asinine update.* And, obviously, Wednesday was the next morning…

Andrea held up a hand. "I knew about the maid, but before we go on, tell me more about Dylan Graham himself. Did you investigate other people in his life who might have wanted him dead?"

"Your brother's gun was at the scene," Jeremy was quick to toss out. "His prints were on it."

Andrea didn't give the impression she'd been affected by Jeremy's sharp response and slowly drew her gaze to Carson.

"My partner is correct, which you know, but…" Carson straightened his tie, cursing internally for showcasing just how uncomfortable he was feeling. He'd expected the chief's question but wasn't fully prepared to feed her the line he'd been given.

"But, Detective Snow, it makes sense my brother's prints would be on his gun. It doesn't eliminate the possibility that the real killer wore gloves." The way she put that out there in such a cool manner, given the stakes involved, earned Carson's respect.

"It doesn't mean that happened either," Jeremy said, jumping in before Carson could reply. "We've already told you your brother's motive."

Andrea exhaled, elongating the silence, and her shoulders tensed. "If you would be so kind as to actually answer my question. Have you considered other suspects?"

If Carson was going to get through this meeting with some pride intact, he had to focus on the facts they did have against Matthews. They had the gun and the journal, giving them means and motive. Opportunity was conceivable because Troy Matthews had been in contact with Dylan Graham just days before his murder. "Mr. Graham left behind his parents and an ex-wife. No children, no current girlfriend, and no enemies that we know of." It was a sweeping statement with zero substance, and he hoped the Stiles PD chief wouldn't call him out on it. The truth was the brass had their killer behind bars and didn't intend on allocating manpower to the pursuit of what they viewed as a frivolous endeavor.

Andrea dipped her head, but a quick shadow crossed her facial features. "No enemies that you know of," she parroted, poking at the raw point in his statement.

"That's right." He resisted the urge to straighten his tie again and overcompensated by sitting up straighter.

"Uh-huh. What about signs of forced entry? It could be that the shooter broke into Dylan Graham's home and killed him."

"For what purpose?" Jeremy volleyed back. "There was no evidence of a robbery. And how would that explain your brother's gun at the scene? Come on."

His partner was such an adolescent, and he'd just opened a mess. Carson cringed, suspecting where this conversation would now go, but he was unable to stop it. Just like a boulder rolling down a hill, the result was going to be disaster. Call it a hunch.

"Then you did an inventory of his home? Who did you verify his possessions with?" A slight blush hit Andrea's cheeks.

"All my partner means is there was nothing to indicate that someone broke into the home," Carson clarified.

"In other words, you didn't investigate this angle at all. And before you say it again, Detective

Friedman, I'm aware you have Troy's gun," Andrea said coolly, a judgment and accusation not far from the surface. She either saw them as incompetent or manipulated. Carson didn't like either one. "Do you have any eyewitnesses that put Troy Matthews at Graham's home the night of his murder?"

"We don't, but that doesn't mean he wasn't there." Carson rushed this out. He wanted to reply before his idiot partner did and made things worse. They didn't need her questioning whether they asked around too. He heard it himself, how this investigation was botched and biased. There could have been another explanation for Matthews's gun and the journal, one that didn't implicate him.

"Huh. Yet you said his time of death was between four and six PM. Not exactly the middle of the night. People would be out and about. Many would be getting home from work, kids from school. They were in class last week."

This woman was sharp, but he'd admire the quality more if her laser focus wasn't on him. He was pissed that he was in a position that made him look incompetent. If only he'd been allowed to conduct this investigation as he'd wanted. Before he could respond, she spoke again.

Andrea uncrossed her legs and leaned forward. "No one reported a gunshot? Was a silencer used?"

Carson shook his head, feeling this meeting slipping right out of his hands. Chief Fletcher had taken it and was shaking it like a dog with a stuffed toy in its jowls. Though she clearly wasn't having fun. The more she stood for her brother's defense, the deeper red her cheeks became. Carson wasn't a fool to mistake it for anything other than increasing anger.

"I'm just a little stuck on this point. A man was shot in the early evening, and no one heard a sound?"

That was the consensus among canvassing officers, but it hadn't been a point that was given much credence. It was obvious a gun had been fired. The bullet in Dylan Graham's cold, dead body was all the proof they needed. "As you mentioned, that is a busy time of day. People are caught up in their agendas. Also remember that Graham was shot in his home."

A slight smirk. "You and I both know the sound of gunfire would travel through the walls of a well-insulated house."

There was no mistaking her judgment of their work, but in this case, it was what it was. "Most people wouldn't know gunfire if they heard it. They'd mistake it for a car backfiring or someone setting off a firework."

"Fireworks in the late afternoon, early evening? Did uniformed officers ask about this when they canvassed the neighborhood?"

"We've disclosed everything we're at liberty to," Carson said. In fact, they'd ended up sharing more.

"Says who?" Andrea volleyed back, and Carson swore under his breath.

He'd been concerned about Jeremy exposing them to inquiries, and he'd just done it himself.

"Detective Snow, is someone else controlling the direction of this investigation?" Andrea angled her head, her lips pursed.

Carson would be shooting himself in the back if he served up his sergeant's name. He was a miserable pissant and nearly a decade his junior, but he held Carson's career in his hands. "As the lead detective on this murder investigation, what we reveal is at my discretion, Chief Fletcher." He squared his shoulders and leaned forward, projecting authority and strength. "No doubt, as a fellow officer of the law, you can appreciate that it is necessary to hold back some aspects in a case from third parties." Even as he prattled all of this off, his conscience was prodding at him like a steaming, hot poker. He also had his pride to contend with, as he wasn't typically prone to being swayed by other people. Yet here he was, letting the sergeant take his strings and make him dance.

"You need to come forward to the defense with everything you have. It's not ethical to hide your hand."

"You are right," Snow said, "to the defense. This meeting was granted as a courtesy."

Andrea's eyes glassed over, and her cheeks burned crimson.

As bad as Carson felt, he had grasped on to his position of control. "Since you are not with the defense or officially assigned to this case, we were under no obligation to share anything with you. Not even as much as we have. I trust you understand our position."

Seconds ticked by on the clock on the wall. Each one a tiny *thunk* taking another potshot at his moral code. He'd never sacrificed his values before now, but he hadn't worked hard all these years to lose his retirement package just as he was getting close to using it. If he violated direct orders and was terminated, there was the real risk of that happening.

Eventually, Andrea dipped her head and stood. She left the room without thanking him for what he had shared, but Carson didn't blame her. In her eyes, he was a snake, which was exactly how he felt. There were pieces of this case that didn't click together, and he was being bullied into making them fit. All to boost Sergeant Durham's image and that of the department. Rubbish. Justice should come ahead of such shallowness. Carson had a tough decision to make. He could carry on being Durham's lackey or stand his ground. All he knew for certain right now was he couldn't continue living like this.

CHAPTER 16

Madison had forgotten about the rental company coming to pick up the chairs at the house until she received Chelsea's text that it had happened. Then again, it wasn't something she had to commit to memory because it would have been taken care of while she was on a flight to Mexico for her honeymoon. Going home after Troy's arrest had been tough with it fully decorated. But the thought of seeing it empty of the chairs felt like more than she could handle. At least she had something to delay her from going home.

The snow had stopped by the time she pulled into the parking lot for Tiptop Movers. They were the company she and Troy had hired to move them. They had done a marvelous job, but what if one of them did take Troy's gun to frame him? It would suggest the plan had been in the works for at least a couple of months.

And if it was someone at the moving company, that could eliminate Richie Klein as a suspect. He'd been in prison up until early last week. Although it was possible he had an accomplice on the outside. It might be too soon to rule anyone out. She smiled at her conclusion, but it was how she worked. Everyone was guilty until proven innocent. It was a point Terry often called her out on. But she was unapologetic in this. Her career and life experiences made her skeptical. She wasn't deluded into thinking that everyone was good and kind with others' best interests at heart. Rather, many were out for themselves. They'd lie and cheat to protect their secrets, and there were no boundaries on how low some would sink.

A few big moving trucks were in the lot, with the company's name and logo emblazoned on the sides. Another one pulled in, and Madison turned to watch them park. Two men were in the cab, and the one in the passenger seat had helped with their move.

She made her way over, beelining to the man she recognized. There were two different approaches she could use. One, go in hot and accusatory, flashing her badge. Two, play it cool and keep her gold shield out of it. Her impulse steered her toward the first, but she wasn't going to take any chance of being found out and stopped by Andrea. After all, Troy's freedom was at stake. "Hi there," she said to the man.

Her casual and familiar greeting was initially met with a side-glance to his partner, followed by a slight bob of his head. He flashed a smile at Madison. "Hello."

His colleague left them and carried on toward the building.

"I think you helped my fiancé and me move a couple months ago. Sorry I can't remember your name." Not that she recalled asking for it at the time.

"Billy Roth."

"Do you remember me?" Playing things cool wasn't her strong suit. Neither was hiding her true feelings, but that didn't stop her from continuing to try.

"Ah." The man scrunched up his face, fine lines creasing into deeper grooves around his eyes. "Maybe? But don't take it personally. I move a lot of people. What can I do ya for?"

"I heard you might know someone I'm trying to reach." Asking immediately about the gun would risk getting Roth's back up. Besides, even if he was the thief and the killer, he wouldn't admit to it, so she decided on another route. She might be able to find something to support her theory of a partnership. "His name is Richie Klein."

Confusion washed over his expression, and he shook his head. "Nope, I've never heard of him. Someone told you I did?"

"You know what? Never mind." She waved a hand, trying to feign the stereotypical blond airhead and hating herself for every second she assumed the role. And she could be wasting her time with Roth. It could have been the other man assigned to their move who was connected to Richie Klein. Or neither of them. It was possible the theory that a mover took Troy's gun was a bust. She turned to leave.

"Hey! You!" A large man in coveralls was closing the distance between the shop and them. He had a meaty finger pointed at Madison. "Who are you?"

"A customer," she shot back, her earlobes heating at his brash approach. "Do you treat everyone this way?"

The man lowered his arms. His ruddy cheeks were balled, and the flesh of his face plump. His thick neck spilled above the collar of his shirt. "I'm the manager here. What can I help you with?"

"I was just talking with Mr. Roth here." She gestured to him, and the bigger man pulled a handkerchief from a pocket and wiped it across his forehead.

"Well, Billy here has work to do, don't ya? Another few hours on the clock." He popped his eyes at his employee.

"I better go." Roth took off, and seeing him leave, Madison wished she'd just gotten right to Troy's Smith & Wesson.

"Is there something I can help you with?" The manager pushed his hankie back into his pocket but left a corner peeking out.

"My fiancé and I hired your company two months ago for our move."

"I appreciate your business, but what brings you here today? It looked like you were asking Billy some questions."

Madison thought Winston was bad with his need to talk everything to death, but this man hung over his employees. She could just cut and run, or voice her concerns as a customer. "Something very important has gone missing." Technically it wasn't missing, but it wasn't in their home.

"Were you blaming Billy for that?"

"Not once." Her temper was heating up. Trying to suppress her direct nature was almost killing her.

"Well, good. Billy's not who you'd lodge such a complaint with anyway. That would be me. You'll need to fill out a form, and then we'll investigate."

His word choice wasn't missed, though at least he was being honest by implying he wouldn't be personally addressing the matter. "And how long would that take?"

"Depends, but I can assure you every one of my employees is bonded. Is it possible you misplaced this item yourself?"

Her earlobes caught fire. "Is blaming customers standard practice?"

"I never said that."

"It was implied."

A few beats, then, "I apologize if I offended you, but if you fill out our form, I'll make sure it gets priority attention."

She could read between the lines and deduced exactly what he meant by *priority attention.* More likely, it was another name for File 13 or the garbage can.

"If you'll just come with me." The manager turned back to the building, but Madison hesitated.

A claim would leave a written record that she was here poking around. If this reached Andrea or Sergeant Winston, she'd have to explain herself. But an even worse possibility occurred to her. She'd rushed ahead wanting to see if she could tie Richie Klein to someone here, but that was a double-edged sword. If she was onto something with the partnership idea, her coming here could have placed her and Troy's lives in danger. Putting her name on paper exposed her to anyone who had access to the office.

The manager raised his eyebrows. "So… that form?"

"Sure, I'll fill it out, but as a detective with the Stiles PD."

"A detective?"

"Uh-huh." She'd rather have the department involved if the worst possibility came to reality. "Though I must say I'm not impressed by your customer service."

The manager grimaced, and she got a sickening feeling in her gut that this little visit was going to bite her in the ass. But as long as it didn't get her or Troy killed, she'd deal with it.

CHAPTER 17

Madison was beating herself up about going to Tiptop Movers. Then for filing a claim and potentially making things worse. But second-guessing herself wouldn't get her anywhere. And people with the moving company might not have anything to do with Troy's gun ending up next to the body of a dead man anyhow.

Ack! A headache was blooming in her temples.

Her thoughts were spinning in circles. *Were the movers involved? Weren't they? Who is behind this? Why? Is Richie Klein out for revenge?* Round and round she went.

Terry hadn't called yet with Richie Klein's location, but Winston may have somehow found out what he was trying to do and shut him down. Nothing would surprise Madison about that man. She wouldn't even be shocked to find out the Braybury detectives had notified him before swooping in to arrest Troy.

She went home, not knowing where else to go. With Troy in jail, she was existing in a world that had tilted upside down, and it had her feeling lost.

Stepping inside their house, she braced herself to see an empty living room. As Chelsea had told her, the rental company took the chairs. What she hadn't mentioned was that she'd returned the room to its normal state. The furniture was brought up from the basement and was back in place. The flower urns were tucked into the corners.

Tears sprung to Madison's eyes.

While it was kind of her sister to do this, seeing it back to normal drilled in how *unnormal* everything was right now. It also somehow amplified her grief about all that had been recently lost. The wedding, the honeymoon, their freedom. Possibly their future.

And she was here, in her empty house, without another heartbeat. No Troy. No Hershey.

She dropped onto the couch and cried, letting some of the hurt out of her system. There was no ignoring the deep ache in her heart. The sadness was so overwhelming, and she needed to process some of it if she wanted to do any good for Troy.

After a few minutes, she blew her nose and gave herself an internal pep talk. *You've got this. Save Troy.*

But what could she try next? She'd gone to Joni focused on the past, and maybe that was the best place for her to remain. The Graham investigation was assigned to the Braybury PD and obviously hit very close to home. But if she could remove Troy from suspicion of Emily Kane's murder, the rest of the case they had against him would topple. Starting with his motive. They said Troy wanted to silence Dylan Graham, but there would be no need if his innocence in Emily's murder was proven beyond a doubt.

And if she was putting her efforts into the past, she had two potential leads in Emily's best friends. Madison would like their opinion on Richie Klein, and while Joni hadn't remembered, one of them might know who he had allegedly assaulted in ninth grade.

She went to the home office and googled Melissa Hatfield. While she might be going by a different surname these days, there was still the chance the query could net a social media account noting her maiden name.

Nada.

She was more confident when she typed *Brooke Morales*. Joni had said they were friends on social media, so she must exist online. And bingo.

Madison clicked the link and looked at the profile picture. It showed a good-looking family of four. The couple was in their forties, and the boy and girl were in the age range of six to eight. From what Brooke showed the world, she had the house, the kids, and the white picket fence. She had a fair complexion, blond hair styled straight and with dark roots, blue eyes, and gold hoop earrings. The man's coloring was darker, with olive skin, brown hair, and brown eyes. Both were smiling, their expressions striking Madison as genuine. Even the children appeared happy.

But beyond this photo, Madison couldn't get anything. Brooke's privacy settings were tight and only allowed friends to see her information and her friends list.

Madison could ask Joni if she knew where Brooke lived, but she had gotten the impression the *friendship* was online and distant. She also wanted to involve Joni as little as possible. That limit had already been reached, as far as Madison was concerned.

Google wasn't offering much more either. No phone numbers came up with either search. Not that it was surprising with so many forgoing landlines and privatizing their cell numbers.

To get further she'd need to pull official backgrounds, and Sergeant Winston would never let that fly.

Madison banged a hand on the desk. So freaking frustrating!

She took a few breaths and called Andrea. The line rang to voicemail. Was that a good sign or bad? Did it carry any meaning?

If she didn't stop her spiraling thoughts, she was going to quickly lose her mind.

She ended the call without leaving a message, and her phone rang immediately. "Andrea?"

"Ah, it's Terry. You do have caller ID?"

"I just didn't look. You have something for me?"

"Not yet, but I know how angry you get when you don't receive updates. I'm still working on tracking down Klein. No luck so far. Not for lack of trying. I even spoke with his parents, who, by the way, want nothing to do with him."

Madison had been debating Richie Klein's involvement, but what Terry just said gave the man more ammunition for motive. He had spent his entire adult life thus far in prison and apparently also lost his family.

"You hear me?" Terry prompted.

"I did." What she heard was Klein seemed more probable as a suspect than before.

"I'm doing all I can. I'm not about to give up."

"I know you never would." Her respect for Terry increased when he told her he was going to take the sergeant's exam, even if she was sad about losing their partnership. But he'd do well with regular hours, which didn't translate to the field. Her gaze drifted to her computer screen, and she opened the tab with Brooke Morales's social media profile. "I hate to ask but…"

"You need another favor?"

"I do."

"When I told you I'd help however I could, I meant it."

She wasn't the only one who had changed since his career decision. He seemed more committed to the job than he'd ever been. These days, he also struck her as more willing to rock the boat *some*. "I'd like to talk with Emily Kane's friends from high school."

"Are you sure that you should, well, get directly involved?"

And there is the partner I know… "I don't have a choice." She could lay out her reasoning but didn't see it making a difference.

"What do you need?"

"She had two close friends. One goes by Brooke Morales now, and the other was Melissa Hatfield. Her last name might have changed since."

"And you want me to find them?"

"That would be great," she rushed out. "I'm not even sure if they're in Stiles or nearby."

"Do you really think talking to them will help Troy?"

"I think it might, and that makes it worth a shot." If she didn't find Dylan Graham's killer soon, Troy would lose everything. So would she. Going at this from the angle of Emily Kane did seem the best way to go.

"Do you mind if I ask how?"

"I figure if I approach this from the Emily Kane case, I'm not going to step on anyone's toes."

Terry laughed. "And since when do you worry about that?"

"True. I just want everything on the up and up. Well, as much as possible anyway. You asked me how I think they might help. Well, I want to hear their take on Richie Klein." She hadn't told him she suspected Klein, but he'd have put it together she did.

"And Troy?"

"I suppose, yes. I also found out that there was a girl in ninth grade that Klein allegedly assaulted. That goes to his character. If I can track her down and get her to talk, that works even more against him."

"I hate to see you getting yourself tied up in all this."

"It's too late for that, Terry."

"Well, the Emily Kane case is closed."

"Is it though? The Braybury detectives are hinging Troy's motive on Graham alleging he should have been sent away for killing Kane."

"Oh, this has the potential of creating a PR nightmare."

"You're worried about public relations when Troy is facing murder charges? You're already turning into a suit."

Terry's end of the line fell quiet.

"I can't apologize for that. Troy's future is on the line, and you just sounded more worried about image."

"I was just making a comment and didn't mean anything by it. I never said it would stop me from helping you. Which I will do, by the way." With that, he ended the call, and she was left to feel like shit. And a tad hopeful.

The doorbell rang, and Andrea was on the front step. Madison moved back to let her inside, a shiver catching her. The temperature had dipped.

"Should I get the wine?" Madison asked her.

"Probably. But if we keep turning to the bottle, we might end up with health problems before this is all over."

"I'll get us coffee." It was three thirty in the afternoon, but it wasn't like she'd be sleeping anytime soon.

"Sounds good."

Madison left Andrea to take off her coat and boots in the entry. She got the coffee machine started.

Andrea dropped onto a stool at the peninsula just as the first pod started filling a cup.

"Tell me the detectives opened up to you," Madison said, and Andrea shook her head. "But they agreed to talk to you. Then they didn't? I don't understand."

"Well, I wish I could explain it."

"Maybe I should just go and—"

"No, you're not going anywhere." The look that Andrea leveled on her was police chief, not future sister-in-law. Her words weren't a suggestion as much as they were an order.

She snapped her mouth shut, the urge to protest very strong, but she'd choose her battles wisely. If Andrea learned Madison was poking around the Emily Kane case, she'd be receiving more than just *a look*. She'd have the chief's full wrath. For as long as she could, she'd appear compliant. Madison grabbed the brewed coffee for Andrea and started a pod for herself.

"Thanks." Andrea took a long, appreciative sip, her eyes closing as if the flavor of coffee on her tongue was melting all her stress away.

And she'd butter her up with coffee... "Don't mention it." Madison got herself a coffee and sat next to Andrea.

"It's all so infuriating, but I don't see what we can do." Andrea was gripping the handle on her mug so tightly, her knuckles whitened.

"Just tell me what they told you." As her own words hit her ears, she questioned where that level of calm had come from.

"As I said, not much. Enough to gather they haven't done much. They saw Troy's gun and the journal and ran it to the DA's office."

"It's certainly how it feels." The back of Madison's neck stiffened with the weight of the entire world being against them.

"Not how it feels, but rather how it *is*. They just gave me the basics. Dylan Graham was killed Tuesday night between four and six PM. There was no sign of forced entry. No eyewitnesses. No one heard the gunshot. And that's assuming they asked around."

"What do you mean *assuming*?"

"Just that. I never got any straightforward answers."

"And other suspects?"

"Huh, well, it was his maid who found him on Wednesday morning. I told you that before. Well, she was cleared. So they at least considered someone else." Andrea grimaced and took a sip of her coffee.

"That's all? Are you serious?" Madison's earlobes were on fire with rage.

"They have their man, as I've said before."

"So they're really not looking for anyone else?"

"Nope, and from the sounds of it, they never did."

Madison was almost too angry to talk. She weighed the little Andrea did say. "You said the time of death was Tuesday between four and six. Well, Troy has an alibi."

"Which is?"

The truth was she and Troy worked Tuesday until five, but she didn't see him until he got home after seven.

"Maddy?" Andrea prompted.

Madison shook her head. "We'll figure it out."

"Then he doesn't have one?"

"That I know of, *but* we also know Troy didn't kill Dylan Graham, so he must have an alibi."

"Whatever it is, it better be rock solid. They are clinging to the fact they have Troy's gun with his prints on it."

Has the whole world gone mad? "Which makes sense. It is his gun."

"Exactly what I told them."

A span of silence followed before Andrea spoke again.

"I just have a bad feeling the Braybury detectives are holding back. Being coerced somehow, possibly. But whatever they aren't saying, I get the feeling it's the key that will liberate Troy."

Madison wished Andrea had never told her that. She had her mission now, and it didn't involve sitting still and waiting things out.

CHAPTER 18

Sleeping as a guest of the Braybury PD wasn't getting any easier. Troy didn't recall drifting off at all last night. Yet he was in the courthouse the next morning anyhow, dressed in a suit Madison had brought him. She was in the gallery, where she'd stay until the arraignment finished. His sister wasn't present because she was meeting with the Braybury police chief, hoping to receive some actual professional courtesy. Troy wasn't holding his breath. If the Braybury detectives were receiving directions, it would be coming from the top.

He glanced at Madison, and she offered him a head bob and pressed smile of reassurance. Her support would get him through this.

A minute later, Troy's name was called, and he and his lawyer, Vincent Park, took their positions in the courtroom. The edges of Troy's vision were fuzzy, as if none of this was real and he was existing in a dream state. The people were nothing but cardboard characters droning nonsensical banter. He really needed sleep.

The man at the bench wasn't someone Troy had crossed paths with before, but his nameplate announced him as Judge Whitaker.

Violet Pollard was the district attorney. She was fortysomething with delicate facial features and had her brown hair drawn back into a tight bun. It sent out the message she was no-nonsense and focused on her goal. Unfortunately for him, hers ran contrary to his.

She laid out the charge against him. "The state is charging Troy Matthews with murder in the first degree."

The judge looked at Troy. "How do you plead?"

"Not guilty, Your Honor." Troy's heart was pounding. He felt like he'd slipped into another reality, not his own.

Park stood and tugged down on his jacket. "All the prosecution has against my client are baseless accusations."

Pollard peacocked herself. "We have solid evidence. To start, Mr. Matthews's gun was at the scene—"

"Enough," the judge intercepted. "This is not the time to lay out the evidence. That is to be done at a probable cause hearing. One is hereby set for Tuesday of next week."

"Defense would also like to request that the defendant be released on his own recognizance,"

Park began. "Surely as an esteemed officer of the law for nineteen years with the Stiles Police Department, Troy Matthews can be granted that request."

"Granted." With that, the judge banged his gavel, dismissing them.

Park turned to him. "You're a free man."

"For now."

Madison was standing in the aisle, watching him, but she wasn't smiling. It was too soon to celebrate, and they both knew that. Next Tuesday, they'd be back in a courtroom where it would be decided if the case would proceed to trial. From there, heaven forbid, his fate would rest in the hands of twelve jurors.

Park gripped Troy's shoulder. "Just hang in there, all right?"

He nodded, appreciating the attorney's intentions were in the right place.

Troy held out his hand to Madison and didn't stop walking. She slipped hers into his palm, and they headed for the freedom of the street. But there wasn't much freedom to be found. A crowd of reporters put their microphones in his face.

"Tell us, why did you kill Dylan Graham?"

"You're a cop. You should be better than this. Why did you kill him?"

"You are a disgrace to the badge."

Madison yanked Troy's arm, likely pulling him in the direction of her car. "Don't listen to a word they're saying."

Too late for that. After dedicating his life to helping people, in one moment, they turned on him. "Let's just go home." He wanted to add *and forget all this happened,* but he was beyond believing in miracles.

"You got it."

They managed to squeeze through the mass and reached Madison's Mazda. He let out his first deep breath once they hit the highway.

"The Braybury police aren't even considering other suspects. Did you know that?" Madison looked over at him, one palm on the steering wheel, grinding on it.

"What do you expect? They've leveled charges against me. As far as they are concerned, case closed."

"No, that's not good enough. You know what I'm like. What any good cop should be like. You revisit all the evidence as many times as needed. You make sure everything lines up before you move on. They're just phoning this in, and you're going to pay for their incompetence. And that pisses me off," she snarled.

He'd always admired her spunk, but they didn't know how long this was going to stretch out for them. He put a loving hand on her leg, and her face softened so much it practically cracked. In that he saw that the emotions behind her anger were fear and sadness. "I'm not sure what we can do about it. Andrea's trying to see where she can get with their police chief, but not everyone is like you, *Bulldog*." He smiled as he served up his pet name for her. Regardless of her claim to dislike it, he got the sense she took it for how he meant it, as a compliment and term of endearment. She was courageous in the face of fear, both an attractive and terrifying quality about her.

"We can't all be perfect." She winked and took his hand, but her phone rang.

The display on the car's dash showed *Sergeant Blowhard*.

Troy chuckled. "That's new. Winston?"

She smiled. "Uh-huh. Like the nickname?"

"It suits."

"It does. Here, I'll just reject him." She reached out to hit the button that would send him to voicemail, but the car hit a bump and she accepted the call instead.

"Madison…? Are you there?"

Madison held a finger to her lips as if suggesting they pretend they weren't. Troy shook his head.

"I'm here," she said. "What do you want?"

"I'm hearing things, and I don't like what I'm hearing."

Madison rolled her eyes. "You should know better than to listen to rumors."

"Well, you know damn well what I'm talking about. I know you do. Now take the time off, Detective. You had the next two weeks booked for your honeymoon. Take advantage of them."

Madison was seething, her chest rising and her breath hissing as it exited through clenched teeth. She hung up on Winston. "*Take advantage?* As if we're having the time of our lives. He's such an insensitive prick. He's probably the one who knew the Braybury cops were coming for you. I just feel it in my gut." She balled a hand into a fist and held it to her stomach.

Troy wasn't going to fuel the conversation. Besides, if Winston was guilty of Madison's accusation, she wouldn't have to worry about him for much longer. Andrea would root him out of the Stiles PD and send him into early retirement. His sister was like him in that way. Only trustworthy people were permitted in her circle.

"What do you think?" Madison looked over at him.

"Whether it's him or someone else, it will get sorted." It was an expression his British mother would say to his father whenever anything weighed on him. Even when he lost his job after fifteen years, Troy had watched those words relax his father's shoulders. He missed his parents and wished they were still alive, that the oncoming car hadn't careened into their lane, but a bolt shot through Troy's heart. If they were here to see what was happening to him now, it would kill them all over again.

"I should have known you'd say something like that."

"What did Winston mean when he said, 'You know damn well what I'm talking about'?"

"It's nothing."

"It's obviously not nothing." He fell silent, intending to use a common tactic in the interrogation toolbox.

"I think he's referring to Tiptop Movers."

"The people who moved us? I don't understand why— Oh." The pieces fell into place. "You went there and questioned them about the gun?"

"Not directly."

"But you are snooping around. Please just leave all this alone. Don't you see you could make things worse—"

"Make them worse?" she snapped. "How is that even possible? From where I'm standing, you've been charged with murder. This is your freedom we're talking about. Also *our* future. I'd think you'd welcome all the help you could get. Speaking of, aren't you going to fight for yourself?"

Her words were a frontal attack and cut deep, rousing his resting anger. "Don't mistake my silence for guilt or indifference. I didn't kill Dylan Graham. The truth will come out." He'd given a lot of thought to who might be behind this. The second he was afforded the opportunity, he was going to slip away and see his hunch through.

Madison shook her head. "Well, then you have far more faith in the justice system than I do at the moment."

He could have argued that. In truth he was running very low in the faith department. That's why he planned to take his and Madison's future into his own hands.

CHAPTER 19

Madison was letting all her anxiety and uncertainty sap her power. She'd also let Troy's adamant declaration of his innocence silence her. How could she then question him about his alibi without looking heartless and like she didn't believe in him? She was also afraid of his answer. After all, a solid alibi could make all of this go away. If he had one, surely he would have already provided that to the detectives. But what if he didn't have one?

She'd have to figure out how to approach the topic. As she tossed around the words she could use, it took immense effort. She tended to say exactly what she wanted without much thought or filter.

They grabbed gyros and salads from Sammy's, her go-to for Greek food. It would count for lunch and dinner, as it was four o'clock in the afternoon. She had suggested eating there, but Troy had said he preferred to go home. She couldn't blame him, but she wouldn't have minded dipping into a brief illusion of normalcy. Forget that the probable cause hearing was hanging over them and that everything seemed stacked against them.

He let her unlock and open the front door, but he stood at the threshold for a few moments, the paper bag with their food in one hand.

"Troy?" she prompted him.

He didn't respond verbally but stepped inside and wiped his shoes. She was about to point out the mat was gone, but it had reappeared. Chelsea must have put it back when she set up the living room, and Madison just hadn't noticed it before. In fairness, her mind had been preoccupied assimilating the main transformation to the house.

"Do you want water or a pop to go with lunch?" she asked him.

"Water would be nice." He barely looked at her, his voice small.

"You got it." She walked to the kitchen to get them both water, plates, and forks. The entire time she puttered, her mind was on Troy. Never in the time she'd known him had he ever struck her as timid. Was the stress of this finally getting to him? In a way, she hoped it was and that he'd snap out of his silence and start fighting for himself. She certainly couldn't surrender to "all will get sorted" and let things lie.

She expected that Troy would have followed her, and they'd eat at the peninsula. When he didn't show up, she went looking for him. She found him in the front room. He was just standing there, breathing heavily, his shoulders rising and falling, his jaw sharply angled, his green eyes a storm unto themselves. She recognized that look, having felt that disappointment and hurt herself.

Madison stepped up to him and laid a soothing hand on his lower back.

He turned to her, sadness in his eyes.

"No apologies, remember?" She was getting ahead of what she was sure was coming and took the food from him.

"What did I ever do to deserve you?"

"You're kidding, right? I'm the high-maintenance one." She laughed, knowing this about herself. How her moods and obsessions oscillated. Her vendetta with the Russian mob had almost gotten her killed on a few occasions and had landed Troy in the hospital for a stint. Yet he was standing in front of her, asking *her* what he did to deserve her. He really was a prince. She was about to lean in for a kiss when her phone pinged with a text message, and the sound ticked up her heartbeat. It was likely Terry with Klein's location or where to find Emily's school friends. Unless he texted to say Winston made him back off. But she couldn't check her message right now, not in front of

Troy. Even if waiting would torture her. She set the food on the coffee table. "So, should we eat? It'll be getting cold by now." Gyros tasted good right from the fridge, but she didn't want him thinking about the alert on her phone.

"You know what? I'm not really that hungry."

"They must have fed you well in…" She stopped speaking, realizing this as one of those instances when she wasn't thinking through her words first. "I understand," she amended. As hungry as she was and how divine the food smelled, she wasn't sure how much she'd dent her meal either. Or whether it would stay down. She took the bag to stick it into the fridge. Before she left the room, from her peripheral, she saw Troy drop onto the couch and massage his forehead.

Part of this might be her fault for rushing him into doing something as normal as eating takeout. If only she could make this nightmare go away. *The text message…*

Her instincts were telling her it was Terry with news that she could act on. *Please, please, please…* But if so, she didn't want Troy to see her face when she read the text or responded. He was smart, and he'd smell what she was up to in a hot second.

"I'm just going to eat in here," she called out to Troy. She wasn't sure he'd heard her over the television that was on now.

His response was delayed but came. "Okay."

She put his meal container in the fridge and took hers to the kitchen peninsula and dropped onto a stool there. Fishing her phone from her pocket, she went to the notifications. It was a message from Terry, and she eagerly read it. She was used to how he tapped out long messages without punctuation and often forgoing capitalization.

> *Hope all went well this morning no update on Klein yet Brooke Morales and Melissa Hatfield still her last name lives in Stiles*

Following this he listed their addresses all bunched together.

She wished she could get up and leave now. It would sure beat sitting around. Instead, she was tethered here unless she could come up with some plausible excuse to leave. Maybe food would help her to think.

She popped the lid on the food container and inhaled the intoxicating mingle of aromas. Nothing compared with spiced gyro meat, onions, freshly diced tomatoes, and tzatziki. She took a bite of the gyro, leaving the Greek salad staring at her accusingly, but it could stare away. She should have ordered fries as a side. Troy was a healthy eater though, and she didn't want to be popping fries in her mouth while he was next to her eating lettuce leaves like a rabbit. Not that it normally stopped her from indulging. She wasn't exactly sure why she hadn't today.

It only took a few bites, and the food started churning in her gut. Probably due to the pent-up stress of the last few days. She put the rest in the fridge and joined Troy in the living room. They rarely watched television because their shifts with the Stiles PD usually kept them quite busy. It might be nice to sit still for a second, though her mind chastised her for even considering a time-out. But if she couldn't go anywhere, she might as well make the best of it. As she sank into the couch, some relief washed over her. All the go-go of late had her exhausted. The program on the screen wasn't one she recognized, but she could exist in stillness for a moment or two.

Troy muted the TV and turned to her. "How was it?"

His question came at her from the random blue at first. "The food?" He nodded, and she said, "Good." There was no need to confess she'd eaten very little, as that would make him feel bad. Again, she flagged herself for pussyfooting around. Troy was a grown man, and he knew she was a strong woman. One who ate fries, no less. She sighed. "I couldn't get much down."

"I can understand that." He kept looking over at her. Obviously, he wasn't too enraptured by what was on the TV. But he was peering into her eyes, doing that thing he was quite skilled at, and reading her mind.

"What?"

"Are you doing all right? I mean overall?"

"I'm fine." She attempted to smile, thinking again how he was interested in her welfare while he was the one facing murder charges.

He bobbed his head, but his gaze was fixed to hers. "Who was the text from earlier?"

"The...?"

Troy pointed to her hands.

"Oh." She had forgotten she was holding on to her phone. There was no way she could tell him it was Terry with information she planned to follow up on, but she hated lying. "It was just Terry. He was checking in." Not a lie, not the complete truth. She still hated herself for toeing the line of deceit.

"That's nice of him."

"Yeah, he's a good guy." *Like a brother...*

"Go ahead and call him if you want. I was just watching a mind-numbing reality TV show."

"You'd think you'd have had enough reality." She smiled at him, an expression he didn't return, but it wasn't one he parted with often anyhow.

"I'll just entertain myself with other people's troubles." He turned the volume back on.

How he could just sit here and do nothing was killing her. Didn't he see that unless they did something, he would be going to trial for murder? After all, the Braybury police already had their guy, case closed, no more looking. A fire was burning in her chest, approaching the boiling point. She started bouncing her leg, and he glanced over at her.

"I've just crossed over from tired to wired," she said.

He didn't say anything as he faced the television again.

Maybe she should just tell him what she was up to, but she didn't see that turning out well. She foresaw a huge fight, and her launching into a barrage of questions about his alibi on Tuesday night. Also why he'd never come right out and told her he didn't hurt Emily Kane.

Gah! Am I now doubting his innocence? This entire situation was a cruel mind game.

She tapped her phone against her leg and fidgeted, trying to get comfortable. But it didn't matter how she positioned herself, it wasn't working.

Troy paused the show this time. "Okay, something's eating away at you. What is it? If you want to text Terry, I don't care. Especially if it stops you wriggling like a worm." He half laughed at that comment.

"Maybe I will." She pecked a response to Terry and thanked him for the info. When she'd finished, the TV program was still paused and Troy was drilling his gaze into her.

"Why are you lying to me?"

"Why do you think I'm lying? You know I detest it."

"All right, maybe you're not full-out lying, but you are skirting the truth. Why did Terry really text?"

Again, she debated whether to fess up. The images of a blowout happening between them rolled in very vividly, but with the way he was watching her, she needed to be forthright. "He was checking in. That's not a lie. But, yes, there was more to it than just that." He opened his mouth to speak, but she steamrolled ahead. "I can't be sorry for wanting to do something. I can't just sit here and do nothing. You are facing murder charges. Life imprisonment." He cringed, but she went on. "We know the Braybury cops are convinced they have their guy. They're done with this investigation. To them, it's case closed. But you're not alone. You have people ready to fight for you, Troy. I am one of them."

"I don't need people to fight for me. Not even you." He flicked the television off and got up from the couch. "I'm going out."

"You're what?" She popped to her feet. "Where are you going?" She was prepared to go with him, wherever he wanted. "You should be resting," she added.

He stopped and leveled a cold stare at her. "A minute ago, you were complaining I was sitting still."

"All right, whatever you're doing, I'm in."

"Nope, you're not. You're going to stay put." He raised a pointed finger, which she twisted, and he lowered his arm.

Her hackles were raised, her earlobes heated. "Never, ever talk to me that way again, Troy Chase Matthews. I'm not someone you can boss around. No one tells me what to do." Her heart was pounding, her nostrils flaring. She didn't remember being this angry before in her life.

"You're right. I apologize."

"Damn right you should apologize." She glared at him. Despite loving him, his current attitude had her wanting to walk out the door.

He closed the distance between them and put his hands on her shoulders, and while she inwardly withdrew at his touch, the softness of his expression and their history had her staying put. "I was out of line, and there are no excuses for what I just did. I'm sorry."

After a few beats, she said, "Apology accepted."

"I just don't want to see you get hurt. Whether you get in trouble with your career or… Well, we don't know who we're dealing with here. Who set me up."

She trembled at that. The fact he was afraid for her safety gave more credit to her earlier fear.

"I'm going to step out, just for a bit, but I'll be back. Trust me. Please."

His earnest petition melted her defenses, and she nodded. Watching him bundle up and go out the front door burrowed an ache in her chest. She probably should have insisted on going with him, but once he got down the road, she had somewhere else to be herself.

CHAPTER 20

Troy had really screwed up telling Madison what to do. He had no right, and it was entirely against his character. He wasn't controlling in the least and admired her free spirit, strong mind, and spunk. But his behavior was only more proof that he needed to get his situation resolved sooner rather than later. If it went on much longer, even his relationship with Madison may be jeopardized. He already saw that she had changed and was holding back, tiptoeing around him like he was a delicate china doll. He saw in her eyes that she had questions she wasn't daring to ask. Was she afraid of the answers? Was her faith in him wavering?

He pulled his Ford Expedition into the parking lot of the Sandman Motel. The headlights of a passing silver Hyundai Accent glared in his rearview and blinded him for a second. While the name of the motel could have been an attempt at joviality, the run-down dive gave it a truly creepy vibe. This was aided by the fact it attracted certain types from the lower rungs of society. Violent ex-cons being one.

When Dylan had called and told him Richie Klein was holed up here, it hadn't come as a surprise. His pitch that they'd get together and it would be like old times was pushing things. Instead of the reunion being appealing, Troy wanted nothing to do with it. Richie was a chauvinist and liked his women submissive, or at least he did twenty-four years ago. Dylan really wasn't much better. But what was the point in telling the detectives any of this? They had their minds made up. Though it did have Troy wondering how this journal made any sense. Dylan certainly hadn't leveled any accusations or threats during his call.

It was obvious something shady was going on. When that was the case as a teenager, it typically revolved around Richie, and Troy suspected now wasn't any different. He had no choice but to talk to the guy if he was going to find a way to clear his name.

Troy knocked on the door for room 8, and it opened with a *whoosh*.

Richie was standing there, a pale image of his younger self. His hair had thinned out, and he was a string bean with little muscular structure. Troy brushed past him into the room, not in the mood for a trip down memory lane or with any urge to become reacquainted with his former friend. "Well, well, if it isn't the cop. Troy Matthews, how have you been?"

Troy recoiled. He had a feeling Richie knew exactly what he was going through. Either from the news, Dylan, or his involvement in all this. It could also be how he knew Troy was police. The last time they had spoken was before Richie's arrest. "How did you know I was a cop?"

"Word gets around."

"Dylan?"

"Yep." Richie shut the door. "We haven't talked in twenty-four years, and there's no, 'How are you, buddy?' 'How did you hold up in prison all those years?' You just let yourself into my room, copping an attitude."

"Enough. Let's not pretend we're buddies. We tolerated each other back then, but a lot of time has passed."

"You're telling me."

If his old friend was looking for empathy, he'd be disappointed. "I should have just asked you a question all those years ago."

"Shoot." Richie crossed his arms, his body language indicating the exact opposite of his verbal response. He wasn't that open to talking.

"I never asked you why you did it." It was a question that haunted Troy on occasion. While he had testified in support of Richie, after the jury passed their verdict, Troy had started having second thoughts. When all this came up about Dylan, they rose again. Richie's character had much to be desired. He could have taken things too far, and hopped up on booze and drugs, it was even easier to imagine.

"Is that you asking me now?"

"It is. What did Emily do to deserve what you did to her? She reject your advances or some bullshit like that?"

Richie unfolded his arms. He tightened his jaw and angled his head. "Maybe you should leave. I've gotten by the last twenty-four years without you in it. You never came to visit once, and now you show up accusing me to my face. No show of support. Rather, why did I do it. You're some piece of work, you know that?"

"Look who's talking. You raped her, Richie, while she was already injured. Then you strangled the life out of her. What the hell were you thinking?"

Richie remained silent.

"Did you kill Dylan Graham too? Set things up to make it look like I did it?" As he spoke, he rummaged through the motel room, not finding much except empty take-out containers and booze bottles. He didn't know what he expected to find, but proof he was behind Dylan's murder would be a good start.

"What the hell are you doing? And are you high?" Richie grabbed Troy's arm, and it had Troy's vision turning red.

"Get your hand off me," he hissed.

"Get out of my room!"

Troy spun and grabbed Richie by the collar and rushed him against the wall, lifting him off the ground.

Richie slapped Troy's hands, a feeble attempt to get him to loosen his grip.

"I am coming for you. You hear me! And you better leave me and Madison the hell alone."

"What... are you... talking about?" Richie sputtered in fragmented gasps.

"Do I really need to spell it out for you? You killed Dylan and did your best to pin it on me, but you underestimated me. What I just can't figure out is why you did this."

Richie's eyes were wide and his face red. Troy let him go.

Richie hunched forward, rubbing his neck and sucking in air.

Troy let him be, watching his former friend beaten down, but with every passing second, he was getting angrier. Still, he waited for Richie to catch his breath.

Richie straightened, leaned against the wall again, this time for support. "What do you mean Dylan was murdered?" He was still rubbing his neck.

"I've said it twice now. Don't tell me you don't read the news."

"I don't."

"How did you know I was a cop?"

"I told you already. Dylan mentioned it."

Troy was heaving for breath. "Before you killed him? And don't try to play all innocent with me. Why did you kill Dylan? Why frame me?"

Richie raised his arms in surrender. "I swear I didn't. I didn't even know that Dylan was dead until right now."

"Well, I don't see you shedding any tears over it, considering you just found out." Not that Troy was buying a word from Richie's mouth. "And just like you did twenty-four years ago, you stand before me and say, 'I didn't do it.' But you were guilty then, and you are now."

Richie looked away.

"You can't even look me in the eye," Troy spat.

He now met Troy's gaze. "I didn't kill Dylan."

"Forgive me for not believing you. And why Emily?"

Richie sniffled. "I was just a kid, and I was high. Things got out of hand and—"

"That's how you justify rape and murder? You've been sitting in a cell for twenty-four years. That's plenty of time to reflect on your crimes, and you come out of prison with pathetic excuses? Exactly like you, though. Why should I be surprised? You're unbelievable."

Richie's face scrunched up, and he threw a punch. Troy juked out of the way just in time and countered. He landed a blow to Richie's chin, and his head was thrown back against the drywall, making a hole there.

Instead of backing down, Richie wailed out, "You don't know who you're messing with!"

Troy was quite certain he did, but he struck Richie again. He doubled over but didn't stay down for long. He sprung upright and hit Troy in the chest and then the cheek. Troy faltered backward, surprised by the strength Richie harnessed in such a small frame, but he was still no match for him. Troy could bench-press his weight.

"I killed her because she had it coming. She was so weak." Richie smirked at his confession as he came at Troy again.

"You like to feel powerful, in control, like some tough guy? Take this." Troy drew his arm back and released, striking Richie hard.

His legs crumbled beneath him, and he fell to the threadbare carpet of the Sandman Motel.

Troy took one look at him and got the hell out of there.

CHAPTER 21

It was only five o'clock in the evening, and the sun had already pulled a disappearing act. Madison drew up on the house of Brooke Morales, and the darkness set the stage for her Christmas decorations to steal the show. Twinkling lights draped a mature cedar tree in the front yard and outlined the eaves and windows. Tasteful lawn ornaments of Frosty and some reindeer were placed in the garden beds.

Madison raised the brass knocker that sat within an oversized wreath on the front door. She was prepared with how she was going to approach this meeting. Hopefully it worked.

The door opened, and a woman in her early forties answered. She resembled her online profile picture, but her hair was a little frizzy around her ears. Before Madison could confirm she was Brooke Morales, two young children between six and eight bounded to the door in a flurry of energy. The boy and girl circled her and sang "Let it Snow" at the top of their little lungs. The woman looked apologetically at Madison.

"Hey now, quiet down, please," the woman said.

The kids ran off into the house but not in a quiet fashion.

"Can I help you?" The woman leveled her gaze at Madison.

"Actually, I'm hoping you can." Madison flashed her badge, laying the groundwork for her attack plan. "Detective Madison Knight. Are you Brooke Morales?"

"Uh-huh. You're with the police? Is, uh, everyone okay?"

"I'm here to talk about Emily Kane," she told her.

"Okay. But Emily? I'm not sure I understand. Her killer went to prison."

"That's kind of what I'd like to talk to you about. If I could come in for just a few minutes…?" Madison peered past the woman, and despite the hour, it didn't smell like dinner was underway yet.

Brooke stepped back to let Madison inside. "Please take off your boots and leave them on the mat."

Madison did as Brooke had requested. The home was open concept and warm. Tinsel and garlands were wrapped around the doorframes with baubles, bells, and bows. A grand

Christmas tree with a million trinkets stood in one corner of the living room with an animated Santa Claus climbing a ladder propped against it. Madison liked the holiday, but it was like set designers from Hallmark movies had their way in here.

"Sit wherever you would like," Brooke told her as she dropped into an overstuffed chair.

The kids swept into the room, chasing each other and squealing.

Brooke got to her feet and held up her hands to them. "That's enough."

Both stopped, mouths gaped open, eyes wide. "Mom needs some adult time to talk to this detective."

A man with a tan complexion and dark features graced the doorway. The one in the family portrait on Brooke's social media.

"Detective?" He narrowed his eyes at Madison.

"It's nothing," Brooke assured him. "But if you could entertain those two munchkins for a bit, that would be great."

"Sure." The man rounded up the kids and left the room but shot Madison a protective look before disappearing.

"Ah. That's better." Brooke let out a long breath. "But now it's so quiet, my ears are ringing." She smiled.

"Your kids, I assume?" They were the children in Brooke's profile picture, but there weren't any photos on display in this room. There wasn't really time for idle chitchat, but showing personal interest could go a long way to relaxing Brooke. And if she was relaxed, she'd talk more freely.

"Yep. No rest for the weary. Seven-year-old twins."

Madison didn't see much resemblance between the two kids. "Oh, twins?"

"Fraternal," Brooke said, reading the implication in Madison's response. "They don't share the same DNA and don't need to look alike or be the same gender."

Madison smiled and nodded. "You learn things every day."

Brooke went to a curio cabinet in the room and withdrew a framed photo from a weaved tote. Madison feared it was going to be more about the twins and prepared to redirect the conversation to Emily.

"Thought you might like to see this." Brooke handed the picture over to her. It showed three teenage girls. One was Emily, the other a younger Brooke, and the third was likely Melissa Hatfield.

"The Trinity together."

"Yeah. How do you know about the Trinity?"

Madison didn't want to drop Joni's name. "It must have been from the investigation." She'd live with the blush of truth. "So that's Melissa Hatfield?" She pointed to the third in the photo.

"That's right. Have you spoken with her?"

"Not yet, but I plan to." A note in Brooke's voice suggested sadness or regret, so Madison asked, "Have you and Melissa stayed in touch?"

Brooke shook her head. "We grew apart after… Well, you know." She returned the photo to the cabinet and sat down. "What do you what to know about Emily? I guess I'm just lost because I thought all that was behind me. Her killer was caught and served time."

From this point, Madison really had to weigh her responses so that she wouldn't potentially cause Troy more problems. "Do you believe that?" Given all the tension between her and Troy, the things he wasn't saying, it caused little sparks of doubt to fire within her. She hated herself for them.

"Why wouldn't I?"

Madison shrugged and said nonchalantly, "Sometimes the wrong person goes to prison."

"Is that what you're telling me? That Richie didn't do this? Is that why you're here? To tell me Emily's killer is still out there, that he's been free all these years?"

Madison gave a tight smile. "I never said that. We're just reevaluating some things, that's all." The use of *we're* was an obvious stretch, not that Brooke knew this.

"Then the police have reopened the investigation."

Madison's heart clenched. She hadn't intended to come here to sway a change in Brooke's mind or stir up the past. Though she should have known it would do exactly that. Just sensing the pain this was putting Brooke through didn't feel good. But Madison had to keep her focus on the bigger picture. Troy was innocent, and she was determined to prove that, no matter what it took. "It's not reopened per se. There's a recent case, that I'm not at liberty to discuss, where some allegations were made. I'm simply following up on those." She hoped that would be enough to soothe Brooke, and based on how she'd sunk further into the chair, it had. Madison asked, "If it wasn't Richie, then who do you think it might have been? Anyone you were suspicious of back then?"

"I don't know. Emily had a lot of guys on the line."

"By that, I take it to mean a number of boyfriends?" Joni had said something similar, that Emily was popular with guys.

Brooke smiled, her eyes taking on a faraway look. "If you want to be kind about it and label them boyfriends. She was… I hate to speak ill of the dead, but she fooled around a lot."

Richie, assuming he was the rapist, may have taken liberties, thinking he was somehow entitled. Then maybe he ended up killing her because she wasn't going to keep quiet about what he had done. Regardless of whether it was Richie or not, the person who was responsible might have been rejected by Emily in the past. "Did Emily and Richie ever hook up?"

"Not that she told me, and she usually wasn't shy about kissing and telling. But if he had made a move, she probably would have slept with him. He was good-looking."

If that was the case, Madison had to wonder why Richie would have raped Emily, assuming he had. But then again, rape wasn't about sex, it was about control. "That was enough criteria for her to sleep with a guy?" Madison didn't mean to sound judgmental, but that was how it came out.

"Hearing you say that sounds awful, but yeah."

If what Brooke was saying was true, Troy wouldn't have a reason to rape Emily either. Madison hated that the thought even creeped in. It still didn't mean that Richie was innocent of killing Dylan and framing Troy. For the sake of keeping an open mind though, she should probably also consider that Richie wasn't guilty then or now. But when she'd asked outright if Brooke thought someone else killed Emily, Brooke didn't have an answer. Madison would need to approach it from another angle. "Were there boys who had a crush on Emily, who she might have rejected in public?" She was thinking that someone's wounded pride may have caused them to snap. As for why they'd come forward now, that part of the puzzle wasn't clear. But one had to keep pulling at threads to get to the truth.

"There were a few, but I remember one guy more than the others. She'd yelled at him and helped the jocks play pranks on him. He was dorky, as we saw him at the time. Bookish. Black-framed glasses, thick lenses. He had bad acne and braces at the start of high school too, which didn't help."

"His name?"

"I'm sorry, but it's been so long— Oh, his nickname was Tinman, due to the braces." Her initial excitement at remembering dulled to embarrassment once she said the childish moniker.

"You don't have any yearbooks kicking around by chance, do you?" Madison was hedging her bets because the woman had held on to the framed photo of the Trinity.

Brooke shook her head. "I'm not nostalgic that way. If it's not of use to me now, I let it go."

Except for that photo with Emily... Though holding on to that made sense. A tragedy had befallen a dear friend. Madison stood and thanked Brooke for her time.

"Wait," Brooke said, "are you sure you can't give me more details about why the police are interested in Emily's case?"

"I would if I could." Madison dipped her head and left, guilt coiling through her for the deceit. Her visit hadn't been official.

She got into the car, and her phone rang. Terry was on the caller ID, and she answered before the second ring.

"I know where to find Richie Klein," he said.

CHAPTER 22

The Sandman Motel was a rat pit. The brown paint on the building's brick was chipped, making it appear speckled, but its lack of aesthetics wasn't what had Madison's attention when she pulled up to the place. The strobing lights of police cruisers pierced the night, and the sight of the Crime Scene van didn't bode well for her gut. Neither did the two unmarked vehicles that were typically assigned to detectives.

She parked and eyed Terry talking to a uniformed officer she didn't recognize. He must have been a new transfer to the Stiles PD, as she didn't see a training officer hovering over him.

"What's going on?" she asked Terry. She didn't trust new people easily, and she needed to cling to all the familiar she could right now.

"DB is all I know. I just got here myself."

Dead body...

"A homicide, ma'am," the uniform told her, and her hackles raised on instinct. This time it had nothing to do with the *ma'am* bit.

A homicide... She trembled and tried to talk herself down. Klein staying here could just be a coincidence. It didn't mean he was the dead guy. She turned to the uniform, Jensen on his patch, bracing herself to ask and get the answer despite having a very, *very* bad feeling. "Victim's ID?"

Jensen shook his head. "I haven't heard yet. But the word is he was just released from prison last week."

Madison's head spun, and all the lights blurred together. It had to be Klein. But if he was dead, he likely wasn't the one who had murdered Dylan Graham. Then who is doing this? Were they pecking off Troy's clique from twenty-four years ago? Would they be coming for Troy, or was framing him all they had planned? "I can't believe this is happening." She could hardly talk, her throat was so dry.

Terry put a hand on her shoulder. "I'll see if I can find out more." He turned to go to the lobby, but Toby Sovereign and Lou Stanford were walking toward them. They must be the detectives from Major Crimes who were assigned to the case.

"Madison?" This was from Lou. Toby was unusually quiet and standing back.

"Who is it?" she pushed out, finding her voice again.

Seconds of dreadful silence. Lou looking at Terry, back at Toby, and eventually saying, "Richie Klein."

"Richie." She staggered and tried to cover it by pacing a bit. And if he was murdered like Dylan, then was Troy safe?

"You really shouldn't be here, Madison," Toby said. "This is a crime scene."

Madison spun and put her face to within inches of his. "Don't feed me that line, Toby. Not today, not ever. Talk to me. Please." She had tagged on the latter bit when Toby's cheeks flushed, and he clenched his jaw.

"He's right, though, Maddy," Lou followed up softly while ushering her closer to her Mazda, Toby and Terry doing the same. "It's best that you are not here, were *never* here," Lou added.

The implication being they would forget seeing her on scene. But why would they do that? Was it to protect her from blowback from Winston? Or did they find something in Klein's motel room that suggested she was in danger? Though, surely, if they had, they'd be saying as much. "Just tell me what happened, then I'll go." She crossed her arms and tilted her head.

Lou faced Toby and sighed. Toby pressed his lips, his go-to when he was about to say something she wouldn't want to hear. She remembered the expression well from the time they were together.

"A nine-one-one call was made, complaining of noise and a disturbance coming from room eight," Toby laid out. "This was just past five o'clock. Apparently, this person also saw a rather well-built man leave the room and get into a Ford Expedition." He let that sit there, but the impact was instant.

A Ford Expedition, Troy's vehicle. Bile rose up her throat, the bit of gyro she had eaten wanting to return for an encore. She covered her mouth and swallowed it back down. Troy had left the house close to five. He had told her to trust him, all the while planning to kill Klein? No, if Troy was caught up in this at all, Klein's death was an accident or happened in self-defense. But where was he now? In either case, he would have stuck around. What the hell was going on? Another wave of nausea rocked her and had her clenching a hand over her gut.

Lou went on. "We're going to keep our heads level and our minds open, okay?"

She nodded, not absorbing much of what was being said. Her mind was a mess.

"Where is Troy now?" Lou asked, his voice velvet, as if the answer didn't harness the power to destroy her.

No, all of this must be a coincidence... Troy had told her to trust him. He'd never have come here to murder Klein. Just like he wouldn't have murdered Dylan Graham. Or raped and strangled Emily Kane twenty-four years ago. Her entire world was spinning, leaving her hopelessly adrift.

"Madison," Lou started, "I realize this must be a lot to take in, but things aren't looking good for Troy."

She met his eyes. That was the understatement of the year.

CHAPTER 23

Madison was trying desperately to reach Troy, but she kept landing in his voicemail. After the fifth time, she left a message, "I don't know where you are, but you need to call me right away. Please, I love you," she added quickly before hanging up. She didn't need to be so blunt, letting her nerves take the lead, but an eyewitness had seen him leave a murder scene. How the hell could Troy spin that to look good?

Come on, Troy, call me back!

Despite attempts from Lou, Toby, and Terry to get her to leave, she was still at the motel. About thirty minutes had passed, though it felt excruciatingly longer with every failed attempt to reach Troy. In that time, Cole Richards, the medical examiner, had shown up with Milo Boswell, his assistant. Madison had seen little of Cynthia, who was determined to work until her baby came, or anyone else with the Crime Scene Unit. There must have been a lot of forensic evidence to process in Klein's motel room. So far, it had been kept off-limits to Madison.

Terry had gone in a while ago and had yet to return with news.

Madison considered calling Andrea to let her know about the situation, but she'd need to explain what she was doing here in the first place. She wasn't going to say anything unless it became fact Troy was in trouble again. But standing out here in the parking lot was ridiculous and getting her nowhere.

She breezed past Officer Tendum, a uniform she knew, who was posted at the door, but froze in the doorway. Once she crossed the threshold, she could potentially contaminate evidence inside that could serve to exonerate Troy. She didn't move any farther, and she didn't have to.

Richie Klein was supine on the floor between the end of the bed and the TV unit. He was of slight build, straggly even, and he'd been badly beaten. Fresh cuts and bruises marked his face and arms, and there was a belt tied tightly around his neck.

When she raised her gaze, five sets of eyes were on her. Those belonging to Richards, Milo, Cynthia, Terry, and Mark Andrews, another tech with Crime Scene. Toby and Lou were currently talking with other guests of the motel to see what else they could get for witness testimony.

She was speechless as she considered that Troy could have done this. He'd certainly be strong enough to overpower a man of Klein's size. But why would he do this? Had Klein threatened to expose Troy like Dylan Graham supposedly had? Guilt snaked through her at the treacherous thought. But how else could she possibly feel right now? Troy had left, insisting that he go alone, no less. Add to that the eyewitness account and the fact Troy wasn't taking her calls.

Cynthia set the camera she had been holding up against her baby bump. It dangled there from a strap around her neck. She walked over to Madison and put an arm around her. "You shouldn't be here."

"Maybe. But I need to know what happened."

"I would have come to update you," Terry said.

"How long do you expect me to wait?" she snapped and felt bad since Terry had been supportive from the start. "I just couldn't wait any longer, that's all." She rubbed her arms, suddenly chilled to the bone.

The room fell silent. She should leave. Her presence was putting her friends and colleagues in an uncomfortable situation, but she needed to know if the man she loved was a killer.

Richards cleared his throat. "Preliminarily, the time of death is between three and six," he offered as if she was there in an official capacity.

No math was needed here. She just needed to tear apart the timeline and consider the facts.

Between the 911 call and the eyewitness, time of death was likely closer to five o'clock. Troy could have been the last person to see Klein alive. That didn't mean he killed him, but what if he had? She shuddered.

Cynthia tightened her hold on Madison. Her best friend didn't know that Troy had stepped out around that time, insisting he go alone and asking for her to trust him, but Madison had no doubt that Cynthia was sensing something. She was skilled at reading her mind and small tells, like Troy. The tremor that had run through Madison would have spoken volumes.

"Cause of death appears to be asphyxiation caused by ligature strangulation," Richards added. "Petechia is present."

Broken blood vessels manifested as tiny dots often on the lips, inside the mouth, and in the eyes when the body was deprived of oxygen.

"The blood you see coming from his ears, nose, and mouth might also be related to the cause of death, though the beating he received left its marks too. As you likely know, it's not easy to strangle someone. It takes strength and determination." Richards's shoulders lowered as he added that last tidbit.

"Thanks." Madison laid a hand over her stomach, turned to leave, and bumped into Sergeant Winston.

"Detective Knight? What the hell are you doing here?" Winston's glare transported from her to Terry. "Hmph. I should have suspected as much. The two of you need to learn boundaries and brush up on protocol. If this isn't your case, get the hell out!" He thrust a pointed finger toward the lot.

"Sorry, boss, it won't happen again," Terry said, heading out.

"You're damn right it won't, and if you don't straighten up your act, you can kiss becoming a sergeant goodbye."

Madison's back was to them at this point, but guilt over putting Terry in this spot crashed over her. The stress became worse when Winston, on their heels, bellowed for Lou and Toby to round up Troy and bring him in.

CHAPTER 24

The man kept to the shadows, careful not to be seen and cautious of being perceived as a threat. The last thing he wanted was a nosy, do-good neighbor making trouble for him. Otherwise, nothing was going to kill the buzz jolting through him. He'd been so patient waiting for his day of retribution, and it had finally arrived. In fact, some pieces were falling together so perfectly, he couldn't even have planned for them. Foremost was the timing. It couldn't have been any better.

He snickered as he ducked behind the tall row of bushes that lined the property of the two-story home that had his interest. Though, more accurately, it was the residents who lived there that truly had his attention.

Not long ago, he watched the Ford Expedition pull into the driveway and the driver get out, but he didn't anticipate the man would be home for long. He must not have returned straight home from the motel. Maybe he'd gone to blow off some steam elsewhere for a bit. But thanks to him, it didn't take much to finish the job. Blessing number two.

Now, just the thought of being here to witness him being hauled away in cuffs was… *titillating*. Yes, that was the perfect word, as the satisfaction stirred all sorts of dormant urges. There would finally be justice.

The lights had been turned on in the home one by one, and Troy hadn't bothered to close the curtains in the front room. The man in the bushes watched him pace the length of the window. There was no way he could know what was coming for him. That made all of this even more glorious.

Another shiver ran through him. Yes, pure bliss. The blindside, the retribution… perfection.

Troy deserved everything coming his way and more. He should be happy that he didn't just strangle the life out of him, slit his throat, or pull a trigger and shoot him dead.

But once death came, his fun would come to an end. Sometimes, suffering was owed, and he was determined to suck all of that from the marrow of his revenge.

Police cruisers turned down the street. Their lights were flashing, but the sirens remained silent. As much as he wanted to stay around, he had to put some distance between him and the house. Too bad because where he stood offered a front-row view. He walked away, slowly, glancing over his shoulder. He didn't expect the police would pay him any attention if he was seen as a man out taking a leisurely evening stroll. They would take issue with him if he was discovered hunched behind a bush.

As suspected, none of the officers paid him any attention. For once, his invisibility was an asset. People rarely saw him or gave him a second glance at the best of times. It was an asset when there was so much he needed to do to set things right.

The police knocked on the front door, despite there being a doorbell.

The door was opened, and two plainclothes detectives stepped forward to talk to Troy. Initially, he couldn't overhear a word being said, but that quickly changed.

"Are you being serious? You're going to—"

"Please, just calm down," one of the detectives said. "I'm sure there's been a misunderstanding, but we've been told to bring you in."

The man from the shadows turned, a lightness in his step, a smile on his face. Justice. But his plans for revenge were just getting started. The man had a fiancé, a detective herself. How would Troy feel when he found out he was the reason she took her last breath?

CHAPTER 25

How the hell can this be happening again?

Troy paced circles in an interrogation room at the Stiles PD. His own colleagues and brothers in blue arrested him, ripping him from his home like he was some hardened killer. This was the second time in a handful of days being treated this way, and it was getting old fast. Could Toby and Lou really think he was a cold-blooded murderer? Toby, maybe, by a stretch. He had wanted to get back with Madison not that long ago, and she had turned him down flat. But, still, there needed to be more to facilitate the arrest than jealousy. And both men had told him they had no choice but to take him in for questioning.

Troy had come to find out that Richie Klein was dead, strangled with his own belt. Apparently there was evidence that led them to Troy. Not that they had yet shared what that was. But Troy had left Richie very much alive. Hurting, but alive. Regardless, Troy knew how it looked. Especially if someone had seen him or his truck there and the time-of-death window lined up. Signs of a physical altercation would have marred Richie's body, just the same as it did Troy's. He had abraded knuckles from hitting Richie, but for a smaller guy, he got in a few good blows himself. He might not have taken full advantage of yard time and the weight room in prison, but Richie was scrappy. Troy's busted lip and throbbing right eye was testament to that.

Police could fabricate motive for him killing Klein, as they had Dylan Graham. They would wrap it up in a neat bow and assume Troy wanted to silence anyone who could turn on him and offer proof he raped and killed Emily Kane. But he was innocent then, just like he was now. Emily had done nothing to him, and he would never, *ever*, hurt a woman. Let alone rape one. As for murders, the only lives he'd taken had been necessary in the line of duty. It was them or other innocent people.

But he was trying to unravel the bigger picture. He had gone to talk to Richie in a quest for answers. Presumably he had been in contact with Dylan for him to know where he was staying. The two of them might have stayed in contact while Klein was in prison. But if it wasn't Richie out for some sort of warped revenge, then who? The fact Troy had no idea terrified him.

The only clear bottom line was this person had returned, bringing the past with them. But why? And who else was in danger? This person hadn't killed Troy, but he had taken out his two friends from that time. If this was just about killing, then Troy should be in a pine box himself. Rather, he was left alive to experience another type of hell.

Speaking of, how would Madison react to him being arrested again? Would that be enough to push her to call it quits with him? While he had been confident in her loyalty before, surely two murder charges would test the resilience of their relationship. And he couldn't answer her calls. He was still reeling from losing his temper with Klein the way he had and needed to cool down.

The door cracked open, and Lou and Toby stepped into the room. Troy stopped his pacing, and he held his breath, almost afraid to hear what they were going to tell him. But how could things get any worse?

"Ah, Troy, we've got some news," Lou began, and the use of a filler word disclosed the news was *bad*.

"Just tell me." Troy would find a way to handle whatever was coming his way. It wasn't like he had much choice anyhow.

"All right. The case is being transferred to the Braybury Police Department." Lou didn't look at him as he told him this but kept his gaze on the floor.

"Pardon? Can you repeat that because I think you just said—"

"He did just say it," Toby said, stepping in. "Detectives Snow and Friedman have already been called and are on their way."

"Why would…?" He was so angry that he couldn't form words. The Sandman Motel was in Stiles PD jurisdiction, so why would the case be transferred out? The fact it was local had been one grace in Troy's favor. Surely, people in his own police department would hear him when he spoke and offered his defense.

"It comes from on high. Sorry. Just be strong. We are on your side," Lou offered, but a quick glance at Toby had him wondering if *we* included him. His eyes and facial expression were unreadable. In the years Troy spent reading people, Toby was closed off most of the time.

"From on high," Troy said, chewing on that. That could only mean one person.

The door opened again, and Andrea entered the room. "If you could excuse us, Detectives, I'd like a few minutes with my brother."

Both Lou and Toby left.

Troy faced his sibling like he would the enemy. "You here to drag me away in chains? Here you go." He held his wrists out to her.

She made sure the door was shut, then went around turning off the video and audio surveillance.

"Hello? Andrea? Did you not hear a word I said?"

"Oh, I heard you. I'm choosing not to react to your anger."

"Well, good for you." Troy flailed his arms in the air, dropped them. He rarely let his emotions take over, but he cut himself some slack.

"You think I'm so evil, but I don't see cuffs on your wrists. You offered them up. I could get you a pair if you'd like." She pulled out a chair and dropped down and indicated the one across from her. "I mean, usually those arrested for murder are cuffed before being dragged in. From the way I heard it, everything was done in a calm and respectable manner."

"Respectable? Try being on this side." He sat, reluctantly, doing so because he wanted to, not because he was his sister's lap dog.

"You really think this is fun for me? I'm under a lot of scrutiny here, Troy. A lot of pressure."

"*You* are?" He clenched his jaw and shook his head. "I was hauled away from my wedding, accused of a murder I didn't commit. Now another one in my own city, for heaven's sake."

Andrea didn't say anything, but her cheeks flushed. She was angry as hell too.

"And I've just come to find out you're handing the case over to the Braybury detectives. Really?"

"I don't have much choice."

"To detectives who hate me already, who are prejudiced." He leaned back and slapped the table with his palm. "You are feeding me to the wolves. Why? For a political move? To ensure you're a shoo-in for police chief next term?"

Her eyes blazed as she leveled a glare at him. “Be happy you’re over there, or I would have slapped you for that one.”

“Real professional, Chief.”

“You’re unbelievable, you know that? I’ve done everything I can to help you. I got you a good lawyer and spoke with them over there. I’m still championing on our behalf.”

“Oh, please.” The words were out, and he was instantly sorry. Her facial expression pinched in on itself. “I apologize. You have been here for me. I’m just… Urgh. I can’t believe this is happening.” As dedicated as his sister was to her career, she’d always put flesh and blood first. The decision to push the Klein case to Braybury must have tortured her.

“Happening? Interesting. This time it didn’t *happen* to you, Troy. You did this to yourself. You were at the Sandman Motel, in Richie Klein’s room. Or does an eyewitness have it all wrong?”

If there was someone who testified to seeing him there, he was screwed. There wasn’t much he could say until he talked it over with Park.

“Everything’s off, nothing’s on the record. This is just you and me having a conversation. Were you in Richie Klein’s room around five o’clock tonight?”

Even though it was just them, he was leery to admit to it. “I should talk with Park before I say anything.”

Andrea leaned back in her chair, and it was as if all the air deflated from her body. "Ah, shit."

"Yeah. Shit. But it will all get sorted, right? I mean that's what we say."

She met his gaze, a single tear beading on her eyelashes. "I'm not so sure it will this time."

His heart sank because he had the same bad feeling.

CHAPTER 26

When Madison got home, Troy's Expedition was in the driveway, but he wasn't there. She tried Troy's number again, and this time it went right to voicemail. A cold sweat blanketed her. That usually meant the phone was off. Had he been arrested or— She didn't want to entertain the alternatives circulating in her head.

Just calm down... Breathe...

She tried Lou's line, and it rang repeatedly. Without leaving a message, she hung up, her insides frozen with fear.

Whoever killed Dylan Graham had likely killed Richie Klein. That seemed to be a fact. Anything else was far too coincidental and unlikely. If Troy was innocent though, that meant someone was out there knocking off the friends one at a time. The only one left was Troy. What if the killer became dissatisfied with just framing Troy? What if he had taken him?

She stood at the end of her driveway, huddled in her coat as the cold winter night blew around her.

If an eyewitness was to be believed, Troy had been seen coming out of Klein's motel room around the same time as the reported altercation. It also fell within the window for time of death. But what if someone was watching Troy and took advantage of the situation? They went in afterward and killed Klein? Not entirely impossible.

Damn it, Lou, why aren't you answering your phone?

She almost hoped it was because he was questioning Troy. It was preferred to Troy being with some psycho. While Troy could hold his own, he was still mortal. The thought of losing him stole her breath.

Her mind was only going to rest when she knew where he was. Even if that meant he was in custody. She pulled out her phone, thinking she'd try Andrea, when she spotted shoeprints in the snow. They were tucked close to the bushes on the property line.

What the...

She moved closer, and the majority appeared to face toward their house. Chills ran through her as she landed on why that would be. Someone had been standing there watching the house. Looking for Troy? Waiting for him to get home?

Her phone rang in her hand and had her jumping. Caller ID told her it was Lou.

"You called? I saw your number as a missed call."

"Is Troy with you?"

"Yeah, he's been brought in for the murder of Richie Klein, Maddy, and the case is being passed over to Braybury."

"What?" she spat. She barely had a chance to be relieved Troy wasn't holed up with some psychopath before Lou whipped that out. The one thing in their favor this time had been the jurisdiction plainly fell within that belonging to the Stiles PD. Troy would have stood a better chance with detectives who saw the evidence and didn't pigeon-hole it to incriminate him.

"The chief felt it was the right call, the *nonprejudicial* call."

That might be, but it felt like a betrayal.

"Madison, you heard me?"

"I did. I'm just trying to process this. Where is he now? Please don't tell me he's already on the way to Braybury."

"He's still here waiting for the Braybury detectives."

"Keep him there until I get there."

"I don't know if—"

"Do it, Lou." She ended the call, her gaze fixed on the shoeprints in the snow for a few seconds. Troy might be in custody, and he *might* have crossed the line by going to Klein's motel room. That didn't change the fact someone out there was watching them.

CHAPTER 27

Madison hustled down a hall at the police station toward the interrogation rooms, suspecting she'd find Troy sequestered in one. She didn't get far.

Andrea stepped out of an offshoot hallway and held up a hand. "Nope, I'm not going to let you do it."

"You don't even know what I plan on doing."

"I'm sure I can guess, but we need to let the judicial process run its course. The Braybury detectives are on their way. It's their case now."

"How can you be so cold? Troy is your own brother."

Andrea grimaced. "You think I'm cold? I'm doing all I can to make sure that everything is followed by the book. The last thing we want is how we handle this coming back to hurt Troy."

Watching her future sister-in-law heaving for breath, her cheeks becoming pink, cooled Madison's temper some. She also had looked out for Troy's best interests all his life, so why would she stop now? It was unsettling just how much these past few days messed with the mind, made her question things she never would otherwise.

"Come with me," Andrea said.

"Can't I just see him for a minute?" Madison wanted answers straight from his mouth, not fed to her through *appropriate* channels. When too many people became involved, the message got messed up in the relay.

"Please." Andrea's softened request had Madison's shoulders sagging.

"Fine."

Once set up in her office, the door shut and locked behind them, Andrea spoke. "Tell me what you know first."

The police chief, like her brother, had a way of reading people. She'd likely deducted that Madison was privy to quite a bit. "I was at the Sandman Motel, and I saw Klein. I assume you heard this much from Sergeant Winston."

"He never said a word."

"Huh." She would have thought he'd take pleasure in pointing it out. So what advantage was there in him holding back from the chief? There had to be one. "Well, he gave me the boot."

"Which he should have. It was an active crime scene, and you had no reason to be there. Speaking of, why were you?" Andrea angled her head.

Madison would be stabbing Terry in the back if she said why. "I'm not sure that's important."

"Uh-huh." Andrea met her gaze, and there was an unspoken communication that buzzed between them. Madison would wager she suspected Terry's hand in the matter. "Why was Troy in Klein's motel room?"

Until now, she'd only surmised he'd been there. Andrea's words confirmed the eyewitness account. "So he was there."

"Yes, which I assume you knew?"

"I had a feeling but didn't know for sure."

Andrea sighed deeply. "Then you might not know this. There was a physical altercation between the two. Before you ask, Troy faired pretty well. Just some minor cuts and bruises."

Madison should be feeling for her fiancé, full of empathy at his suffering, but this was his fault. He went to the motel. And then the hell he put her through not answering his phone. She shot to her feet and paced the office. "What was he thinking? And how did he even know where to find him?" She stopped moving and gripped the back of the chair.

"Good questions that I'd love the answers to, but Troy's not talking."

"You're kidding me? After all of this..." Madison's earlobes were sizzling as her temper ratcheted up. He refused to speak even though he had to know what this would be putting her and Andrea through. Right now, she could strangle her fiancé herself.

"He's a complicated man."

"One that I could throttle."

"Get in line." A subtle smile, inserting levity as the only tether linking both women to sanity.

Madison had seen Troy retreat inward before. He did it when there were a lot of emotions at play, primarily grief or anger. So which spurred him to keep quiet now? Was the man she had given her heart to a killer? She couldn't really believe that, no matter how often the doubts slithered in. She'd continue dismissing them until she had no other choice, but the evidence against him was stacking up. He had no business being in Klein's motel room. Which brought her mind back to the convenient timing. Someone was watching them. Had that someone followed him to the Sandman Motel and taken advantage of a volatile situation? "Something bigger is going on here. Troy's not a killer." *Maybe if I say it enough times, it will squeeze out all doubt!* "You should know that someone was watching our house from the bushes near the road."

Andrea shifted in her seat, sitting up straighter and leaning forward. "What? How do you know that?"

"There were shoeprints in the snow, and they were facing our place." Madison had called Cynthia on the way here, and she was going to send out Mark to make casts of them.

"Then someone is keeping tabs on Troy. But why?"

"That I don't know, but it's likely the killer. Since the prints were fresh, I'd say they wanted to be there to witness the aftermath of their handiwork."

"They followed Troy to the Sandman Motel, killed Klein after Troy left, and positioned himself at your home to see Troy arrested," Andrea said, laying it all out. "But who hates Troy this much, and how does it all tie to Emily Kane's murder from twenty-four years ago?"

"Also, why now?" Madison added her own question to the list. She wasn't going to disclose that she'd had her suspicions that Klein was the one who had murdered Dylan Graham and framed Troy. It would draw attention back to why she was at the motel.

"And does it have a correlation to Klein getting out of prison?"

"It must. Not that I know how." Madison played over her earlier thoughts, about this person keeping an eye on Troy and how that might factor into the night's events. "Who called nine-one-one?"

"It came from a payphone near the motel."

"A payphone? I was told that the caller lodged a complaint about noise and a disturbance, but it didn't come from someone within the motel?"

"No, from the payphone right out front."

"That doesn't make any sense. Did the person leave their name?"

Andrea shook her head. "We just know it was a man."

"So the call didn't originate from the Sandman Motel *and* was made anonymously. From a payphone, no less." Her mind was going wild trying to get the reason for this and could land on only one. "The caller must be the killer. We need to see if any cameras cover that payphone."

"Wait. Before we leap to conclusions—"

"No leaping, Andrea. I'm looking at the facts. It was the killer who called nine-one-one. He followed Troy to the motel, waited for him to leave, went in after, killed Klein, then called it in."

"Then he got lucky no one beat him to calling nine-one-one. He risked being caught killing Klein."

"You know what the Sandman Motel is like and the clientele it attracts. None of them are going to willingly call the police there. I'm surprised there was even an eyewitness who described Troy and his truck."

"Well, that was the motel clerk, but I hear what you're saying."

That was Madison's first time hearing the identity of the eyewitness. For a place like the Sandman, it made sense it was an employee and not a guest.

"What you're suggesting is that Klein being killed was opportunistic. The killer hadn't planned ahead. After all, how could he have known ahead of time Troy was going to Klein's motel room?"

"Exactly." Her heart was racing, as it felt like pieces were starting to click together. First off, they were looking for a man. That would also align with the size of the shoeprints next to their hedge.

"This makes whoever it is one scary bastard."

"But his spontaneity might start to work in our favor. He could have left behind valuable evidence. To start, calling from that payphone. He didn't want his cell phone to be traced back to him, but in his rush to call nine-one-one, he may have overlooked surveillance in the area."

"My God. I'll make sure we check on cameras immediately. But what if this guy tires of stalking Troy? What if framing him for murder two times isn't enough?"

"I'd thought the same. Troy could be in trouble."

"He's in police custody. He set Troy up to face life in prison because his death wasn't enough for him. This guy wants Troy to suffer. The only other friend in that group, Barry Weir, is already dead." Andrea's eyes met Madison's. "But if something were to happen to you… He could be coming after you next."

Her chilling words sent shivers through Madison. It didn't matter how many times her life was threatened, it never got easier to think about.

CHAPTER 28

Troy was at a loss for words. If he could just reverse time, he never would have gone to see Richie. Nothing good had come from hanging out with him as a teenager, and apparently nothing good came from it now. He used to like Richie enough, but he was never Troy's favorite person. Richie and Dylan used to be tighter, while Troy and Barry were.

It had been a stretch to think that Richie had killed Dylan, but it was the only answer Troy had come up with. His visit to Richie was just supposed to confirm his suspicions, not set off another series of events that would land him behind bars again.

Vincent Park was circling the room as if a vulture over carrion. Troy had given his account, and even the skilled attorney wasn't hiding his concern well. But Troy had been with Klein within minutes of his murder, and there was a perceivable motive. The Braybury police already thought Troy was guilty of raping and killing Emily Kane because of Dylan Graham's journal. He could foresee that's where they'd leap with Richie's murder, but he'd see soon enough if he was right.

Lou had dropped off a couple bags of potato chips, but Troy left them untouched. *Salted cardboard.* He couldn't think about eating anything right now. It had to be going on ten o'clock at night by this point.

There was a knock on the door, and Detective Snow entered with his partner, Friedman.

Both men bobbed their heads in greeting to Park, who sat in the chair beside Troy.

"You haven't even been out of jail for twenty-four hours. You miss the bars?" Detective Friedman sneered.

"Enough of that adolescent behavior," Park chastised. "Let's stick to the facts of the case before us, shall we?"

"Fine. You want facts? How about your client murdered again." Friedman leveled a pitiful glare on Troy. It was clear his intention was to appear menacing, but the younger detective was like a Chihuahua trying to present itself as a bullmastiff. Laughable.

Snow cleared his throat. "Mr. Matthews," he said evenly. "A call to nine-one-one reported a disturbance in Richie Klein's motel room around five PM. Where were you at that time?"

At least one of the detectives seemed more reasonable this go-around, but his friendlier approach still wasn't going to work to make Troy talk.

"If you could just answer my question," Snow prompted.

"And why should I? It's clear you think you already know what I'm going to say." Troy didn't have tolerance for small talk and speaking for the sake of hearing his own voice.

"You were at the Sandman Motel," Snow said. "Will you confirm that?"

"Sure." A skirt around confirming or denying, but it was the best Troy felt like offering.

"I'll take that as you were there." Snow leaned forward, clasping his hands on the table in front of him. "Why were you there?"

Troy didn't respond.

"What happened inside his room?" He gestured to the cuts on Troy's face.

Park looked over at him and nodded subtly. Silent encouragement to talk.

"We had a disagreement."

"Looks like more than that," Friedman inserted, cutting Troy off.

Not a fan of being interrupted, Troy cast him a grimace that had the detective shifting in his chair. As he thought, all bark, no bite. "He was alive when I left him."

"But, just for the record, did you get into a physical altercation?" Snow asked.

His words reminded Troy that Andrea had turned off all the surveillance in the room. Park had reengaged it when the detectives walked into the room. In this situation, it was for his protection as much as anything. "That's right."

"We appreciate your honesty," Snow said, and it had Troy recoiling. He didn't like being patronized any more than having his speech clipped. "Going back to the beginning, how did you know where to find Klein?"

Troy didn't miss the detective's tact was to deploy diplomacy. He could have demanded an answer, but he sugarcoated it. "Dylan told me."

"Just before you killed him?" Friedman spewed out, and Snow glanced over at his partner and shook his head. "What?" he spat back at Snow.

"Mr. Matthews, please continue," Snow encouraged.

Now they are trying out good cop, bad cop… "I don't know if I feel like talking anymore."

Friedman snorted. "You don't really have the luxury of—"

Snow drilled Friedman with a look that had the detective snapping his mouth shut.

Thank goodness for small miracles, Troy thought.

"The choice is yours, Mr. Matthews, but things will move along faster if you cooperate with us," Snow said.

Troy glanced at his lawyer, who blinked slowly as if to encourage him to speak.

"That phone call you brought up," Troy began, putting his focus on Detective Snow while completely ignoring Friedman, "was Dylan calling to let me know that Richie was staying at the Sandman. He was wanting to arrange a reunion of sorts."

"Of sorts?"

Troy had misspoken by adding that, but it was no doubt colored by his personal feelings toward Richie. "I was never really tight with Richie."

"Yet you testified to his character," Snow pointed out.

"I didn't want to think he could have done that to Emily."

Friedman smirked. "Didn't want to think that, or knew he didn't because you—"

"Detective Friedman, I ask that you stop resorting to accusations against my client, or you need to leave," Park retorted.

Friedman's cheeks fired red, and he pushed his back against the chair and crossed his arms like a sulking child.

"I must say I'm not sure why you're telling us the details of this phone call now. Why not tell us before? Do you think coming forward will benefit you in some way?" Snow asked.

"My private phone conversations are none of your business. That's part of the reason I didn't tell you before. The other is, listening isn't exactly your strong suit."

Friedman looked at him through narrow slits but surprisingly kept his mouth shut.

"Why did you go to see Richie Klein?" Snow's voice was level and calm, surprisingly nonjudgmental.

Troy considered whether it was beneficial to come forward with his reason. He could clam up or dance around it.

"You can tell them," Park said to him.

"I thought that Richie might have killed Dylan and framed me."

Friedman made a show of rolling his eyes.

"So you went there to confront him," Snow said.

"I guess you could say that."

Snow leaned forward. "And you saw this being a peaceful exchange, even though you believe he set you up for murder?"

"I went there to talk."

"A moment ago, it was to confront him," Friedman fired back.

Troy clenched his jaw. That slip highlighted the benefit of keeping quiet.

"Please just help me understand," Snow said. "What was Richie Klein's motive to kill Dylan Graham? It sounds like they were good friends. You just told us Dylan wanted to arrange a 'reunion of sorts.'" Snow's eyes narrowed as he spoke, his tone more accusatory than a moment ago.

One Braybury detective was as bad as the other. Both had their minds made up against him. Snow just did a better job of hiding that fact sometimes.

"My client is being cooperative, Detectives," Park said, "and it would be appreciated if you showed some respect for what he's saying. Not twisting it to serve your purposes."

"No one is twisting," Snow said. "I haven't said anything your client didn't say first."

"You're making assumptions. It was never said that Graham and Klein were good friends," Park countered.

Snow pulled a face. "Why else would he want to get together with Klein and include Troy in the mix?"

Park smiled. "Do you hear your own words? They reveal you accept Troy's account of the phone call for you to assume that Graham and Klein were friends. If you accept that, then release all charges against my client and let him go."

"We have no way of knowing what conversation took place. We're just going by what your client is telling us," Snow volleyed back.

"Precisely. Yet the entire motive you concocted against my client in the Graham case is that the victim threatened to expose him. So which was it? Your story or the truth that my client just shared? That the call was nothing but

Dylan Graham calling to arrange a reunion? After all, I can't imagine he'd want to do that if he thought Troy a rapist and killer." Park sat back, tugging out on his suit jacket.

Score one for Park!

Silence followed the lawyer's reasoning because it was undebatable.

Eventually, Snow said, "We still have the journal, but going by what your client just told us, Dylan wanted the three of them to meet at the Sandman Motel."

Park nodded.

"Then I ask, Mr. Matthews, why would Richie Klein hold ill will against Dylan Graham? What would be his motive to kill him and frame you? Please, help me understand your thinking." Snow set this out with a cool, professional detachment and sat back in his chair.

Park gestured to Troy to respond.

"I thought it was possible Richie held us responsible for his going to prison, as if our testimony failed him."

"So he killed Dylan but thought he'd just get you sent away?" Snow countered.

"No one can know exactly what a person is thinking."

"Except you presumed to do that with Richie Klein," Snow volleyed back.

"Oh, please, it's no different than you and your partner with the Graham investigation," Park put in.

Snow glanced at Park but said to Troy, "It wasn't just a calm discussion though, was it? You and Klein got into an altercation. Punches were thrown."

"Is there a question in there?" Park huffed out impatiently.

Troy's heart thumped with a fresh infusion of adrenaline. "Why are you so set on putting me away? What scares you about looking at the actual evidence?" Park reached out to touch Troy's arm, but he shrugged him off. "If you actually looked at the evidence, you'd know I'm innocent of both murders. Richie was alive when I left him. I haven't seen Dylan in years. You couldn't have found forensic trace tying back to me in his home."

Snow stiffened. "We have looked at the evidence. Murder scene one: your gun was there. Murder scene two: an eyewitness puts you there, as does your own testimony."

"Or was your first murder Emily Kane?" Friedman interjected. "If we were to exhume her body, would we end up finding forensic proof against you?"

"Let her rest in peace. Let her family." Troy's nostrils flared with every intake of breath.

"Things are getting out of hand here, Detectives," Park stepped in. "We all know you don't have enough grounds to facilitate a warrant for such a thing, so let's refrain from the threat, shall we? Let's focus on the here and now.

And from what I'm seeing, there is no concrete proof my client was involved with the murder of Richie Klein. I suggest you let him go."

"Let him go?" Friedman spat. "You've got to be joking."

Detective Snow's face twitched, so slight it was barely perceptible, but it was a flicker of vulnerability in his otherwise tough demeanor. Maybe Snow wasn't as against him as it would seem. It was hard to tell. The detective seemed to wobble back and forth. It could be someone controlling his strings, as his sister had suggested, but why? To make headlines? After all, a SWAT officer charged with murder one was guaranteed to make headlines and shine a spotlight on the Braybury PD. "You're not so sure about my guilt, though, are you?" Troy asked, directing the question at Snow.

The detective's eyes snapped to meet Troy's, but he said nothing.

There was a knock at the door, and Snow called for the person to enter. Lou came in and handed a piece of paper to Snow, then shot Troy an apologetic look on his way out.

Snow read the page, and once Lou left, he said, "You ever hear of Rapid DNA testing, Mr. Matthews?"

"No." Dread twisted in Troy's gut.

"It's more recent technology, but our crime lab in Braybury has the ability. It gives us results within one to two hours. According to the report, saliva was found on the vic, and it was yours."

"I told you that—" Troy stopped talking when Park shook his head.

"My client told you that he was in that room and hasn't denied a physical altercation with Richie Klein. It is feasible some of his DNA found its way onto the victim. It doesn't mean that Troy Matthews killed the man."

Snow leveled his gaze at Troy. "The DNA was taken from Richie Klein's belt. The same one that was used to strangle him."

Troy could feel the noose tightening around his own neck.

CHAPTER 29

Madison stirred awake, finding herself on the couch under a throw blanket. Her face was pressed against a pillow that smelled of Troy's woodsy cologne. She hugged it to herself and sat up. It was still dark outside, so she hadn't been out for long.

A cooking show was playing on the television across the room, and she reached for the remote and turned it off. As if she had any hopes of becoming a gourmet anytime soon. Her sister and best friend would tell her she could do whatever she applied herself to, but being a master chef wasn't one of her aspirations. In fact, her only one at the moment was to free the man she loved from jail.

It was unthinkable that they were in this position a second time in a handful of days. She would have stayed at the police station if her presence could have made an ounce of difference, but Andrea had sent her home. That was probably the wisest course of action because she didn't trust her reaction at seeing the Braybury detectives. Andrea said even the police chief for the department was tight-lipped. So much for extending professional courtesy. But they were convinced they had their man in the Graham case. With Troy back in the spotlight, they'd be more than certain.

If only she could ask Troy what he'd been thinking to his face. She'd like to read his facial reaction, what was going unsaid. She was still angry with him. He must have left the house planning to see Klein, yet he insisted on going alone and didn't trust her enough to confide his plans. Quite a slap in her face, as all she was doing these days was trusting him. Didn't he appreciate the tough position he was placing her in? For a man who deliberated outcomes to the nth degree, how could he not have foreseen the possible repercussions of confronting Richie Klein? Though how could he have anticipated that someone would kill him after he left? Either way, the situation was driving her mad. Troy must have seen a strong advantage to going to the motel, but what? Did he suspect Richie Klein like she had, or at least considered him holding the key to unraveling the puzzle?

Her phone rang, and she scrambled to answer, following the trill and finding her phone tucked into the side of the couch. The clock read 7:30 AM. She must have slept through the night. It was Andrea calling.

"Tell me you have good news," Madison answered.

"I have some, but it's not exactly what you're wishing for. Troy remains in custody in Braybury, but there is a camera on the motel that offers a sight line to the payphone from which the nine-one-one call was made."

With Andrea's news, the fog in her head lifted. "Did we get the killer's face?"

"Not that far yet. We have a warrant though, and officers will be presenting this to the owner this morning."

"We need that footage as soon as possible."

"Trust me, Madison. It's a priority."

She didn't care for the way Andrea's voice darkened at the tail end of her dialogue. There was an incoming storm. "There's something else you have to say. What is it?" She barely managed to squeeze out the question, terrified of the answer, though unsure how things could get worse.

"Troy's DNA is on Richie Klein."

"You told me they were in a fight. That would make sense."

"It was on the belt around Klein's neck."

That statement initially came as a blow, but she conjured an innocent explanation. "And where did the belt come from? Was it Klein's or had the killer brought it...?"

"It was believed to have been taken from Klein's pants."

"That's easy to explain, then. They were fighting, and Troy was struck, spittle or blood flew, hit Klein's belt while it was around his waist."

"It is possible, but in the context of everything… well, it's not looking good."

Madison struggled to come to grips with what Andrea had just told her. It wasn't just the forensic tie between Troy and the murder weapon. It was how they knew this already. "DNA takes weeks to months to process. How could they know any belonged to Troy?"

"It's called Rapid DNA testing, and it's sometimes disputed."

"Then we'll dispute it."

"I'm talking a margin of error between ten to twenty percent."

"Sounds significant to me."

"I don't want to latch on to a dream. Now, the process does destroy the DNA sample, whereas the traditional method does not."

"Then it can't be retested. We'll have his lawyer call it into question. There might be some hope in that."

"I've been told they only used a small sample, not the extent of what they had."

Of course they didn't… It seemed no matter how things progressed, they were always pushed back into a corner. "I need to talk to Troy."

"I'm sorry but…" Andrea left her words dangling there, and a tingling sensation spread across the back of Madison's neck.

"What?"

"He doesn't want you to see him right now."

Ouch! She kept her faith in him despite the recent odds and was determined to do all she could to help him, yet he refused her. Some nerve.

"That's not the entire message though," Andrea rushed out. "He told me to let you know he's safe and not to worry. They have promised to isolate him from other inmates now that some might know he's a cop. He also knows you believe in him and said that he knows you *very* well."

Madison was trying to process all that Andrea had said and pluck apart why she emphasized that latter bit. If she wasn't losing her mind, Andrea was saying Troy wanted her help. Knowing her very well, he'd be aware that she couldn't sit back and do nothing about the accusations against him. The point was he didn't want her squandering precious time talking to him when she could be getting answers.

"You heard me, right? He knows you very well," she repeated.

It hadn't been her imagination jumping into the rabbit hole. "I heard you loud and clear."

"Good. Now, just be careful."

"I will be." Before heading home last night, Madison had adamantly refused protection detail. She had pointed out that she'd faced off with the Russian Mafia and survived. Andrea had tried to tell her even cats ran out of lives. Madison still ended up getting her way. It wasn't that she didn't have a healthy regard for her well-being, but she wanted the freedom of movement. She didn't need a police detail knowing she was poking around. And now that it seemed Andrea was permitting it, she wouldn't want that conflict arising either.

"You should also know that the arraignment for the Klein case is this afternoon at three thirty. It's unlikely he'll be released without bail a second time."

Madison had some money from her grandmother that might cover it, but Troy might be safer behind bars than on the street. "Let me know what happens."

"I will."

The call ended. Andrea hadn't questioned why Madison wouldn't be at the arraignment. It was unspoken that she'd be busy trying to get to the truth. For the police chief, the less she knew, the better, the more deniability.

But as Madison sat there, she wasn't sure where to start. The shoeprints outside confirmed a stalker. There couldn't be an innocent explanation for their existence. Was he out there now, keeping watch over the house while she was inside?

Goose bumps traipsed along her arms, but giving in to fear would get her nowhere. She had to think like a cop. As she'd pointed out to

Andrea last night, she had survived the Russian mob. Dimitre Petrov had *men* at his bidding. This killer was *one* man. Though he remained faceless unless the security camera from the Sandman Motel came through. If only she could determine the motive for the murders and framing Troy. Then she might get one step ahead.

Only one thing seemed clear: this was all connected to Emily Kane. It came down to Dylan Graham's journal and the accusation against Troy. Whoever the killer was, they were drawing attention to that night.

Think, think, think…

She tossed over in her mind what she had gleaned so far. Emily had been a popular girl with a lot of admirers. According to her friend Brooke, she'd slept with a lot of guys and kept the bar low. If a guy was good-looking, Emily would give it up for them. But Brooke had also told her about an awkward kid nicknamed Tinman. If Emily had rejected him, that could have provided motive for him to rape and kill her, but how did that extend to Dylan Graham and Richie Klein? In addition, to Troy Matthews? One would think if Emily's killer was still free, they'd remain quiet. So maybe this person didn't kill Emily, but it still landed Madison short of a motive for the present-day crimes. They had to have some connection to the past.

But as Madison's thinking cleared up, she realized the Dylan Graham crime scene came with a built-in defense for Troy. She couldn't believe she hadn't thought of this until now. Shock must have shut down logic, but the existence of the journal could exonerate Troy of killing Dylan. The Braybury detectives claimed that Dylan Graham threatened to turn Troy in to the police. If that was the case, and Troy had been willing to kill to protect himself, he would have ransacked Dylan's place. He would have searched for anything that Dylan might have had against him. He certainly wouldn't have left a journal hanging around, with a glaring accusation, for the police to find. Her hypothesizing had just chipped away at a key piece of evidence for the Braybury detectives.

And was there only one journal in the entire home? She'd only heard of one. Did that mean Dylan was new to the habit of recording his thoughts? Given the impression she'd gotten from Andrea, the Braybury detectives alluded that Dylan had been struggling for years with guilt over believing Troy had killed Emily. That alone suggested that Dylan would have lots to write about. In that case, there should have been boxes of journals. If only there was some way to find out. There was no way the BPD was going to tell her. Being allowed into Dylan's home was an even bigger ask. But Dylan had left behind people who knew him well, including an ex-wife. If anyone would know if Dylan was distressed, it would be the woman he had lived with.

There might be a reason to be hopeful. Then again, maybe she'd confirm the detectives' suspicions. There was one way to find out. Madison had to track the ex down and speak with her.

CHAPTER 30

If Troy never saw the inside of a jail cell again, he'd be happy. His neck and back were curled into a corkscrew, and a headache pounded behind his eyes and at the base of his skull. At least he wasn't being held in the drunk tank with puking alcoholics, hallucinating druggies, or strung-out prostitutes. But he'd been stripped of his clothing and provided an outfit from the Braybury PD. If he hadn't felt like a criminal before, the garb he was wearing certainly sent home the point. And while he might not have company in his cell, he was left with an endless parade of thoughts.

He should be in Mexico, just stirring awake next to his new wife. How drastic a turn had his and Madison's lives taken. He couldn't be blamed for how this mess started, but the one revolving around Richie Klein was all on him. He should have known anything involving Richie would stain him, just as being associated with him had years ago.

It caused Troy anxiety to think he had even stood in open court and attested to Richie's good character. He had done so somewhat reluctantly at the time. Over time, he excused himself as a teenager who hadn't found his way. Richie was someone he hung out with, drank with, pulled odd pranks with. He was one of the three who were always around, and for all of Richie's weaknesses, he struck Troy as loyal to his friends. That spoke a lot to Troy, but it didn't necessarily mean he'd ever trusted him.

And after facing Richie all these years later, any doubts Troy had about his innocence were wiped away. He had raped and murdered Emily Kane and confessed to as much. It wasn't just his words. It was on display in his eyes and his body language. He even struck Troy as being proud of what he had done. What a sick freak!

And just like then, Richie had pulled him into his web. If it hadn't been for Richie landing the first blow, Troy wouldn't have retaliated. There wouldn't have been a fight. There wouldn't be forensic evidence of him in Richie's motel room. An eyewitness still might have seen him, but not necessarily.

As for his DNA on Richie's belt, that was easily explained away, but the Braybury detectives weren't willing to take his side. All it would take was spittle flying from Troy's mouth or some of his blood—they didn't disclose the source of the DNA—when he was hit. That could have landed on the belt. Simple. But the detectives didn't even seem open to considering this. Again, they were set in the belief they had their guy.

There was a curdling in Troy's gut that told him the judge he'd appear before this afternoon would feel the same way. Once the presiding judge learned Troy was facing a second murder charge within a week, he'd be happy to smell fresh air again before he died.

Madison. His head pounded harder at the thought of her. She was his only hope of getting out of here, but would she be able to find the necessary evidence? It would take more than theories and the sprinkling of doubt. If he was to be set free, Madison would need to catch the killer. There was no way around that. And even though he knew she was as tough as nails and could hold her own, that didn't mean he didn't worry about her welfare. In the past when she stubbornly took up a vendetta with the Russian Mafia, it dang near killed him. First, mentally and emotionally. Second, literally. But there were times he thought they'd kill her, and that would be it. She'd be gone from his life forever.

But it was that toughness he counted on now. That and her tenacity. Like a dog with a bone, the basis for his pet name for her, Bulldog. Hopefully, Andrea passed along his message just as he had said it, and Madison received the implication. If she did, he might stand a chance of getting out of here before a trial started.

Might. It all came down to what she could dig up and who she could corner. She wouldn't have the benefits of the Stiles PD behind her. Andrea couldn't be tied to whatever Madison did, or her career would be in jeopardy. It was best that she knew nothing of what avenues Madison pursued. And thinking along those lines, he wished he had an idea where her intuition was taking her now. He didn't doubt she held faith in his innocence, but where was she looking for answers? Where was she going to start? What was her reaction when she found Troy had gone to visit Richie? He should have asked his sister if Madison was shocked or surprised. Knowing her response would tell him a lot. Did she suspect Richie of Dylan's murder, as he had? Either way, he could trust that she would do something regardless of whether she received his implied message. She wasn't one to sit idly on her hands and do nothing. He'd be a fool to think so. She fought for her loved ones and the underdogs.

Troy rubbed his temples, wishing the headache would ease just a bit, but it was unlikely. He couldn't stop thinking, and the more he did, the more his head throbbed.

He was obsessing, but how hard could it be to uncover who was behind this? It had to be simple, as answers often were.

This person was connected to the past, more specifically to Emily Kane. At least presumably that was the link. This person had it out for Troy and his friends, but again, why kill them and leave him alive? Dylan was shot, a quick death. Richie was strangled, a little more drawn-out and horrific. But it was as if he really wanted Troy to suffer. And whoever it was had done a good job of it so far. At this rate, Troy would lose the woman he loved, the job to which he'd dedicated his efforts, and spend the rest of his life behind bars.

Who could hate him so much? He could rack his brain for hours and maybe never land on the answer. He'd spent his adult life in law enforcement, and that built up inherent enemies, but that number decreased when focusing on his past, namely Emily Kane.

He dismissed this line of thinking, as it would lead him nowhere. The facts were all that could help him. Usually he'd grab a marker and start laying it out on a board, but he did his best to bullet-point them in his head, even if they were out of order.

Fact #1: Connected to the past and Emily Kane

Fact #2: Got a hold of my Smith & Wesson

Fact #3: Killed Dylan and framed me by leaving gun at scene

Fact #4: Dylan's journal mentioned I was the one who killed Emily, not Richie

Fact #5: Richie knew nothing about Dylan's murder and ended up murdered after I left him

It was that last fact that niggled him. Richie was murdered after he left him, and by what the detectives had told him thus far, his time of death was within the window of his being there. That was too close to be coincidental. If it hadn't been for the fact that Richie was strangled with his belt, Troy might second-guess that he'd left him alive. So if the timing wasn't coincidental, it was likely opportunistic, as Snow had even mentioned. That meant the killer would need to be nearby to take advantage of the opportunity.

His eyes popped wide. The killer had been watching him and saw him go into that motel room. Did he know about the fight though? He probably would have if he saw Troy leave. Then he would have moved in and killed Richie, probably thanking the stars for his timing. Though no one testified to seeing anyone else enter the room, or so Troy could only assume, as the detectives were fixated on him.

But how had this person known Troy had gone to the motel? The only answer was he had a stalker. He didn't recall anyone standing out to him within the past few months. He had to think back that far, as he was quite sure that's how long his S&W had been missing. Even when he suspected Richie, he saw the hole in his theory that Richie would have been in prison, but Troy didn't rule out that he could have worked with someone on the outside. But now, any of his suspicion against Richie was wiped out, leaving an unknown third party. Also, the gun being taken that long ago was an assumption. It wasn't like Troy reached for it with any sort of regularity.

But this person would have likely been in the neighborhood and hanging around their house to follow him to the motel.

Madison.

Again, she entered his mind. This person may have been watching him, but he'd also have seen Madison. Maybe him losing his relationship with Madison wasn't enough for this sicko. What if he wanted Troy to suffer more by targeting her? The thought chilled him, while at the same time, rage ran hot through his veins. And he'd be able to do nothing to protect her as he sat helplessly behind bars.

He strained to think harder, searching his mind for anyone's face that he'd seen repeatedly—seemingly out of place. All his mind served up was the image of a silver Hyundai

Accent. *What the…* But then the thought daisy-chained and provided him with context. He had seen this type of vehicle a lot in recent days, but he'd dismissed it as meaningless. Now he wasn't so sure. One had been behind him when he pulled into the motel's parking lot last night. It had driven on, but it moved slowly.

He hopped to his feet and raced to the bars. "Guard, I need to talk to Detective Snow immediately."

CHAPTER 31

The man from the shadows was out in the daylight. The clock on his dash told him it was just a few minutes after nine, but he'd been circling the block since six AM. He was taking a chance that someone would see him, but in his favor was the fact people were so caught up in the minutiae of their lives, they rarely paid attention to what was going on around them. He couldn't be more pleased with how things were working out, but his job was far from being done. Even though seeing the morning's news headline on his phone had thrilled him, Troy deserved to suffer more than "a fall from grace," as the reporter had pegged his latest arrest.

It only drilled home that Troy needed to really hurt, and he knew exactly how to make that happen. He drove past the house again, slowly, but not creeping along suspiciously. The blue Mazda was in the driveway. All he'd have to do was create a ruse to get into the house or find his own way inside. He knew she was alone. No friends or family or fellow cops to protect her, and the chocolate Lab they had wasn't there either. It must have been staying elsewhere. Likely the original arrangement for while they were supposed to be honeymooning somewhere.

He gripped the steering wheel tighter. The very thought of Troy going on with a happily-ever-after pissed him off to no end. He wasn't worthy of such a reward for his transgressions, for the secret he'd held on to all these years. He had to have known what he had done when he took that stand and prattled on about how great of a person Richie Klein was. *Bullshit!*

Troy would get his full due, but he wasn't going to risk messing it up by acting too soon. It had to be the perfect timing for the ultimate impact. And he was a patient man. Or he could be.

He tapped the brake at seeing the blond cop come out the front door, headed to her car. She was walking fast and with purpose. That couldn't bode well for him. He'd done his research on her. Madison Knight had made her own news on several occasions. In her most recent moment in the spotlight, she'd taken down members of the Russian mob in a warehouse explosion down at the docks. The consensus of the news articles painted Madison as someone criminals wouldn't want to trifle with. What a power couple she and Troy had made. Too bad that was all over now.

He pulled into the driveway a few houses down and watched as she came to a stop sign and turned right.

There was a churning in his gut, and it never lied to him.

Madison was a threat to him, and threats were best eliminated sooner rather than later.

CHAPTER 32

It hadn't been hard to locate the former Mrs. Graham. Her first name was Belinda, and she lived in a higher-income neighborhood in Stiles in a gray-brick side-split.

It was just after nine thirty when Madison pulled in front of Belinda's home. Troy was due in front of a judge less than six hours from now. It felt an impossibly steep climb that she'd pull off finding the real killer in that time. Hopeless even, but she didn't have the luxury of wallowing. Troy needed her. And hopefully she wasn't the only one who had his back, and the motel security camera would capture the face of the killer making the 911 call.

She got out of her car and rang the doorbell. A dog was the first to answer. Big, from the deeper tone to his bark and the shadow crossing the sidelight. Footsteps padded toward the door, and it cracked open.

A woman stood there wrapped in a cream cable-knit sweater and blue jeans. Next to her was a chocolate Lab, and the sight of it had Madison missing Hershey. She should pop by her sister's place for a visit at least, but that might confuse him if she didn't take him home. Unfortunately for her, Hershey was best left at Chelsea's for now, so Madison had the freedom to do what she needed. Besides, Hershey would have full-time company with Madison's three nieces home for Christmas break.

"Can I help you?" the woman asked.

Madison had debated whether she'd identify herself as police or not, but without doing so, she didn't know why the woman would speak with a total stranger. "I'm Detective Madison Knight. Are you Belinda Graham?"

"I am." Her blue eyes narrowed, and she gripped the doorframe of the screen door a little tighter, her knuckles turning white.

She could appreciate the woman's hesitance at having a cop showing up at her door. Especially considering she would have had recent experience with news of her ex-husband. "Would you have a few minutes to talk about Dylan Graham?"

"Sure, but there's not much I can tell you."

"I'm sure you told the Braybury detectives all you know, but I just have some follow-up questions." A flicker crossed the woman's eyes that didn't sit well with Madison. If she was right, it was telling her the detectives hadn't spoken with Belinda.

"Okay." Belinda backed into her entry, which for the size of the house on the outside was rather compact. The big dog didn't help much.

The Lab came over to Madison, sniffing her legs, and she petted him. "Beautiful dog. What's his name?"

"*Her* name is Cindy."

"Hey, Cindy, hey, girl." The dog was younger than Hershey, her paws still needing to be grown into. Her ears were soft and velvety and made her homesick for Hershey and for the way things were before those Braybury detectives stormed into her wedding.

"You said you have questions about Dylan," Belinda prompted, snapping Madison out of the little bubble into which she'd retreated.

"Yes. I apologize for the distraction. I've got one myself."

The woman smiled but didn't ask after name or age as was typical of a fellow dog lover. She must have been more preoccupied by what had Madison at her door. "If there is somewhere we could sit down, this conversation might be best suited to that."

"Sure." Belinda gestured toward a doorway that led to the front sitting room. It had a large window facing the street and was furnished with comfortable-looking furniture. Much like her attire, Belinda's home struck Madison as homey and cozy.

Madison sat on a stuffed chair that swallowed her up. She wasn't tall or huge to begin with at only five foot five and of average weight, but in this chair, she felt tiny. The feeling wasn't welcome when she needed to exude power. She shimmied to the edge of the cushion, but it beckoned her to sit back. She refused to comply.

Cindy came over and set her muzzle on Madison's lap, and she petted the dog's ears.

Belinda sank into a matching couch and snapped her fingers for the Lab to lie down. Cindy complied, dropping at Madison's feet. Dogs really rocked. They sensed when a person needed comfort.

"First of all, I'd like to offer my sympathies on the loss of your ex-husband," Madison said.

"I appreciate that." She shook her head, and her jaw took on sharp lines. "You know the police didn't even bother to inform me. They told his parents, and they passed along the message to me."

The skin on the back of Madison's neck tightened. It was as she suspected a moment ago. "The Braybury police never spoke to you?"

"Nope. Not one word."

Anger pooled inside her. They really did a botched-up job of investigating Dylan Graham's murder. It was like they stopped trying to find a killer the second they had Troy's name. *And his gun…* But Madison preferred to forget that part. "I'm sorry to hear that."

"Me too. I might have had something to offer." A tear traced down her cheek, which she quickly wiped away.

Madison sat straighter. This visit could pay off. "Were you and your ex still close?"

Her blue eyes had turned deep indigo, and she met Madison's gaze and nodded. "We never had children, but we got together young and did a lot of growing up together. We met in college and got married after graduation."

That would have been after Emily's murder. If he had been upset over what had happened, surely that would have been evident to a new girlfriend. Harboring a secret like that, presumably thinking the wrong friend went to jail, would have changed Dylan. And while Belinda had entered his life after the murder, there would have been giveaways that told her he was troubled. Belinda had likely never met Troy either. "You must have hit it off," Madison said.

"We did. He had this quiet confidence about him. Over the years, he lost the quiet part and became proud."

Her description didn't fit someone who was struggling with the past or harboring deep regrets.

Belinda went on and offered, "It's ultimately what pushed me away. He was working all hours. Don't get me wrong, he was making a lot of money and was an important man, but there's more to life, ya know?"

Madison nodded. "What did he do for work?" She realized her slip when the woman's eyes narrowed.

"Shouldn't you know that as a police detective?"

"Right. I apologize for that. Just a mind slip." Madison put a fingertip to her left temple and smiled, hoping that would suffice to skim over the blip.

"Huh, well, the troubles started when he made partner."

A lawyer maybe... Following this avenue would likely reveal someone who had an issue with Dylan Graham, but would they also have a tie to the past? It was possible and a path Madison might do good to explore. Dylan could have taken on a recent case that bore a connection. She made a mental note to find out where Dylan had worked.

"What is it you'd like to know? I'm doing all the talking, and you said you had follow-up questions."

"Ah, yes. When you met Dylan in college, you said he had a quiet confidence, but did he seem dark or depressed in any way?"

Belinda shook her head. "If he had been, I never would have been attracted to him."

"I suppose not. Did he ever mention the name Emily Kane to you?"

Belinda sat back farther into the couch and clasped her hands in her lap. "He did. It wasn't easy for him to talk about her, but she was raped and murdered just before college started. He didn't speak about her much, but he did testify at the trial in support of his friend. Not that it did his friend any good. I think that whole experience really helped Dylan know what he wanted to do with his life."

Madison tried to pick apart her last sentence to make sense of her meaning but wasn't sure. "What do you mean by that?"

"Oh, just that he wasn't sure that Richie... That was his name, right?"

Madison nodded.

Belinda added, "He didn't think he necessarily killed that girl."

That had Madison's heart picking up speed. She tried to suppress the flush of anxiety that made her body quake. "No one wants to think that of a friend."

"I guess that's true." Belinda bobbed her head.

"How did Dylan feel when Richie was sentenced to twenty-four years?"

"He didn't really give much of a reaction, just said in an off-the-cuff manner that Richie must have done it if twelve people saw it that way. But as I said, it helped him know he wanted to be a lawyer and stand up for people."

So he was a defense attorney... But it was hard to accept that Dylan had spoken in Richie's defense and was nonchalant about accepting the verdict. Something seemed off there. There might be more here she hadn't anticipated uncovering. Had Dylan raped and murdered Emily Kane? The concept was a wild-card theory, but it occurred to her, nonetheless. If that was the case, it made it more likely the killer held him accountable for that night. But why take revenge all these years later? And how did that explain Richie Klein's murder and Troy being framed? There were obviously things she was missing. "It doesn't sound like Dylan was too upset about what had happened to this girl." She did her best to keep judgment from her tone.

"He didn't like to talk about her, but I'm sure you can understand why. It wouldn't exactly be something you'd want to dwell on."

"Then you wouldn't say he seemed bothered or haunted by it at all?"

Belinda shook her head. "After the verdict was handed down, he didn't really say anything more."

Strange behavior to be sure, and it could be indicative of him bottling up his feelings. It could just as equally be evidence that Dylan Graham had indeed let the past go. None of that accounted for Dylan journaling. "During the time you were married, did Dylan ever journal or speak with a therapist?" Madison could only imagine what her therapist, Tabitha Connor, would have to say about all that had transpired this past week.

"Not that I ever saw. You have to appreciate the man I was married to was a hardened defense attorney. He represented the scum of the earth and did it with a smile on his face when he got them off. Even when it was clear they were guilty."

This made Madison more suspicious about Dylan Graham's past. Had he watched on as his friend was sent to prison for a crime he himself committed? Or had the pair worked together? And bringing this to the present day, where did that leave Troy? And how did it explain this journal Dylan supposedly wrote in? Did he take up the habit of penning his thoughts after his separation and divorce? But surely, if the Emily Kane murder weighed on him, Belinda would have known. She would have seen something in the man she went to bed with night after night for years and had known since college.

"Is there anything else, Detective?" Belinda asked, cutting through Madison's thoughts.

"No, that's all." Madison stood to leave.

"Sorry I couldn't have been of more help."

"You were. More than you know. Thank you."

Belinda shut the door behind her, and Madison took a deep inhale of the cool December air. She came here thinking she'd get some clear-cut answers and was leaving somewhat befuddled. She wasn't convinced that Dylan Graham had been the great man Belinda had painted him to be. Madison would wager he'd had his secrets. Whether that was involvement in the rape and murder of Emily Kane, she didn't know. What she had, though, was the Braybury detectives telling her about a journal, in Dylan Graham's handwriting, alleging that Troy was Emily's rapist and killer. But according to Belinda, Dylan hadn't shown any signs of being aggrieved by the past.

What am I missing?

Then the answer hit her like a bullet between the eyes.

CHAPTER 33

Detective Carson Snow was at his desk, and he flipped through the forensics reports from the Klein case. There was proof in black and white that Troy Matthews had been in the motel room. Though he didn't need lab reports to confirm something Matthews hadn't denied. In fact, he'd been forthcoming, once Carson got Jeremy to shut up for two minutes, about the fact he went there to speak with Klein. He didn't even deny that they got into a scuffle. Matthews had also disclosed his suspicions about Klein being Dylan Graham's killer. Carson could see how he could make that assumption, especially if he served time for a crime he didn't commit. He might hold his friends responsible if he thought their testimonies let him down.

Matthews had also confessed that he was never certain of his friend's innocence but justified standing up for him in open court. He said it was what friends did for each other.

Carson appreciated the loyalty even if it was offered blindly. And Matthews hadn't said it in as many words, but Carson swore it was written in his eyes that he now believed Richie Klein had raped and murdered Emily Kane.

Of course, that was in Troy's favor, but he'd only alluded to it. Maybe Matthews was tired of pleading his own innocence when his claims kept getting slapped down. Carson couldn't blame him there, but he was just doing his job. There was evidence working against the SWAT team leader, and Carson couldn't just ignore that because the man carried a badge. The law was the law, but he was having a hard time swallowing this as justification. He appreciated there were shades of gray with every case, too, and that crime scenes were rarely a distinct black and white. In fact, when they were, that was when he had doubts.

Take the Dylan Graham case. The suicide letter at a murder scene was keeping him up at night. He'd flipped it over and over in his mind, trying to rationalize it. Maybe Graham had decided to kill himself and wrote the letter, but before he could carry it out, his killer had beat him to it. It was a stretch, but not entirely impossible. He'd learned a long time ago that anything was possible no matter how seemingly unlikely. Often the more unlikely was the truth.

He didn't know Matthews before he hauled him in for Graham's murder, but there was something honest and pure about the man. There were times he considered that Matthews had been framed.

It was clear Matthews felt the same way, not only because he suspected Klein but because he went so far as to seek him out. Had he killed him? Maybe even by accident, a physical altercation that got out of hand, or self-defense? But Matthews never claimed any of that. Then again, how would a tightened belt around the neck support that? No, Klein had been deliberately murdered. By Matthews? Carson wasn't sure, but his opinion mattered little when faced with eyewitness testimony. Uniformed officers had returned to the motel clerk, and he identified Troy Matthews from a photo array as the man who went into Klein's motel room. At the same time, they inquired if he had seen anyone else enter room 8 after Matthews had left. No one had. This was a request Matthews had made, and it hadn't paid off for him. Just like nothing else had.

As Carson sat watching the clock move forward, it was only a handful of hours before Matthews would be back in front of a judge. Matthews was going to be crucified. A second murder on the same day he had been released on his own recognizance from a previous homicide charge… It wouldn't matter who was sitting on the bench. Any judge would lock him up, and if he or she set bail, chances were it would be astronomical.

At this point, though, Carson's hands were tied. The evidence mounted against Matthews was present and held. An eyewitness account and his DNA on the victim. Going back to the Graham case, his gun and a journal entry providing feasible motive for the two bodies in the morgue.

For Carson, it came down to whether Troy Matthews raped and murdered Emily Kane as opined in the journal. Carson's gut told him Matthews wasn't the type. And why murder a man days before his own wedding and another after being freed on his own recognizance? None of that made sense either.

Same with the 911 call about the disturbance at the Sandman Motel. Why would a passerby, not someone staying at the motel, have a reason to call? And on a payphone, no less. Everyone had a cell phone these days. If Carson were to guess, the caller wanted to remain anonymous. The reason for that could only be sinister. He'd discussed all this with Chief Fletcher from the Stiles PD, but they were still waiting on video footage that covered the payphone. Even so, a face only got them so far. Without a suspect to start with, they'd need to hope he was in a facial recognition database.

None of this was sitting well with Carson, but taking a stand for Matthews was far more complicated. Sergeant Durham wasn't taking meetings with him but had passed a message through his assistant. He viewed disagreement on par with insubordination, which wouldn't be tolerated. Durham didn't want detectives who thought for themselves, he wanted minions to do his bidding.

As was often the case when he faced a moral dilemma, Carson looked at his daughter's photo.

The phone on his desk rang, interrupting his internal war. "Detective Snow," he answered.

"Detective Knight, and I need you to listen to me."

Carson admired her gumption and how she was the type to tell things how she saw them. He could discern that much from the few dealings he'd had with her. "I'm listening."

"First of all, how many journals did you find in Dylan Graham's home?"

"Just the one."

"Hmm. Well, you need to have the handwriting in Dylan Graham's journal compared to samples of his known handwriting. With Graham being a lawyer, there should be a lot of documents to pull from."

So she found out he'd been a lawyer, though why should that surprise him? Carson could be offended that she assumed they hadn't bothered to do this, but her straightforwardness toned down his response. "That's already been done. The results aren't what you want to hear."

"Oh, I'm not saying that Graham didn't write it. I'm saying that he was *forced* to write it. The comparison is to see if it shows any signs of duress."

Carson sat back, thrumming his pen against his desk. "I can appreciate why you'd want to believe that—"

"No. It's not some wish. It's called being thorough, Detective. I…" She stopped speaking there, but what she wasn't saying caught his attention.

"You what…?" He sensed she'd done something and was close to making the admission when she'd gone quiet.

"Did you even speak to Graham's ex-wife?" she pushed out. "Even look into his personal life? Or did you just decide you'd pin the murder on Troy? Run with the convenient finds in front of you?"

His cheeks heated at the accusation. Probably for how accurate it was, for the fact he was being forced to be the person he despised, and she was calling him out for it. "You take care of your investigations, Detective, and I'll handle mine."

"Huh. Sounds like you didn't bother, then."

Carson had a feeling Madison was doing more than running on assumptions. She'd likely spoken with the ex-wife, tramped on his and Jeremy's toes. "You shouldn't be interfering in a Braybury homicide investigation, no matter how close you are to the suspect."

"Suspect," Madison scoffed. "Don't you mean *accused*? Because that's more accurate."

A few beats of silence stretched across the line, which Carson broke because he was just uncomfortable. He could see himself through the same lens as Madison and didn't like what he saw. "Is there something I can do for you?"

"Just your job. Have that handwriting analyzed again, maybe by someone different. Have them see if there's any evidence that he wrote it under duress."

"And why would I do that?" He knew he was being stubborn and proud, but it stung how accurate her assessment was of him. Somewhere along the line, he'd lost his backbone.

"Because Dylan Graham didn't journal. Not ever."

"Says who?"

"You just told me a minute ago there was only *one* journal in his home. Don't you find that odd?"

Carson didn't respond, but her words confirmed she had been poking around.

Madison went on. "Let's just say you do. You should anyway. But he also never gave any indication that he was haunted by what had happened to Emily Kane. He never voiced his accusation about Troy to anyone."

He wasn't going to ask how she knew this, and he was going to let it pass. Let her do what he couldn't. At least someone out there was free to be Troy Matthews's champion and approach things objectively. His daughter's face was staring at him, and he felt the judgment and turned the frame down. "Are you suggesting the killer forced Dylan Graham to write the accusation against Troy in a journal?"

"That's what the evidence tells me. Someone out there wanted to frame Troy for Graham's murder, give him motive. The existence of a phone call between Graham and Troy was an added bonus for this guy."

"If this person is set on revenge, as you make it sound, why not kill Troy?" Carson was barely grasping on to the case against Matthews. He could feel it slipping through his fingers.

"This person wants him to suffer. He might see prison as a greater punishment than death. Troy has dedicated his entire life to being an officer of the law. To have all that work called into question, to be publicly humiliated and sent away to prison… that is a death all its own. It just doesn't end as quickly."

Being a lifer himself, Carson could appreciate what she was saying, and her case had all his doubts blossoming. "That blasted suicide note."

"The what? What did you just say?"

He snapped his mouth shut. His thoughts had been so thunderous, he'd spoken out loud.

"What *suicide note*?"

He was cornered. It was time to come clean. "There was a suicide note left at the scene of Dylan Graham's murder."

"There was— *What?* Are you kidding me? And you charged my fiancé with murder? I'll have your badge."

Carson deserved all her wrath and more, but it wasn't hers that held his future in the balance. Once the chief found out that he'd let the suicide note slip, he'd probably rally for his badge. He just might get it too, as Carson would be guilty of divulging sensitive case information he'd specifically been ordered to withhold.

"Talk to me. Now."

Carson had to try to backpedal out of this one. "It seems Graham was intending to take his life. It's just that the killer beat him to it." Carson pinched his eyes shut. There must be a spot reserved for him in hell at this rate.

"Troy. That's what you really mean when you say *killer*, isn't it? I mean you have officially charged him."

Again, Carson was saying all the wrong things without meaning to do so, but he wasn't going to touch on her comment. "The victim suffered a gunshot that was not self-inflicted. The angle doesn't support that, and your fiancé's gun was retrieved from the crime scene."

"Convenient," she muttered. "Can't you see this is a frame job? What did the suicide note say?"

"'I'm sorry for past sins but take these with me now. To the grave.'" The words flowed from his lips without a thought of his future with the

Braybury PD. To hell with it. Madison deserved to know. Maybe Carson could turn things around, or at least do a wholehearted job from this point forward.

"Make sure it's analyzed too. Either again or for the first time. And is there any way to determine if the same pen was used on the note and journal entry? Also if it was written at the same time?"

"I'm sure there is."

"Good. Get it done or I will."

"I'll have this rushed through. You have my word."

Madison ended the call without a thank-you or goodbye, and he couldn't blame her. He wasn't owed basic pleasantries. He'd become the type of cop he'd always hated. Righting his daughter's picture, he promised her and himself to turn this around. He'd do what he could to get to the truth. He might not get his retirement package, but he'd be going out with some dignity.

CHAPTER 34

Madison's earlobes were sizzling with rage, and tremors crackled through her entire body. Before Detective Snow's slip, there hadn't been one word about a suicide note. If he had disclosed this to Andrea, she would have passed this along. But Andrea did express feeling the Braybury detectives were holding back. Was the suicide note the extent of it, or was there more? Honestly, she wasn't putting anything past Detective Snow and his partner anymore.

She wasn't blind to the fact there were corrupt cops out there. Some within her own department were entangled with the mob. She did her best to ferret them out, though she considered it a work in progress. But what did Snow or Friedman stand to gain by prosecuting Troy?

Madison was still sitting in her Mazda outside of Belinda Graham's house, and she probably wasn't fit to drive as intoxicated with rage as she was.

Snow probably thought by promising to do his actual job by having the writing analyzed again, he was going above and beyond. Unfreaking-believable.

Madison didn't remember the exact words of the suicide note, but the gist was enough. Something about apologizing for past sins he'd take with him to the grave. While this could be twisted to correlate to the journal entry, did it carry further meaning? As she'd suspected after speaking with Belinda Graham, did Dylan play a role in Emily Kane's rape and murder? She expected the killer had told him what to write, likely holding him at gunpoint, but maybe he didn't dictate the exact words. Or was it as Detective Snow said, and something had Dylan Graham becoming suicidal? If the letter was legitimate, did that mean the journal was too? Or was one authentic and the other not?

The variables were plentiful, but two facts remained. The killer had a grudge against Troy, and Emily Kane's murder had resurfaced. Why after twenty-four years though? It made her think it tied in with Richie Klein's release from prison. If not, had he been triggered by something else more recently?

Was it someone who didn't think the right man served time? Or *enough* time? But if they thought Richie Klein was innocent, why kill him? And what made him think Richie wasn't guilty? Was it Emily's killer himself returning?

Though why resurface after getting away with it all these years? There was obviously a lot she was missing, but the clock was ticking.

It was ten forty. Troy was due in front of a judge in less than five hours.

Gah. It was maddening.

In an ideal world, she'd follow up with Emily's other best friend, her parents, and Dylan Graham's place of work. It was possible someone involved with a recent case was connected to him in the past. She'd need Terry's help to delve into that.

Her phone rang, and caller ID told her it was Andrea. "Tell me we have his face," Madison answered.

"Yes, the footage caught it, but the quality is crap. It's very grainy and made worse by zooming in, but the lab's working on it."

"Which one?" Madison didn't exactly have much faith in Braybury at the moment.

"Braybury. Listen, Madison, that's not why I called. I heard from Troy a moment ago. Before you ask, he's fine and hanging in there, but he thought of something. He also believes someone has been watching him, and you too."

The footprints in the snow told Madison that, but what had convinced Troy? "Why?"

"He's noticed a silver Hyundai Accent on a few occasions. Most recently last night when he was turning into the Sandman Motel."

Madison shifted up straighter in her seat. "That can't be a coincidence."

"I don't think so either."

"Check the Department of Motor Vehicles for any registrations that fit those parameters."

"That's been done. There are far too many to act on. Where are you right now?"

She looked at Belinda's house and noticed the curtain fall back straight. Belinda had been watching Madison, likely curious why she hadn't left yet. "You probably don't want to know."

Andrea didn't touch on that but said, "Why do you always have to play the hero?"

"This time, Troy needs me to be, and I'm not going to let him down. Please understand that." She glanced in her rearview mirror and caught the glimpse of a silver car, though not able to make out its make and model, but it was probably her imagination getting carried away. Weren't silver and white the most popular colors for vehicles? "I'll be careful," she eventually assured Andrea and ended the call. At least her future in-law didn't insist on sending officers out to watch over her.

It wasn't until the call ended that she realized she hadn't told Andrea about the suicide note. She'd been rather distracted by the news Andrea had shared. But she wasn't going to let this sicko dissuade her from getting to the truth. She hit Terry's contact, counting on his willingness to help her again.

CHAPTER 35

"Hot from the crime lab." Jeremy Friedman swooped around Carson's desk and dropped a folder on it.

Whenever Carson didn't think his partner could be any more annoying, he proved him wrong. Before the unpleasant interruption, Carson's mind had been on both the Graham and Klein cases, even though most of his focus should have been on the former. They needed to gather all the evidence from the Graham case together for the DA. The probable cause hearing was next Tuesday. While that was a week away, it still demanded their primary focus. "What is it?"

"The print results."

"Just a tad more clarification would be great." His thoughts were all over, and he couldn't make sense of the little his partner had said.

"Right. I forget you're getting up there." Jeremy tapped a finger to his head and dropped onto a chair facing Carson's desk.

"It's from the articles on Emily Kane that Graham had printed and stowed away in his desk. You had initiated the request."

"That was fast." He'd made the call to the lab after hanging up with Madison. He'd asked about the printing and for the handwriting analysis to be revisited. Carson opened the folder, but before he could get the results, Jeremy took the punch line.

"Only a couple of prints on them. They belonged to Dylan Graham."

A couple of prints... Carson chewed on that and didn't like the flavor. "That makes no sense. Those articles were printed from his printer, which has already been verified, so logic would dictate his prints would be all over them."

"You have the report." Jeremy went to lift his feet onto Carson's desk, but Carson fired a glare at him that prevented that from happening.

"Regardless, so few prints doesn't make sense. The killer must have handled the printouts with gloves." Carson was really starting to lean toward all of this being a frame job against Matthews.

"Did the... *What now?*" Jeremy scrunched up his face, looking like a petulant teenager, and it made Carson want to smack him.

"We need to look at the evidence objectively. If you do, you must admit everything is clean and convenient."

"That's right. Matthews pretty much did our job for us."

Carson smirked. "You really believe that of a career cop? That he would be so careless about covering his tracks?" It was just another lingering anomaly torturing his conscience.

"You know where the chief and sarge stand on this. You want to go against them? I don't."

Carson could go into the fact their first responsibility was to the badge, not earning anyone's approval, but why waste his breath? Jeremy was ambitious, with his eye on climbing rank, and it was impossible to get there without playing the game. Or so Carson was learning for himself.

"I don't understand why you wanted the articles printed anyhow."

"Let me explain it to you." Carson told him his running theory that the killer manipulated pretty much everything on scene. He even admitted that he questioned whether Matthews was the man they were after.

"Huh. So you are working against the sarge?"

"I never said that. I'm looking at the evidence."

"Matthews faces a judge for the Klein murder this afternoon. Now you choose not to stand your ground and doubt he's a killer. Sort of the final hour, don't you think?"

"You're right. I should have said something long before now, but I was too busy being told to shut up and put up." Carson was done being manipulated by the higher-ups. "There were things that stood out about the Graham case from the start. I never should have dismissed them. I whitewashed my conscience by focusing on the seemingly solid evidence against him."

"Yeah, like his gun at the scene," Jeremy slapped back.

"Like that. But surely you must see there is room for doubt when considering all the so-called evidence against him."

Jeremy shrugged and blew out a breath. "I don't know."

In other words, Jeremy didn't want the conflict. "We owe it to Matthews, to the people of Braybury, to conduct a fair and just investigation."

"Did you tell all this to the sarge or the chief?"

"I'm prepared to. Soon. I'm still waiting for some other results."

Jeremy's eyes narrowed. "Why didn't you mention your doubts to me before? What has you thinking Matthews is innocent anyhow?"

At least his partner's ego seemed to be stepping down. Carson shared how the suicide note niggled, also about the journal and his theories there.

"We need to determine if the journal is legit, then. If it's not, there might be foreign fingerprints on the cover. I doubt the killer handled it with gloves from the day he bought it. I mean, it's worth a shot anyway."

Carson smiled. "Nice to see you stepping up, Friedman." Their sergeant and the chief might not be of the same opinion, but that was on them. Carson got on the phone with the crime lab and requested that the journal cover be tested for prints. They were already working on the handwriting analysis, and he was told there was a way to date the ink. Graham's journal entry was dated a few days before his murder. It would be interesting to see what the crime lab turned up. Carson was in the mood to call everything into question. After all, if the brass was going to shit on him, he might as well make it rain.

CHAPTER 36

Madison Knight was in the passenger seat of a Stiles PD department car, while Terry was behind the wheel. It was an unusual arrangement, as she normally drove, but that could be said of what brought them together too. They were across the street from the house belonging to Dawn Summers, Emily Kane's mother. Her father had split not long after Emily's birth, leaving the mother to raise her alone. Dawn had married a man named Phil five years ago.

"It's not going to be easy in there. She lost her child twenty-four years ago, but I doubt it's something you ever get over." Terry turned to face her. "Are you sure you want to do this?"

"I don't think we have much choice. Emily's murder is tied in with what's happening now. If we stand any chance of getting Troy out of jail, a trip to the past is necessary."

"If you're absolutely sure…?"

"I am. Trust my gut." She threw that latter bit out with a smile. Her *gut* had been the topic of many conversations between them. With general predictability, he'd give her a hard time about how she followed her feelings over tangible evidence. But her intuition never let her down.

"All right. I'll let you have this one. You are going through a rough patch."

Huh, what do you know? "That's putting it mildly."

He shut off the car, and they got out and headed to the house. When Madison had called Terry and asked for his help, he'd been more than willing. He said his week was off to a slow start. A good thing considering their job dealt with major crimes, most often homicide cases. When Terry had picked her up at her house, he said he wanted to keep this to the length of a lunchbreak. Longer than that and he feared Sergeant Winston would become curious about what he was up to.

Madison pressed the doorbell, and it chimed a cheery ditty.

"Let me take the lead in there, though, okay?" Terry said to her quietly as they waited for someone to answer.

Madison hadn't agreed to those terms up front, but she could understand Terry's request. She wasn't here officially. But while she'd been told to stay away from the cases against Troy, an argument could be made this didn't apply. They were here about a twenty-four-year-old *closed* case. In fact, maybe it was time to share this thought with Andrea. She wouldn't be stepping on the toes of the Braybury detectives but working to solidify proof that Troy had nothing to do with Emily's murder. If she could pull that off, Troy's motive to kill Dylan Graham would crumble.

The door opened, and a beautiful woman in her forties stood there, arms crossed, head tilted, a pleasant resting smile in place.

"Dawn Summers?" Terry lifted his badge.

"That's me." Summers drew her gaze from Terry to Madison, and she felt empty-handed not holding up her shield but would play it Terry's way for now.

"We're..." Terry cleared his throat. "I'm Detective Grant, and this is my partner. We have some questions relating to your daughter's case."

I guess he is acknowledging me as if I'm here officially... Though he left out my name.

Summers bunched her sweater at the collar. "My daughter's killer went to prison. I don't understand what is left to talk about."

"If we could just come in for a moment," Terry beseeched her.

Summers worried her bottom lip, and Madison was convinced she was going to turn them away just as she stepped back and gestured for them to enter.

"Would either of you like tea? I was about to make one," Summers said.

"No, but thank you for asking," Madison said, speaking up.

Terry accepted the offer in typical Terry fashion. He really did balance her. She was always in blitz mission mode, and he was more laid-back and low-key. He'd argued before that if you were present and really listened, people were more willing to open up. In Madison's experience, no one dispensed with their personal information easily.

Summers took them to the kitchen, in the rear of the house. She gestured toward the adjacent dining room. "Sit at the table if you'd like. I'll bring the milk and sugar over."

"Thanks," Terry told her as he took a seat, and Madison sat next to him.

Summers grabbed a second mug from the cupboard and dropped in a tea bag. An electric kettle clicked, and she poured the boiled water. Next, she set a timer on the microwave for three minutes and brought everything over to the table. "What is it you are here to say after all these years?" She lowered onto a chair. "That he should have served more time? The guy who did this got out last week, but my sweet Emily will never feel the sun on her face again."

Her comment drew Madison's attention to Summers's face. The pain of losing her daughter in such a violent way had carved lines in her brow and around her mouth. Darkness shadowed her eyes. But her words highlighted something else. Before coming here, she and Terry established their purpose was to see if anyone related to Emily hadn't been happy with the verdict twenty-four years ago. The theory being this person's bitterness was the basis for the recent murders. They were here for all of two seconds, and Dawn Summers had expressed her discontent.

"We are sorry for your immeasurable loss," Terry told her.

"Thank you. People think I should be over it by now, but I still feel her loss as fresh as the day I received the news. The only difference is I need to think about it for a moment to conjure up its full intensity." Summers rubbed her arms as if fending off a chill. "I used to think that made me a horrible mother, but my therapist told me that it's normal with the passage of time. And healthy."

Despite Summers's words, Madison wondered just how much she had moved on. The evidence pointed to a man, but it didn't mean Summers wasn't working in harmony with one.

"You must believe Richie Klein should have gotten life in prison," Terry said, clearly picking up on what Madison had.

"Yes. And I realize he was just a child himself at the time, but he raped and strangled—"

The microwave beeped.

Summers took the tea bag out of her mug and set it on a plate she'd brought over. Terry did the same and added milk and sugar to his. Summers took hers with just a rounded spoonful of sugar.

"Do you ever wonder if they got the wrong man?" Madison asked.

Summers peered into her mug. She didn't blow on it or attempt a sip. "I have worked to release all my doubts. Regardless of who did this, she deserved better."

"Do you believe that justice was served, at least?" Madison countered.

"Honestly? I'm not sure I'd ever be satisfied. Emily was my only child. Please just tell me what you'd like from me."

Madison looked at Terry, letting him broach the territory that bordered on the Graham and Klein cases. Regarding the latter, it didn't seem that Summers had heard the latest news from that morning about his murder or she might have shown more relief.

Terry said, "Your daughter's name was brought up in a recent case—"

"Really? Why?" Her brow furrowed.

"I'm not at liberty to say exactly," Terry said, toeing a line. "Does the name Dylan Graham mean anything to you though?"

"It sounds familiar. Did he testify for that Klein kid at the trial?"

"He did," Terry affirmed.

"Well, I was in quite a daze back then. I was also very angry that his friends had the audacity to stand up for him after what he did to my girl."

It seemed Summers was quite set in her opinion that the right man was sent to prison, but she'd also expressed she wasn't happy with the sentence. The question was, did she harbor ill will all these years toward Klein's friends for trying to aid his case? The footprints near the hedge on her and Troy's property line were too large for a woman. It had also been a man who had called 911, which led to the discovery of Klein's body. But as Madison considered a moment ago, Summers could be working with one. "How does your husband feel about all this?"

"Phil wasn't in my life back then."

"He must still have an opinion," Madison volleyed back.

"Oh, he does, and he wishes I'd just let the past go and move on with my life. He just doesn't understand what losing a child does to a mother. Do you have children?"

Madison shook her head. "But Detective Grant has a daughter."

Summers gestured toward Terry. "Then you can imagine."

"I don't think I can," Terry said. "Not to the full extent. But what were things like at home for Emily back then?"

"She was the life of the party." Summers fell quiet, likely as it sank in that Emily had been killed at one. She blew on her tea and took a sip, then added, "She had two close friends she was always hanging around."

Based on what Summers told them, it was unlikely that her husband would be involved in any sort of revenge scheme. Not if he wanted Summers to let go of the past. It sounded horribly insensitive, but the man must have had redeemable qualities, as they'd been married for five years.

"And what about boyfriends?" Terry asked. If he had taken a second longer to ask, Madison would have. She had what Joni and Brooke told her, but the mother's perspective could be telling.

"She had a few from what I gathered. I was caught up in dealing with my own issues. Her stepfather and I were going through a rough time. Not long before her high school graduation, we called it quits."

"I didn't realize you were married before Phil," Terry said.

"I never married the man, but we cohabitated with his fifteen-year-old brat of a kid, Dameon, and he was a little demon."

Madison noted the rather clinical term for living together, but her skin prickled at the mention of Emily having a stepbrother and Summers's label for him. "A little demon?"

"He was constantly getting into mischief. Surprised that he never got himself arrested. He'd cut class and pull pranks that bordered on dangerous. But what did it for me was he was obsessed with Emily." Summers mocked shivers, but Madison felt some making their way down her spine.

"How was he obsessed?" She shot Terry a side-glance, realizing she was approaching a line here. Dameon might have reason to come forward to vindicate Emily's name, especially if he didn't think the sentence fit the crime.

"He'd just stare at her while we ate dinner, and sometimes when we had family movie night. He even made her a mixtape, which she threw at his head."

"How did he take that?" Terry asked.

"I thought it was going to end very badly, but Dameon just picked it up off the floor and told her that one day she'd appreciate him."

The words and the way Summers served them chilled Madison. It brought her mind back to what Brooke Morales had told her about Emily Kane, the fact that she slept around. Madison might have been close with an earlier theory. Had someone Emily rejected done this to her and not Klein? But where did that leave the present-day murders? What would be Dameon's motive to kill Graham and Klein and frame Troy? But as her mind posed the question, it served up the answer. He was obsessed with his stepsister or, from his perspective, in love.

Troy and his friends banded together to speak on Klein's behalf. Their character testimonies could have made the difference between a life sentence and the one that was doled out. "How did he react to Emily's murder?" she asked.

"He was gone by then. Well, out of our lives anyway."

None of this assured Madison that Dameon wasn't who they were looking for. "What's Dameon's last name?"

"Babcock."

She stood and thanked Summers for her time and saw herself out.

Terry followed behind and unlocked the car for them. Once inside, he got the engine started and the heat turned on. "Mind telling me what you're thinking?"

"Can't you see it? Dameon, the stepbrother."

"Yes, what about him?"

"You were in there with me, right? He loved Emily. He might not have hurt her, but if he's continued holding on to her all these years, there's no saying what he wouldn't do. Especially if he didn't think Klein received adequate punishment for his crime. We came here looking for someone who felt that way, and we may have found one."

"Exactly, *may* have found one. She told us she has no idea how he took the news of the verdict. That doesn't mean he didn't take it well. But even if he didn't, it's twenty-four years later. One would think he'd have moved on by now."

Warm air finally started kicking out the vents, and Madison held her hands in front of them. Her fingertips were frozen. And she was giving thought to Terry's words. A sane person probably would have moved on. She might be trying to see a killer where there wasn't one.

"What's his motive?" Terry asked.

She could repeat herself, that he felt an injustice had been done, but added a new theory. "He obviously had romantic feelings for her as a teen. A mixtape tells us that. Her murder stole his opportunity to be with her."

"I don't know. It feels like a stretch."

She smiled.

"What?"

"It's what you always do. I share my thinking, and you knock it down. It feels like old times."

"You realize *old times* was just last week before you decided to— Never mind."

"Yeah, I know. Take time off to get married." She looked down at her engagement ring, the princess-cut diamond winking at her. Mocking her? It should have been joined by a wedding band. She shook aside the sadness that was edging in. "It feels longer ago than last week. With you moving on to become a sergeant, we might not have many disagreements left."

"Ha. If I become your boss, we'll have plenty."

It was one thing to consider Terry as a sergeant, another to label him her boss. She did her best to put that tidbit out of her mind. "Yeah, well…"

"I mean, you aren't getting sentimental on me. Are you, Knight?" He smiled at her.

"In all seriousness," she began, not even touching on Terry's question, "we need to track down Dameon Babcock and have a little talk. That's the only way we'll know if he has motive or can be ruled out."

Terry's face fell serious. "You mean *I'll* have a little talk with him."

She shook her head. "Actually, *I* will."

"That's not going to happen."

"Then we will do it together. Dameon is in our jurisdiction. Our interest at this point is seeing if he may have hurt Emily."

"Bologna. You know that's not what you're after at all. You just made it clear to me you consider him a suspect in the recent murders. The ones belonging to the Braybury PD," he stressed.

She hitched her shoulders. "Then we find something else to bring him in."

"Huh, and we can hold him without pressing charges for forty-eight hours."

"I like it when you talk dirty to me." She laughed, feeling it in her chest. Nothing brought her more happiness than seeing scum land behind bars. And if this particular scum framed Troy, it would bring her immense joy.

CHAPTER 37

Madison knew that Terry needed to get back to the station before Winston noticed he was gone longer than the length of a lunch hour, but they had a stellar lead in Dameon Babcock. She could feel it.

Terry looked him up in the onboard computer. "Clean record. Also, no vehicles are registered to him. Weapons, as you know, is another database I'd have to check."

"He doesn't need a gun of his own. If this is our guy, he took Troy's, but you heard about the silver Hyundai Accent?" She was running on a hunch he had because he mentioned no registered vehicles.

"I did."

"So that's why you're here helping me? You are worried about me and thought if you came along, you could also keep an eye on me. And don't say, two birds, one stone."

"You bet I'm worried about you. Troy's been framed for two murders, and whoever is behind this is unhinged."

"Bless you for seeing that."

"That we're looking for some unhinged whack job? Doesn't that go without saying?"

"I was referring to your faith in Troy's innocence."

"Not a doubt in my mind. But all of this stinks of revenge. Those types are notably unpredictable. They're governed by emotions, and we know how—"

"Don't even start." She smirked at him, knowing her partner was going to make a jab at her because she let her feelings guide her often.

"Anyway, you get what I'm saying."

"I do, but I choose not to dwell on it. Yes, the guy's dangerous, but we need to have a chat with this Dameon Babcock. Due diligence. Either he's who we're after or he's not. If you need to return to the station, I understand, but I'm doing this with or without you."

"Urgh. You can be infuriating. But, yes, I should at least show up, be seen around."

"I understand."

"But you wait for me before talking to Babcock."

"You're already sounding like my boss."

Terry didn't say anything to that and got them on the road in the direction of the station. "I hate that you're going through all this. You guys should be on your honeymoon."

"Teaches me for taking time off."

Terry angled his head and looked over at her as he slowed for a stop sign. "There's no correlation."

She nodded, but she wasn't sure she believed that. After all, she gave in to believing she'd have a happily-ever-after. That had been blown to bits. "Troy is set to face a judge in a matter of hours. At this rate, we have little chance of stopping that," she said, feeling so powerless.

"You can't know that for sure. Just keep the faith." Terry pulled away from the intersection.

"You sound like Troy and his sister with their 'it will all get sorted.'"

"Sounds very British."

"Actually, it does." She'd have to ask Troy to tell her more about his parents. All she knew was that they'd died in a car accident several years ago.

"They're trying to keep positive, and I know you are doing your best." He gave her a smile, but it faded as his eyes caught something in the rearview mirror.

"What is it?"

"You might not want to know."

"Tell me." A bad feeling washed over her. She looked over her shoulder but didn't see anything.

"There's a silver Hyundai a few cars back. It might just be a coincidence. It's not like they're rare."

"No, it's him." Adrenaline flushed through her. "We need to figure out how to flip this around and corner him."

Terry didn't say anything.

"Terry," she prompted.

"This can't be happening right now." He gripped at the steering wheel and glanced upward.

He must have been thinking ahead, of how a chase would become part of the record. He'd have to defend himself to Winston. But if he only realized it wasn't possible to please everyone all the time. Even rule followers ticked people off on occasion. "This could be our only chance," she petitioned.

"I stepped out for an hour. Now I'm going to have to explain how I got involved with a car chase. Assuming it comes to that."

Just as I thought… "If it helps, I'm sure Andrea will have your back."

"You're sure? I'm not. She has her own career to think about. The last thing she'd want is to be seen as taking liberties or creating her own rules. The guy in the Hyundai seems caught up in the Graham and Klein cases. These belong to the Braybury PD. There's your black and white that I know you're typically fond of."

Madison rolled her eyes. He was undeniably like a brother. He effortlessly shifted between gentle teasing and provocation. "This is our chance to get this guy, Terry."

He smacked the steering wheel.

"Just test it out," she said. "Make a few turns and see if he follows."

Terry signaled, pulled into the right lane, and took the corner. She held her breath as she looked through the side mirror. An Accent slowly came into view. The driver's face was obscured by a glare across the windshield, and tinted plate covers wiped out any possibility of getting the license number. But she smiled. "We have cause to pull him over. Tinted plate covers." They were illegal in the state.

"Here goes." Terry eased to the side of the street. He must have been planning to let the Accent pass and then pursue.

What felt like painstaking minutes later, the car came alongside them and pulled ahead. Madison tried to get a look at the driver as the vehicle passed. The buildings were reflecting on the passenger window. "Son of—" She clamped her mouth shut. Terry hated swearing, and he was here as a favor to her and Troy. Risking his own neck, no less, and not just a reprimand from Winston. This killer was clearly following her. Was he content stalking from a distance, or was he planning to come for her? She didn't have a death wish, but she wasn't afraid either. She'd love to strangle this clown with her own hands for what he'd already put Troy through, not to mention the lives he took. But she didn't want Terry caught up in this web too, his life put in danger.

The car passed, and the rear plates were obscured too.

"I should call this in," Terry said.

"No."

"What do you mean no? A second ago, you practically begged me to corner this guy."

"I've had time to think. You call this in to dispatch and let them know you're going to pull over a silver Hyundai Accent for illegal plate covers, and that will get back to Winston. He'll wonder why his major crimes detective is concerning himself with such a thing. It won't be long before he puts it together and knows you're helping me."

"If we're doing this, I want it on the record in case..." He left the end of that sentence to dangle. Her imagination kicked in, but she didn't want to dwell on how this could turn ugly.

Madison put a hand on his arm and shook her head. "Which is exactly why we need to back down and let others handle it from here. I'm going to call this in and say *I'm* being followed."

He nodded. "Okay."

She made the call to dispatch and texted Andrea after hanging up.

> *A silver Hyundai Accent is tailing me. Called it in.*

Her phone pinged back immediately.

Just watch your back. Good move on stepping down.

Madison could only take minimal satisfaction in Andrea's words. She had removed them from the pursuit for Terry's sake.

Sirens wailed in the distance, their volume growing louder as the cruisers blazed past her and Terry. With any luck, they'd catch up with the driver, and Madison would finally have some real answers.

CHAPTER 38

The man was happy for the forethought of blacking out his license plates. It had served him until now. He first heard the sirens, then he saw the whirling lights in his rearview mirror. This was Madison's doing. He'd been spotted, and he could only hope that she didn't see him through the tinted car windows. Though even if she did, she was unlikely to recognize him anyway.

The cruisers narrowed in, tight to his bumper. The officers were signaling for him to pull over. *Yeah, right.* This game would end on his terms, and that time wasn't now. That would ruin everything.

He pressed his foot heavier on the gas, and the car lunged forward. Even still, he feared his horsepower wasn't a match for the police vehicles pursuing him. If he was going to get away, he had to make this about smart thinking. And he had no intention of being caught.

He reached for the silver chain around his neck, the plan to kiss the silver cross pendant he always wore, but he found it missing. Panic rose in his chest. He never took it off, even to shower. It meant the world to him, a gift from his sister many years ago.

Its absence threw off his concentration, and one of the cruisers banged against his bumper. The impact rocked the car. He overcorrected, and the passenger side washed over the curb and came close to striking a few pedestrians. Their screams pierced the air, but instead of causing him further panic, they invigorated him.

A police officer called over a loudspeaker, telling him to pull over.

Instead, he pressed the gas harder, now having regained control over the vehicle. The light at the intersection ahead of him turned yellow. The car in front of him braked, but he steered around it. Cross traffic came through, and a pickup truck almost T-boned his car. He squeezed past on a hope, a prayer, and a flattened foot on the gas.

The maneuver and the timing managed to distance him from most of his pursuers. Only one cruiser was on his tail now, but they were a ways back. He took a turn that would take him through the downtown core. Risky, as he might pick up more cops, but he had to try a Hail Mary. Working for him was the noon traffic. It was heavy but moving. He'd try to blend in among all the other silver cars.

What he didn't count on was winter road work ahead. Signs were telling him to merge into the right lane.

"Shit!" He slapped the steering wheel and creeped forward. Things were moving too slow. He was going to get caught.

He looked past the orange blockade on the left, and a dump truck and backhoe taking up a chunk of the intersection. Unusual for this time of the year, but whatever. It seemed most of the work was concentrated on just a small portion of the road, and there was room to skirt alongside.

Here goes...

He took the left turn and saw the flailing arms of construction workers in his rearview. To hell with them. If anyone was having a bad day, it was him. He kept going, hoping this had been the key move to his getaway.

Glancing back again, he saw no sign of police cars and breathed some relief. He kept driving until he reached the outskirts of the city and took a gravel road toward a train underpass. No one would find him there. He'd be safe.

Madison Knight, on the other hand, not so much. She was as good as dead. She just didn't know it yet.

CHAPTER 39

Madison couldn't believe it when the report came back that the Hyundai driver had given the cops the slip. She and Terry were at her house in the driveway. "That was our chance of catching this guy."

"He'll be back." Terry's cool tone drilled it home that this man was unlikely to give up easily.

When he turned up again, it would be for her. Bring it on. "I hope you're right. Next time, he's going down."

"I don't know how you can be so blasé about this. You have a killer stalking you. That clinches it for me. I can't leave you now. Forget it." Terry was shaking his head.

"You could land in real trouble with Winston."

"It is what it is. Your life is in danger. This guy won't stay away for long, and he'll be angry now."

"Good, in some ways. We're running out of time." Her gaze drifted to the clock on the dash. It was twelve thirty. Troy's appointment before the judge was racing toward him like a locomotive on tracks. She needed to derail it soon if he was to stand a chance. "I'm not just going to wait around though. Let's have a chat with Dameon Babcock. Who knows? He might be the Hyundai driver. I know you said he didn't have a vehicle registered to him, but he probably has friends who he could borrow from."

"All right. Let's do it." He was about to put the car into gear when Madison's phone rang.

Caller ID told her it was Cynthia. "Tell me you have the killer's face," she said.

"Slow down, woman."

"Right. Hello. How are you? Tell me you have the killer's face."

"Oh, Lord." Cynthia laughed, and it must have been stress, but Madison did too. Her friend cleared her throat. "Okay, his what now? Oh, the man who called nine-one-one. I'm not handling that. It's with the Braybury PD crime lab, but I haven't heard anything. I was just calling to make sure you're okay. I heard you were being tailed by the suspected killer."

As if there was any doubt that rumors flew around the department… It hadn't taken any time to make it up to the third-floor crime lab. "I'm good, but he got away." She purposefully left Terry out of it.

"Please, just be careful."

"You sound like Andrea."

"Well, everyone is worried about you."

"Not the Braybury detectives. They're incompetent, and the cases are as good as closed for them."

"They're not all that bad."

Madison passed a side-glance at Terry, who was likely to overhear every word. With all the excitement, she still hadn't let Andrea know about the suicide note. Cynthia and Terry would find out first. "They withheld evidence from the Dylan Graham murder scene. There was a suicide note there. A *suicide* note," she stressed, and it had Terry looking over at her with his eyebrows raised in surprise. She added, "How does that not alert them there's something wrong with the picture? That maybe what they see isn't straightforward?"

"I can't answer as to their thinking, but they have decided to share the evidence list from the Graham case with us."

"They have?" This revelation would have made her fall over if she wasn't already seated. Though it was about time. Did it also mean they were finally going to revisit the evidence with an objective eye, not biased preconceptions? Had it been her phone call to Detective Snow, or prep for the probable cause hearing that revealed all the gaping holes? "What prompted this change of heart?"

"It might be best not to question it and just take it as a win."

A bigger person would do that, but their previous roadblocks still pissed her off. All the while, Troy was left to wilt in a jail cell. "It's a win if the evidence frees Troy. How's that coming along?"

"The strongest evidence against Troy in the Graham case is his gun being the murder weapon and left at the scene. Now, I don't want to get your hopes up…"

Madison was blanketed with chills and sat up straighter. "Please, just spit it out." Her friend was a pro at delaying news to build suspense. One would think *that* was her job.

"His prints were on the weapon—and, yes, I know it's his gun—but there's a new technology that makes it possible to determine *when* prints are left."

Madison let that sink in. "Good. Then we can prove that Troy hasn't recently touched the gun."

"Theoretically."

"This could get Troy out of jail. Please, get on that. I love you!" Madison's eyes beaded with tears. This tidbit felt like a beam of light in an otherwise depressing landscape.

"You bet I will. And I love you and Troy."

Madison would never get through this without loyal and supportive friends like Cynthia and Terry. She was overwhelmed with gratitude. But it was enough that Terry was risking his job by helping her out. "Maybe you shouldn't get involved. I could call Detective

Snow and ask him to take care of this. I've spoken with him a couple of times." Her phone call and when she had brought Troy a change of clothes.

"Just leave the Braybury PD to me."

This wasn't an argument she was going to win, so she let it go. "Did they send you any findings on the Klein case?" She may be greedy for asking, but there was so much on the line. She added, "I know you collected, but I'm sure you had to pass it along."

"You're right on both counts. They even sent me some… updates." There was hesitancy in her friend's admission.

"What is it, Cyn?"

"Did you know Troy's DNA was in Klein's room?"

"I heard his DNA was found on the belt that strangled him. But Troy was in an altercation with him, so its presence is negligible."

"Okay, so you heard that."

"Uh-huh. Is there anything that doesn't point to Troy?" Her insides were quaking.

"Well, he doesn't wear or carry around a small silver cross on a silver chain, does he? I've never noticed him with one."

A glimmer of hope snaked in, even if premature. She didn't know exactly how Cynthia's question was relevant yet. "He doesn't, but was one found in Klein's room?" She took a guess.

"After you left. It was under the bed."

"More like after I was forced to leave."

Cynthia went on without touching Madison's comment. "Klein's blood was on it, and based on where it was found, it suggests it may have come off during a struggle. Troy not having one is great news." Her voice lightened with her last statement. "Though I suppose it could have been Klein's."

And just like that, hope entered in and left just as quickly. "Blood from anyone else?"

"No. There were some prints but, before you ask, no hits in the system. I hesitated to tell you about it at all because I'm not entirely sure where it gets us."

"Not sure? Assuming the silver cross was not Klein's, this is proof someone else was in that motel room. After Klein was bleeding. Ask me, and it belongs to the killer."

Just how do we get him...?

CHAPTER 40

Detective Snow should have stood his ground from the first moment he doubted the evidence at the Graham crime scene. But at least he was absolved of guilt over the car chase. Or he liked to believe so. The truth was, if that person had framed Matthews, there was a chance they could have apprehended him before now. That's if the Braybury PD brass hadn't been so manipulative and controlling about how the Graham case was to be handled. He'd heard about the pursuit from Chief Fletcher and respected how the woman kept a calm, even tone as she'd brought him up to speed. Anger was underlying but well disguised by someone skilled at diplomacy.

Really, though, Carson couldn't have done anything about a silver Hyundai Accent. Matthews had told him he suspected the driver had been tailing him for months, but silver Accents weren't exactly a rare sight. Pair that with no way of narrowing it down, a registration to a viable suspect was impossible to find.

Carson did wonder if Matthews's admission was conveniently timed. After all, now he was facing a second murder charge. While he'd alluded to someone framing him from the start, why not mention this car before? Though Carson could accept the mind was a mysterious thing and didn't always serve up information when it was most convenient. The fact he was even questioning Matthews's integrity on this must be residual from having a narrow-minded sergeant. So now Carson was skewing things to fit his agenda? Heaven help him if he ever ended up being *that* cop.

Sadly, all Carson had were anomalies and nothing concrete to vouch for Matthews's innocence. Yes, there was someone stalking Madison. This person could have done the same to Matthews. Again, it was back to Matthews's inability to offer one solid suggestion for someone who would frame him. The man wasn't even helping himself.

Carson got up and filled his coffee cup in the bullpen. As he stirred in two sugars and a splash of cream, he watched the mini whirlpool, feeling like a victim of one himself. And maybe he was being ridiculous trying to fight the current. It would be easier to go along with the sergeant's and chief's directions. Troy Matthews would stand trial for two murders. Carson would continue working at the Braybury PD and collect a pension when he aged out.

Argh. If only it was that *easy.*

Every time he thought of the career SWAT officer facing a jury of twelve, his fate in their hands, he felt nauseous. He had faith in the justice system, but he had seen it fail. The trial would be rigged against Matthews. No one warms to the story of a cop turned rogue. For good reason. Who wanted armed men and women creating their own rules? The world would be in a worse state than it already was.

He returned to his desk and sat with his coffee and his thoughts. The cubicle warren where Homicide was located was rather quiet. Detectives dealing with paperwork were on their lunch breaks. It offset the unpredictability of following leads in the field when grabbing something to eat was infrequent at best. Jeremy had slipped out five minutes ago, but Carson had declined his invitation to join him. Stepping away offered separation so one could return with a fresh perspective. Carson saw sticking around today as a sort of penance for not listening to his doubts before now. He was also one of the rare detectives who liked paperwork almost equally to being in the field. Possibly more.

There was order and logic to facts printed on a page. Black and white, and it didn't get much clearer than that. While interpretation was sometimes called for, he was assured by the fact science didn't lie. That's what people did. So between seeing and smelling dead bodies, delivering notifications and breaking the hearts of loved ones, and sourcing and questioning suspects, paperwork was a gift with this job.

There still wasn't an update on the second round of handwriting analysis. He'd take an ETA over nothing. He called the lab, and the phone was answered on the third ring by a tech he knew. "Loretta Harmon, how are you today?"

"Uh-huh. I'm great, as always, but you didn't call to shoot the shit. You never do."

Loretta had a fantastic sense of humor, but her abilities in the field and the lab were second to none. Her eye for detail had been responsible for locking up countless bad guys.

"You got me," Carson admitted.

"You know it. Let me guess, you're following up on that handwriting analysis, take two?"

"You read my mind." He smiled, thankful for someone like Loretta in the lab.

"Good timing, as I just got it back from a second analyst. He confirms the handwriting was that of Dylan Graham. But you were interested in knowing if there was any indication it was written under duress. He noted stress is to be expected in a suicide note, but that typically wouldn't translate to someone simply recording their thoughts in a journal. With that said, given the entry accused someone of rape and murder, the expert confirmed that could explain the tightened and straighter handwriting there."

Loretta's penchant for detail was killing him. "There were signs of duress in the suicide note *and* the journal entry?"

"Yes. But this finding is not sorely conclusive that Dylan Graham was forced to write what he had."

It wasn't exactly what Carson had wanted or expected to hear. He was hoping this would be the magic bullet that would help Matthews's case while also sticking it to his sergeant and the police chief.

"That's not what you were hoping for."

Loretta, the mind reader. "Not really. What about the ink though? Did that get us anywhere?"

"That it did. The testing tells us that both the suicide note and the journal entry were written the same day."

Carson chewed on that. The journal entry had been dated a few days prior to his murder. Suicides were typically executed within moments of the thought to commit the act. Yet both were written on the same day. This shattered their entire basis for motive against Matthews. "Graham may have been forced to write and backdate the journal entry."

"It's possible. I have other news for you too. You were asking about fingerprints on the journal. There were a couple of Graham's, but there was one unknown partial."

Carson perked up but quickly deflated. "It could have happened before Graham bought it, or it belonged to the cashier who he paid for it."

"I'm not sure about that. The partial ties to a print left at the Klein murder scene."

"I'm listening."

"Uh-huh, I bet you are. It was pulled from the silver cross."

The one found under the bed in Klein's room at the Sandman Motel. The same cross that had Klein's blood on it. It must belong to the real killer. It's the only thing that could explain the matching prints between it and the journal. That also made it most likely that the killer brought the journal to Graham's house. Presumably he wiped it down and handled it with gloves after buying it, but his cleaning job obviously hadn't been thorough. "This is good news."

"If you think so. I just deliver the facts."

"Which makes you indispensable." He'd kiss her cheek if she was in front of him and it was appropriate.

"One more thing. I received a call from Cynthia Baxter with the Stiles PD crime lab. We met at a forensic conference a couple of years ago. She's asking for a favor as a professional courtesy."

"What does she want?"

"She requested the prints on the Smith & Wesson used in the Graham murder be tested for age."

"You can do that?"

"Oh, yeah, science is advancing every day."

"Cool. Do it."

"You know it."

"Thank you," Carson said before ending the call. He sat back in his chair and swiveled, the coffee in his cup left to cool. He had enough to cast doubt on Matthews's culpability. Now he just had to convince his sergeant and the police chief. Then, just maybe, he could have the arraignment for the Klein case postponed or canceled altogether.

CHAPTER 41

Madison decided that running around behind everyone's backs was ridiculous. Andrea knew very well that she was trying to uncover whatever she could to help Troy's case. Technically, she and Terry weren't looking into the cases belonging to the Braybury PD, as they were focused on the past and Emily Kane. She explained this to Andrea over the phone after the car chase.

"That's just a workaround. You know I do see that," Andrea replied, not fooled for a minute.

"I understand that, but let us carry on. If it comes down to it, it's better to ask for forgiveness."

"Except in cases where you've already asked permission and been denied."

Madison had already confessed their visit to Emily Kane's mother and that their next stop was to talk to Emily's former stepbrother. She laid out their thinking on the matter. How he might have been upset over the trial, and Klein's recent release might have stirred up the past for him. She even added the caveat that this was contingent on him even caring about any of this anymore. "Does that mean you're ordering us to leave this alone?"

"I never said that."

Madison resisted the urge to smile, as her voice would betray the fact she was gloating.

"But it's not me you need to ask permission from anyway."

"I disagree." Madison glanced over at Terry in the driver's seat. It was still an odd feeling seeing him behind the wheel when she normally did the driving. "As I said, the Emily Kane case never belonged to the Braybury PD. In fact, it was originally investigated by the Stiles PD."

"Right. And *closed*. The guilty party has already served twenty-four years."

Clearly, her concern was public perception and how this would look for the Stiles PD. Madison had never been a fan of politics, but it was a game that Andrea was forced to play. "Please, Andrea. Think of it this way. Emily's name came up in the Graham case. An allegation against Troy, more specifically. Aren't we within our rights to investigate that and disprove it?"

Andrea's end of the line fell silent, and Madison took it as a victory, but she'd let the chief speak first.

After several seconds, Andrea said, "Fine. Go ahead. Officially. I will inform Winston, so he knows that Terry has been momentarily reassigned."

"Like he ran the fact the Braybury police were coming to arrest Troy past you?" Madison hurled the words, as her anger was running the show.

"Just keep things clean, Knight."

Ouch, she wielded the surname… "Are you with Troy?" From her understanding, Andrea would be taking him a suit to wear when appearing before the judge. Cue the dog and pony show, but if dressing up could sway the person on the bench into taking it easy on Troy, so be it.

"Yes, and his lawyer. I stepped out of the room to take your call, but he's staying strong. He is worried about you though."

That warmed Madison's heart, but she wouldn't expect any less.

"So, I'll repeat myself. Keep it clean *and* keep safe."

"I'll do my best."

"Listen, I've got to go. Detective Snow just arrived, and I'm not sure what he wants." With that, Andrea ended the call.

Madison wrapped her cell phone in her palm and turned to Terry. "We have the green light to pursue this."

"And Winston?"

"Andrea's taking care of him." As she spoke, her words were full of venom and menace. If only her *taking care of him* entailed giving him an early retirement. It felt good to disclose her next step to Andrea and clear things so that Terry wouldn't get himself into trouble. Her request to Andrea could have gone another way, but thankfully it hadn't.

"All right, then. We get to the address on file for Dameon Babcock and have ourselves a little talk."

Madison chuckled at Terry's phrasing and the funny voice he'd used. "Sounds like a good plan. Though since I'm back to official capacity, maybe I should drive. Oh, I'd also like to pick up my service weapon and cuffs from the station too."

He looked over at her before merging into traffic. "No, to driving. And do we really want you armed?"

"Like it or not, buddy. And don't get used to playing chauffeur." Her joyful volley landed with a thud. She'd been so caught up working with him, she'd briefly forgotten their time as partners was limited.

They swept past the station for her gun and cuffs, and then she drove them to the address on file for Babcock. No incident, and no more sightings of a silver Accent. That was both a relief and disappointment.

Dameon Babcock lived in an apartment building on the edge of downtown. No silver Hyundai Accent in the lot, but there was underground parking too. The structure wasn't a lockout, so they just loaded onto the elevator for the tenth floor.

Madison knocked on the apartment marked 1025. It felt righteous being back, the weight of her gun in its holster, handcuffs within reach.

Footsteps padded toward the door, followed by the metal cover on the peephole sliding across. Madison stuck her badge in the dome. It might help, but it might not. Thankfully, a second later, the security chain and the deadbolt were being undone.

"Yeah?" It was Dameon Babcock. Madison recognized him from his license photo with the DMV.

"Detectives Grant and Knight," Terry squeezed in there, shooting Madison a side-glance.

To start, he was driving the department car more often. Now he was taking the lead in the field. *It won't be long before he* is *the lead, period...* That thought soured in her stomach.

Terry went on. "We'd like to speak to you for a few minutes."

Babcock leveled his beady eyes at her, and she wasn't sure what to read from them, but he gave her the creeps. He licked his lips while looking at hers, and that didn't help the feeling.

She glared at him, hoping he'd take the hint and cool it. "What is this about, Officer?"

"*Detectives*, as I just said," Terry corrected with far more patience than Madison could have mustered.

"It's about your stepsister, Emily Kane," Madison pushed out as she stepped toward the door.

Babcock hesitated but ended up backing into his entry to allow them inside. "What about her?" He rubbed his arms.

"Do you have somewhere we could sit for a minute?" Terry asked.

He gestured toward a ratty couch in the living room that was off the tiled entry. The threadbare carpet was stained, and the entire place felt unclean. Madison remained standing, but Terry sat in a chair while Babcock lowered onto the couch.

"Emily was murdered twenty-four years ago. Surely you know that." Babcock danced his gaze from Terry to Madison and back again, but in the end settled it on Madison.

The way he kept looking at her gave her chills. "We know that. We want to know how you felt about Richie Klein going away for her rape and murder." She was rarely one for mincing her words, and she wasn't about to start now. Babcock could be the guy they were after. She wanted to determine if that was true as quickly as possible. If so, she'd waste no time hauling his ass downtown and getting Troy out of jail.

"How did I feel?"

"That's what I asked." He was either slow or putting on a show that he was simpleminded.

"I liked Emily."

"We heard that much." Regardless of his mental state, he could be behind the murders and framing Troy. She did well to remember that. "Do you think the police got the right guy?"

Babcock rubbed his forehead and shook his head. "Maybe. I don't know. But Em didn't deserve what happened to her." His voice cracked on this statement, and Madison noted the shift between her full name and an abbreviation. That suggested intimacy. One he still must feel toward her.

"Were you close?" The question was a baited hook.

Terry glanced over at her, as if to point out she was hogging the interview, but her drive for answers was pushing her forward. She had more at stake. After all, her future with Troy hung in the balance. At the end of the day, Terry would go home to be with his wife, Annabelle, and their daughter, Danny, and Madison would face an empty house.

"Yeah, we were."

Tingles danced down Madison's arms, hairs rising in their wake. That was a different story than she'd heard from Emily's mother.

"How close?" Terry asked, edging in.

"I loved her, but we were brother and sister in a way, so… But after Dad and that lady broke up…"

"That lady being Emily's mother," Madison inserted, cringing at the disrespect.

"Whatever. She never liked me. She treated me like I was either a nuisance or invisible."

"That must have made you mad," Madison volleyed back.

"I cared more about what Emily thought."

Madison's mind slipped back to the thought he'd started but had abandoned. "Did you ask Emily out after you were no longer her stepbrother?" She took some liberty here, as his father and Emily's mother had never legally married, just cohabitated.

"I did."

"And what did she say to that?" Terry said.

"That it would be too weird for her."

"She let you down gently, then?" Madison's mind wasn't far from one of her earlier theories that the killer might have been someone Emily had rejected.

"She was decent about it." His facial expression belied his words. The corners of his mouth twitched, and his jaw tightened.

"Did you know Richie Klein?" she asked.

"The guy who did this to her? Yes. He was an ass."

Madison snuck in a quick look at Terry. Babcock's bitterness toward Klein was a flag.

"Why is that?" Terry asked.

"He didn't respect women at all. There was a rumor he assaulted a girl in ninth grade, but it was hushed because his father paid off the girl's family to keep quiet about it. Not that it stopped the assault from surfacing at trial."

The bribery part was new. It had Madison seeking out a chair to sit on. It was abhorrent that a father would offer, and that another would accept. "Do you remember her name?" She held out hope he would. He had recalled the arrangement.

"I don't. Just the story surrounding it."

"But it's safe to say that you hated Richie Klein *and* his friends?" Madison snuck in the latter bit, planning to gauge his reaction.

Babcock's eyes ignited. "Anyone who was a friend of Richie was scum."

Madison bristled. "Sounds like quite the sweeping judgment. Did you even know the other guys?" She took offense since one was her fiancé and another a respected friend and cop who had fallen in the line of duty. She couldn't speak to Dylan Graham's character.

"I knew enough," he hissed.

His eyes were clear, and so was his mind. The stupid act had been just that. The man in front of her could have committed the recent murders and tried to pin them on Troy. "Where were you today between eleven and noon?"

"Here."

"Can anyone prove that?" She eyed him with scrutiny.

"Nope."

"Do you have access to a silver Hyundai Accent, Mr. Babcock?" Terry asked.

"I don't own any cars."

"That's not the question my partner asked you," Madison shot back.

He stared at her. "No. I don't 'have access to a silver Hyundai Accent,'" he parroted Terry's words.

She held eye contact with him, not believing a word coming from his mouth. "Then you weren't in the downtown area following us?"

"What? No. I told you, I was here."

People had lied to Madison's face so many times, she'd lost count. She didn't extend trust easily as a result. "I'm afraid it's going to take more than your say-so. If we tracked your phone's GPS, is it going to back up what you just told us?" She hoped she effectively called his bluff, because getting a warrant authorized for that would ignite a shitshow of epic proportions, considering the circumstances. She was cleared to talk to Babcock from the angle of Emily Kane, but this was encroaching on territory belonging to the Graham and Klein cases. She was fine going there on the down-low, but a warrant wasn't that. Besides, they didn't have enough to substantiate one anyhow.

Babcock shifted on the couch. "Fine, I was downtown, but it's not what you think."

"I'll tell you what I think. Troy Matthews, one of Richie Klein's friends, is facing two murder charges. One for Richie Klein, and one for Dylan Graham. But it was you, wasn't it? You set him up." After laying that out, she found herself standing, and her earlobes were on fire.

"I didn't do that."

"Come on, you're joining us at the station." Terry was now standing in front of Babcock, gesturing for him to stand, his cuffs dangling from a finger.

Babcock moved like he was going to comply. Instead, he hopped over the arm of the couch and disappeared down the hallway.

Why do the bad guys always have to run? But she had no idea what Babcock had planned. There wasn't really anywhere for him to go. He was headed deeper into the apartment.

"Come on, Mr. Babcock, the show is up. Time to come with us," Terry called out and shook his head at Madison. "Where does he think he's going?"

"Haven't a clue." Then she heard a window opening and the clanging of metal. Her eyes popped open wide. "The fire escape."

She bolted toward the hallway, but Terry was quicker. No surprise.

"Stiles PD! Stop!" Terry's cries were going unheeded as the clanging continued. He ducked through the open window, but she came to a standstill.

She was in Babcock's bedroom, and photographs of a teenage Emily littered the walls. He had drawn hearts around her head on some of them, but what got to her attention the most was the enlarged poster-size print of Emily Kane tacked to the ceiling above his bed.

Madison swallowed the bile that came up her throat and called in for assistance.

Dameon Babcock needed to be stopped. It was official that he was mentally ill and clearly obsessed with Emily Kane twenty-four years after her murder. But did he kill Dylan Graham and Richie Klein and frame things so Troy would take the fall?

CHAPTER 42

Madison and Terry were back at the station with Dameon Babcock. It had taken Terry a few minutes to catch up with him. They were currently watching him from the observation room through the one-way mirror. Babcock was sitting at the table in the interrogation room, pulling at the already-peeling laminate top.

"We need to stick to questioning Babcock about the car chase this afternoon," Terry said. "But if we can put him there, we'll hand him over to the Braybury PD."

She appreciated that her partner was just reinforcing the game plan he'd come up with. But Madison's goal was to free Troy. If the questioning took them over any perceived line, so be it.

The clock wasn't slowing down. If they were to save Troy from another arraignment, they needed to pull off a miracle. Her phone rang, and she answered.

"You're at the station with a suspect, Maddy. Talk to me." Andrea rushed all that out the second Madison picked up. No greeting, just right to the point.

Obviously, Winston was aware of her presence. And here Madison thought she'd successfully avoided him. It would seem he was doing the same. That suited her fine. The man could set her off at the best of times, and the last thing she wanted was another lecture about respecting boundaries. Clearance from the police chief aside. She'd like to see how he'd handle it if the roles were reversed, and this was personal for him. She doubted he'd adhere to any rigid rules. "I am. Terry and I are quite sure this guy was the one tailing us and was chased through downtown Stiles. He put lives at risk." She thought it would only help her case to point that out blatantly. "I ran this past you before we went to his place," she added.

There was a huge sigh from Andrea's end of the line. "You're right, but now I think I've messed up. I suppose I didn't give myself over to the hope this... What's his name again?"

"Dameon Babcock, Emily Kane's stepbrother for a time."

"I just didn't consider exactly where this might take us. That this Babcock guy might be the one who framed Troy."

"Okay, so what do you want us to do?" Madison could appreciate that Andrea's mind would be all over, but it didn't make it less frustrating to deal with her.

"What's he saying so far?"

"We just spoke to him at his apartment, but he wasn't eager to come in and talk more. He did admit being downtown during the time of the car chase. Thus far, we haven't been able to put him in the silver Hyundai. But there's motive. He's already expressed his dislike for Richie and his friends from the time, including Troy," she said his name for emphasis.

"Man, this is really getting close to the line."

"I know. If we're going to cross it, we'll hand him over to Braybury." Not to say she wouldn't push the boundary line.

"You bet you will. So you think Babcock has motive?"

"We just know he doesn't think Richie paid enough for what he did. But, Andrea, the creepiest thing about all this and makes me think we have the right guy… This Babcock is obsessed with Emily Kane, even now. He has pictures of her in his room. We're talking about a forty-year-old with photos of a teenage girl lining his bedroom walls. He even has a blown-up photo of her over his bed." It didn't matter how many times her mind turned over that fact, her gut curdled.

"Pictures?"

"Yep. And according to Emily's mother, he was in love with Emily as a teenager."

"Love or obsession, something that's stood the test of time. I'm still reeling from the news about the pictures."

"Makes two of us."

"Okay, well, push this guy, but try to tiptoe around the murders. As you said you'll hand him over. I'm counting on your word here, Madison."

"I hear you."

"Good. Now, I didn't just call because I heard you had Babcock downtown. I've got some good news. Troy's arraignment has been postponed."

"Is he free to go?"

"Not yet. But Detective Snow came forward with some new findings that cast doubt on the case against Troy. Something about the journal and fingerprints. But what matters is Troy is no longer facing a judge this afternoon. There's a chance he might not even have to. That's if everything starts coming together."

Madison bit her tongue on the *new* findings bit. It had likely existed all along, but the detective hadn't taken the time to investigate. But it sounded like her call had helped steer Snow in the right direction. "What about the journal and fingerprints?"

"There were some anomalies with both apparently."

Madison smiled, giving herself a second to revel in that. Maybe Detective Snow wasn't the enemy and incompetent, after all. Was he finally doing his due diligence? But she was curious about one thing. "Did he tell you or Troy's lawyer about the suicide note at Graham's scene?"

"Just in the last hour. Vincent Park, Troy's lawyer, is having fun with that one, I tell you. I wouldn't be surprised if Troy's home in time for dinner."

Madison was smiling. "That would be good news."

"You know what? Scratch what I said about tiptoeing with this guy. Snow can hold back, so can we."

Madison's chest lightened at that comment. "You're sure?"

"Yes. Go at this Babcock with whatever you have. As far as I'm concerned, Snow brought this on himself by holding back the suicide note all this time. A suicide note at a murder scene, no less," Andrea muttered the last bit under her breath, clearly ticked off.

"You got it." She ended the call and turned to Terry, who was watching her. "Troy's arraignment has been postponed, no new time scheduled, but they are holding him." As much as she hated to think of him still behind bars, it was better than him facing a judge again.

"That's good news. What else did she say?"

"We can go at Babcock however we see fit. Including approaching him outright as a suspect in the murders. Snow came through and got the arraignment postponed, but he hasn't exactly been playing fair from the start."

"Ah, so the chief feels justified in not toeing the line now."

"When you put it like that, it doesn't sound good."

"But it doesn't change the point." He held up a hand. "Not that I'm in disagreement."

She nudged her head toward the one-way mirror to Babcock, who had stopped delaminating the table and was sitting back, arms crossed and looking bored. "Let's go break 'im."

"That's the Maddy I know." Terry chuckled and followed her next door.

She dropped into the chair across from Babcock. Terry took up his usual spot against the wall behind her. "We just wanted to talk to you, Mr. Babcock. Why did you run?"

Terry jingled his change before Babcock could answer. It was something Terry did that often threw suspects off their game.

"You think I've done something, but I haven't."

Madison settled into her chair and opened the folder she brought in with her. She didn't take anything out but made a show of looking at what was inside. It was an intimidation tactic to make Babcock think they had a bunch gathered against him, but his clean record up until this point didn't provide fodder with which to rattle him. She let seconds stack up in silence before she broke it. "You ran from us. Before that, you told us you were downtown during the time of a car chase through the city. Were you running then too?"

"What? I don't know about any car chase, but I was downtown earlier today."

"When?" She'd play along for a bit, but patience was never her strong suit.

"Around noon. I grabbed a burger from Sally's."

"How did you get downtown?" she countered.

Terry kept jingling his change, and the noise was even working on her nerves today.

"I walked."

She smirked and angled her head. Sally's would have been a manageable walk from Babcock's apartment, but she wasn't letting that derail her. "You're sure you never borrowed a friend's car?"

"I walked," he repeated.

She pulled a photo taken from CCTV at one of the intersections. It showed the silver Hyundai Accent tearing through. "Where did you get this car?"

Babcock leaned forward and studied the picture, then looked up, brow furrowed, the mask of confusion. "I've never seen that car before."

"Uh-huh." Madison leaned back, leaving the photo to stay put. "Can you prove you had that burger at Sally's at the time you said?"

"You could ask the person I ordered from."

"Then you paid cash? No digital payment trail?"

"No." Babcock lowered his head, as if he were timid, but Madison wasn't buying his act.

She placed a photograph of his bedroom on the table, steering away from the chase. "You were in love with your stepsister, Emily." Though labeling his obsession as love settled like acid.

Babcock reached for the picture and pulled it to him. "I already told you that."

"After all these years even. You must really miss her." Madison didn't want to get too carried away in her thoughts about that poster above his bed. It was clear that he fantasized about Emily, his mind taking him on perverted journeys into the past as he nodded off to sleep at night. She wasn't going to think about what else he might be doing.

"She never deserved what happened to her. I told you that. But Richie was owed what he had coming." Babcock's cheeks flushed bright red, and he clenched his jaw.

"*Had coming*? So you set things right? You killed him?" she countered.

"Killed him? What? I meant time in prison."

Apparently, he was back to playing dumb. "You mentioned how you hated Richie and his friends."

"They tried to help Richie get away with murder." He shifted in his chair and sat straighter. He drilled a fingertip into the top of the table. "As it was, their testimonies likely shortened his sentence."

"Richie Klein was also only seventeen years old." As she leveled this out, she was torn between feeling any empathy for a child and the gravity of his crime. Usually she adhered to a black-and-white approach to life, and not that she didn't think Richie deserved to pay for what he had done, but he also wasn't fully in his right mind either.

"He knew what he was doing," Babcock seethed.

"You're right he did." She was siding with Babcock to see what emotion she could stir to life.

"He should still be in prison, and his friends should have shitty lives."

She prickled at that. Did he truly not know about their murders or Troy's charges? She shook the thought aside, chalking it up to a chronic liar who was trying to throw the spotlight off himself. Sometimes he presented himself as stupid, and other times he seemed sharp. At this point in an interrogation, normally Madison would pull out photos of the victims. But she didn't have any from the Graham or Klein crime scenes. Instead, she'd approach it from another angle. "Where were you last Tuesday between four and six?"

"Last week? I can't remember that far back."

Terry stopped jingling his change, and it had Babcock looking past Madison to him. Then Terry started up again.

"Oh, please. You don't have a job that you might have been at?" She closed her mouth, unsure why she tried to give him an alibi.

"I'm in between jobs at the moment."

"So you're unemployed," she fired back, and Babcock's eyes narrowed. He was proud, and Madison doubted he'd take rejection well. Based on what Emily's mother told her, Emily hadn't been a fan of her stepbrother. The mother also made him sound persistent back then.

"It's just temporary," he eventually said.

"Sure. Where were you last Tuesday evening?" She raised her eyebrows, stressing again that she wanted an answer.

"I don't know."

"Were you catching up with Dylan Graham?"

"I haven't seen Dylan since high school."

She could push him on this, but she'd use his own act against him. "And what about Richie Klein? You see him when he got out of prison?"

"Only the pic online with the news report."

That statement had the skin tightening on the back of Madison's neck. It supported the fact that Babcock was apprised of the news. "Then you know that he is—"

"Dead? Yeah, I do, and I'm not shedding any tears over the fact either."

"Huh. When did you last see him?"

Babcock sat back and smirked. "I see what's going on here. You're looking to pin their murders on me, all so you can set that cop free. Well, I'm not letting that happen. Lawyer," he dragged out.

Madison glared back at him, Terry stopped jingling, and they both left the room.

She shut the door behind them. "He's our guy, Terry. He told us he ate at Sally's and denied seeing the Hyundai Accent. Not exactly a strong defense. He suddenly has amnesia for the time of Graham's murder. Before we can ask for an alibi for Klein's, he yells for a lawyer. Come on." Madison clenched her jaw and paced down the hall, turned back. "He did this, Terry."

"Except for we need more than a gut feeling. Can we tie him to either murder scene? To your house, either the shoeprints outside or to Troy's gun?"

She let out a deep breath, feeling boxed in a corner, and she didn't particularly care for the feeling. "We get clearance to obtain his fingerprints and DNA, go from there."

"I'm afraid we might need more before a judge would sign that warrant."

"Then let's start building our case against him. He says he was at Sally's. We go disprove that."

"And if we can't?"

"Then we'll figure out something else." She led the way from the police station, her heart racing. As much as her mind was set on finding justice, her conscience niggled. Was she guilty of trying to make the evidence fit her narrative, just as the Braybury PD was guilty of toward Troy?

CHAPTER 43

Sally's was a burger joint in the downtown core that was the Starbucks of beef patties. Their menu was diverse, and every item was customizable. They even offered a breakfast burger that was a quarter pound patty with an egg over easy and a slice of cheese. The menu version came with a slice of tomato and an avocado spread. Seven hundred calories, not accounting for the bun.

Madison was the first through the doors. Terry was right behind her and sniffing at the air like a hound dog.

"I'm remembering that I didn't eat lunch," he said.

"I bet you are, but I doubt they have anything on the menu for you." Like Troy, her partner didn't venture far from healthy eating.

People of all ages were lined up to the door, all eager to get their meat on a bun "just the way you like it." The chime on the door was triggered again behind them.

"Since we don't have all day." She pulled her badge and held it in the air. "Stiles PD coming through."

"Step aside, please," Terry added, softening the request, and it had Madison shaking her head. They really balanced each other out.

The crowd parted, but the woman at the counter continued prattling off her order. Madison tapped her on the shoulder and showed her badge. "Stiles PD. We need to speak with the cashier here." She nudged her head toward the freckled twenty-something manning the till. She wore the Sally's uniform, which was sunshine yellow, and a visor with Sally's scripted logo embroidered in red thread.

"I'm not going anywhere. I've been waiting in line for twenty-five minutes. Two more won't kill ya." She eyed Madison up and down, and Madison was just about to pounce, when Terry touched her shoulder.

She spun toward him. "What?"

"Just let her place her order." He pressed his lips in a silent plea that she wouldn't cause a scene.

"Fine." Madison gestured for the woman to proceed, and after she shot Madison a cold glare, she did just that.

A few seconds later, the employee called out, "Next!" as if Madison and Terry weren't standing right in front of her.

"Stiles PD. Do you recognize this man as being in here at noon today?" Madison showed the woman a photograph of Dameon Babcock.

"I..." Her brows turned downward as she looked past Madison and Terry to the never-ending line, but she wasn't the only server behind the counter. "We're really busy. Can you come back?"

"No, we can't."

"Then what can I get you?" She poised one of her hands over the keyboard of the ordering system and adjusted her visor with the other.

"Just a bacon cheeseburger with fries. Mustard and—"

"You tell that to the person who builds your burger when your order's called up." The woman pointed out two people in Sally's uniforms who were hustling from the grill to the condiments and toppings bar. "Anything else?"

Terry put in an order for a veggie patty.

The woman told them their total. "How are you going to pay?"

Madison was tapping her foot. She was hungry, but they hadn't come here to eat.

"Here you go." Terry handed over enough cash to cover both orders.

"Thanks," she told him, then lifted her phone in the clerk's face. "Do you recognize this man?"

This time, she looked at it. "The guy looks familiar. Next!" she called to the people behind Madison and Terry. One of them moved up and stepped on the heel of Madison's shoe. She turned and didn't say a word. They backed up again.

"When did you last see him?" Madison asked the clerk.

"Not sure, and I don't have time to chat. Next!"

A woman in her forties came around from the back. She stepped up to the counter. "I'm Cathy Blackwell, the manager. Is there a problem here?"

"Damn straight there's a problem," Madison pushed out. "We're with the Stiles PD and have questions about one of your customers."

"Sure. Let's talk in the back office." Blackwell flashed a placating smile that, despite getting her own way, rubbed Madison wrong.

"Ah, we have burgers coming," Terry said.

"I'll make sure they're brought to you." She signaled to one of the workers, who seemed to catch her message. They hadn't specified their toppings yet, but spit might be an added condiment.

Blackwell led Madison and Terry through a rear door to a spacious office. Despite smelling of grease and onion rings, it was tidy and organized. There was a desk, a computer, a filing cabinet, and several framed photos of Blackwell. The manager running in a marathon, in a swimming competition, and one of her on a mountaintop standing next to a woman who looked like her. Blackwell was certainly the adventurous type. If Madison wasn't in mission mode, she might ask who the woman was.

Blackwell sat behind the desk. "What is it that I can help you with?"

There was no place for them to sit, and Madison just got started. "We need to know if a certain man came in today."

"That should be easy enough to figure out. I'm assuming you are interested in a particular time?"

"We are." Madison was a little taken aback by this woman's efficiency. "The lunch hour between, let's say, eleven thirty and one."

"Sure. Let me get up the footage from that time." Blackwell clicked on her keyboard.

Madison shot Terry a side-glance. People typically made them jump through hoops for any little thing. This manager was a refreshing switch.

There was a knock on the doorframe. It was one of the servers with their burgers. Again, what they would have on them remained to be seen, but it was food and it smelled heavenly.

Madison took hers and thanked the girl, who responded with a curt, "Uh-huh."

Terry got a smile, though, before the woman left the room.

"I have it here," Blackwell said, turning her monitor to face them. "Oh, let me get you chairs." She was gone for only a few seconds before she returned with two. "This will make it easier to watch and eat."

"Thank you," Terry told her.

"Don't mention it." Blackwell returned to her seat and must have hit a button, as the feed started up.

There were so many people that were in and out, and there was no sign of it slowing down. "You guys do a healthy business," Madison said.

"Never a dull moment. We're very fortunate."

Madison's stomach was anxious, and she wasn't sure if she should bother unwrapping her burger or not. Eventually the smells tempted her enough.

The video continued playing out. Terry didn't seem to be having a problem eating, and he polished off his burger in less than five minutes. She couldn't resist any longer and peeled hers out and took a mouthful. No mustard, but heavenly, nonetheless. There was a reason Sally's was a popular burger spot.

Madison ate slowly, straining to see if she could pluck out Dameon Babcock among the throng of people. She ended up finishing her burger before he came on screen. Her disappointment couldn't be masked. Dameon Babcock wasn't the stalker in the Hyundai Accent, but did that clear him from being the killer?

CHAPTER 44

"We need to let Babcock go," Terry said from the car's passenger seat. Once again, she was behind the wheel. "There's not much sense pushing him when we don't have a case against him."

It's too bad creepy isn't enough, Madison thought. "He wasn't following me or involved in the pursuit, but what if we are looking at two people, two motives?"

"The odds are against that. I know that you want Troy out of jail, and I can't blame you. I want that too, but Babcock's not going to do that for us."

She slapped a palm against the steering wheel. They were still parked on the side of the street near Sally's. The burger she ate was sitting in her gut like a boulder.

"I'm open to suggestions here, but it's not looking good," he said. "There's no way a judge will sign off for us to collect Babcock's prints or DNA."

She hated that he was right. "Okay, but there has to be something…" She racked her brain to conjure up that *something*, then landed on two ideas. They were threads that hadn't been fully tugged on. She faced him in the passenger seat. "We can check with the Sandman Motel and see if the desk clerks or housekeeping recognize Dameon Babcock hanging around."

"Okay, but I worry about it being a time suck. Just because Babcock obviously wasn't tailing you."

"Please, Terry, we need to try to see if we can connect Babcock to Graham and Klein. This is one way of doing it." She could hear the desperate peal to her voice, but it wasn't to be helped. She was desperate.

Terry held up his hands in surrender. "Fine. And with Graham?"

"We source out friends, coworkers, and neighbors and see if any of them saw Babcock hanging around recently."

"All good, but what about your neighborhood, even your old one. Whoever shot Graham needed to get Troy's gun."

This reminded Madison of two things left to fall through the cracks. At least she hadn't followed up on them or heard any more about them. She pulled out her phone and called Cynthia.

"Hey, is everything okay?"

"That's one way of answering the phone," Madison countered.

"I'm sorry, it's just been, well, a strange week, not that I have to tell you."

"Did you hear that Troy's arraignment for the Klein case was postponed for now?"

"You bet I did. A great start."

"I'm calling about Troy's gun box," Madison said, rushing into the reason for her call. "Did you get any prints off it?"

There was silence, followed by a sigh. "Only Troy's. I wish I had better news."

Madison supposed that shouldn't come as a surprise. The killer likely would have worn gloves. He had to have some brains to set all this up. "Okay. What about the shoeprints outside our house?"

"A man's boot, size ten." Cynthia gave Madison the brand, but it didn't mean anything to her. Cynthia added, "Nothing distinguishing about them, as they are available in any department store."

If they were high-end or sold at a specialty boutique, they might have a chance of tracking down the buyer. "Well, at least we know. Thanks for the update."

"Don't mention… it." A yawn broke her speech, and Madison felt for her pregnant friend.

"How are you doing, Cyn?"

"Me? Don't worry about me right now. I'm good."

"Good to hear." Madison ended the call.

"I'm guessing by your frown and what was said, nothing there?" Terry asked.

Madison shook her head.

"Well, we're back to trying what you suggested. Though, I'm saying it again. The chances Babcock is the killer and not your stalker are unlikely."

She'd leave his last statement untouched. "Thank you for working with me on this. Now one angle I haven't been able to pursue was a visit to Graham's workplace."

"For what purpose?"

"At one point, I wondered if Graham was working on a case that put him in contact with the killer. Obviously, this would be someone from his past too."

"Hmm. I'm not sure I like this. It's edging too close to the Graham murder case. Technically, we're not working that."

"Technically," she volleyed back.

"The chief didn't give us carte blanche to do as we wish," Terry said. "She just extended us some rope with Babcock."

"This is about Babcock, though, right? He could have hired Graham's firm for something."

"I suppose if we limit our questions to him…"

It was obvious Terry wasn't comfortable pushing against this line, and he had his future as a sergeant to consider. "You know what? You let me take things from here. It will be no skin off my back if things go sideways." She spoke braver than she was. Her badge meant everything to her, but so did Troy. Right now, he took priority.

"That's what you say now, but you're poking around for a killer. If that isn't Babcock, who is currently in holding, that potentially puts you in grave danger."

Grave danger... Leave it to her partner to put things into such a drastic perspective. "I'll be fine. Besides, you should get home to Annabelle and Danny at a decent hour. I don't want to hold you up."

"You wouldn't be. I'm here for you, Madison. Well, you and Troy."

She was touched by his loyalty and commitment to help. "We appreciate that." It felt both good and bittersweet to talk on Troy's behalf. "But I think we should split up, Terry. We'll cover more ground more quickly."

"All right, but I'm still not entirely sure what you're thinking here. Babcock isn't the stalker but is the killer? Yet you want to know if he was slinking around. All this despite the fact two people being after you is extremely unlikely."

"Sometimes life involves the long shots."

"I'll give you that. Unfortunately, it doesn't matter how creepy it is that Babcock pinned up pictures of his dead teenage stepsister. I'll hit Graham's workplace, and you go to the motel."

"If you're sure."

"What partners are for," he said.

She nodded and took them to the station, where Terry signed out another department car.

CHAPTER 45

As far as Madison was concerned, Babcock wasn't walking until they exhausted their options. It was what had her back at the Sandman Motel, a choice she instantly regretted when she pulled into the lot. The night before came flooding back with flashing lights and Richie Klein's dead body. She recalled the dread she'd felt when she hadn't been able to reach Troy. Then how that grew when it seemed the evidence pointed to him. She still didn't understand why Troy had risked coming here. Even if he suspected Klein, did Troy honestly expect that Klein would confess to murdering Dylan Graham and framing him?

Madison went inside the motel's office. It was decked out with seasonal decorations, though the ambience tarnished any cheer. Cheap chairs with cracked faux leather revealed beige foam padding, and the artificial Christmas tree sat crooked.

A scrawny man sat at the desk and stood to greet her. "Room for one?"

She could imagine she looked rough, not having slept much this past week. Her short blond hair probably resembled a bird's nest, but did she really look like she'd be the type to stay here? She flashed her badge, and the man's shoulders sagged. "I'm Detective Knight, and you are?"

"Not interested." He mocked laughter.

"Huh. Not what I was looking for," she said in all seriousness. "What's your name?"

"Carl."

"Well, Carl, do you recognize any of these men?" She brought up an array that included Dameon Babcock and three others who looked like him on her phone. The job made this process necessary. A single photo could be seen as coercion by a defense attorney.

Carl took her phone from her and held it to within a few inches of his face. "They just look like a bunch of average Joe Schmoes to me."

"Any of them come here?"

"Not sure."

"Hanging around or visiting a guest?"

Carl looked up from the phone and out the window toward room 8. "Does this have to do with that murder from yesterday?"

"You're a smart man, Carl. No one can pull one over on you." She smiled, though her every word was bitter sarcasm, and took back her phone.

Carl crossed his arms. "I've been told not to say anything." He leaned down and pulled a card from a shelf behind the counter. "This is the motel's lawyer. You have questions, you need to talk to them."

"But they're not going to be able to help me, Carl. This is your chance to be a hero."

"Yeah, I'm not falling for that. Working here might be shit, but it puts food on the table and beer in my hand." He continued to hold out the attorney's card, and Madison didn't even need to look closely to see that it belonged to a law firm she was quite familiar with. Her ex-boyfriend, Blake Golden, owned the place. The Sandman Motel wasn't the image of the firm's typical clients, but the owner must have money to have Blake's firm on retainer. And that suggested their hands were dirty with other matters than this fleabag motel. Blake made his living repping the scum of society who had thick pocketbooks. Though sometimes he did pro bono work and accomplished good. It was why Madison had let her guard down at one time and allowed herself to be swayed by the lawyer's charms.

"Thanks a lot." She didn't take the card and left.

The motel may have instructed their employees not to talk to the police, but they couldn't control their customers. It was possible the people who had been here last night had already left, but it was worth a shot. She started with the first room that had a car in front of it.

A woman with bloodshot eyes answered. She was either drunk or high, though Madison's guess was the latter. She showed her badge. The woman reversed into the room but never closed the door. Madison wasn't within her legal rights to follow, but she was tempted.

"Excuse me, I have a question for you—"

"What do you think you are doing?" It was Carl from the front desk. He was hurrying toward her across the lot without a coat.

"I'm just talking with your guests."

"More like harassing. Are you going to make me report you?"

Madison turned toward the man. Being told to leave when she was potentially close to a solid hit against Babcock stoked her anger. "I'm not harassing anyone, just asking questions."

"Which some would see as harassment. These customers have already given their statements to the police. Please leave." He accompanied the request with an outshot arm and a pointed finger in the direction of the road.

If this were any other case, Madison wouldn't let Carl boss her around. Considering that she was operating in a somewhat gray area, she relented and walked toward her vehicle.

"Thank you very much," Carl said, serving back the sarcasm.

She got into her car and drove down the street where she pulled over and parked. She smacked the steering wheel. Would they ever catch a break that would have Troy released free and clear? It was a miracle that Detective Snow had stepped in and got his arraignment postponed, but she wasn't putting full faith in the man yet.

She pulled out her phone and texted Terry to let him know she had no luck at the Sandman Motel.

She gave it a few moments, anticipating that he'd respond quickly, but he didn't. She'd have to wait and see whether that was good or bad. Until then, Madison had another thread she hadn't completely tugged. Melissa Hatfield, Emily Kane's other best friend, might have something to say about Dameon Babcock. It may even help them build a case against him. Guess she would see.

CHAPTER 46

Madison knocked on Melissa Hatfield's front door. She lived in a modest bungalow, and unlike Brooke Morales's home, the place showed no sign that Christmas was even acknowledged. With the holiday less than a week away, it was a good bet that Melissa didn't celebrate.

Footsteps padded toward the door. A good-looking woman in her early forties answered at the same time Madison's phone pinged with a text message. She'd let it be for now.

"Melissa Hatfield?" she asked the woman.

"That's me." Her eyes narrowed, and her mouth tightened, telling Madison she was curious for an explanation.

"I'm Detective Knight." Madison showed her badge and tucked it away just as quickly. "I have some questions for you about your friend Emily Kane and her stepbrother, Dameon Babcock. Do you have a few minutes to talk?"

"Dameon? That's a name I didn't think I'd ever hear again. Which would have been a good thing." Melissa ushered Madison inside, during which time, Madison quickly checked her phone.

The message was from Terry saying that he had no luck at the law firm and was heading home unless he heard from her. Babcock would be getting cozy for a night in holding unless something Melissa told her swayed her suspicions from him.

"Would you like a tea or coffee?" Melissa looked over her shoulder as she went deeper into the house.

"A coffee would be nice. Milk and sugar." She would put Terry's belief to the test. Accept the offer in the expectation that Melissa would speak freely with her. Though Melissa already seemed geared to talk. Come to think of it, she'd been rather friendly to a cop who showed up out of the blue. Brooke may have tracked her down to let her know a detective came around asking about the past. If so, Melissa would have expected her.

"You got it. The living room is to the right. Get comfortable, and I'll be right back."

"Will do." Madison did just that.

The living room was decorated in shades of white and cream with splashes of red and yellow. Unlike the brightness of Sally's yellow, this hue was soothing. Even elegant. It added to the mature feel of the space, like no one should dare consume food or beverage in there. No sign of a television either, though she suspected a piece of artwork on the wall was one in disguise.

Madison sat in a white chair.

"Here you go." Melissa returned and handed Madison a coffee and had one for herself. She dropped into a round-backed chair with silver studs.

Madison thanked her for the coffee and took a tentative sip. It wasn't bad.

"I must admit I was expecting you to show up at some point. Brooke called and said you had questions for her. I haven't heard from her in a very long time, so it was nice to catch up some too. She never mentioned anything about Dameon though." As she said his name, Melissa's lips curled as if she were going to vomit.

Between this visceral reaction and her initial response to hearing his name, it was a good bet Melissa wasn't a fan of Dameon's. "You obviously don't like the guy."

"That's putting it mildly. The guy was creepy, always hanging around and watching Emily. I'd say he was obsessed with her. Honestly, I'm surprised he wasn't at the party that night."

Madison would tuck that fact away, though she wasn't sure it mattered. She couldn't see Babcock hurting Emily. It was easier to imagine him lashing out at anyone he saw doing her wrong. Still, she said, "I understand that his father and Emily's mother had separated by the time of her murder."

"Oh, they had, but Dameon still latched on to Emily any chance he got."

"Emily had a lot of boyfriends from what I've been told."

Melissa smiled. "Yeah, you could say that."

"How did Dameon react to that?"

"Nothing outward or anything. Emily didn't make a secret of sleeping around, but that didn't stop him from essentially stalking her. Actually, I remember one time that a jock was bragging about having sex with Emily in the locker room. Rumor got around that Dameon beat him up. It got him suspended from school."

Madison stiffened at the character account. Dameon was protective and could be provoked to violence in defense of Emily's honor. While that had been twenty-four-plus years ago, it was obvious that his obsession with Emily hadn't ended. The pictures in his bedroom told them that much.

"Why so many questions about Dameon, if you don't mind me asking?"

Madison weighed whether she should answer. She probably shouldn't, but she said, "I'm just exploring possibilities in light of current investigations."

"Oh. Does this have something to do with Richie's and Dylan's murders? I've seen the news. Her name come up or something?"

Madison nodded.

"Huh. I'm not sure I understand, as her killer was caught. Speaking of, I also read that Troy's being charged for Dylan's and Richie's murders. Ask me, that's nuts. He was always… well, dreamy, if a girl were inclined that way." She smiled at Madison. "But he was a nice guy. It was actually surprising that he even hung out with the likes of Richie and Dylan."

Madison prickled at the mention of Dylan in this context. There had been her passing hunch that he was involved with Emily's rape and murder too. "You didn't like either of them?"

"Not at all. They were both somewhat chauvinistic. Richie more so, but Dylan never discouraged his offhanded comments. Troy and Barry would. I heard what happened to Barry through the news. Did you know him?"

"Quite well."

"I'm sorry for your loss. It doesn't seem to matter how much time passes, the loss of someone you care about cuts deep. I'm still not entirely over what happened to Em. At this point, I don't think I ever will be."

"Well, I am sorry for your loss too." Madison offered the genuine sentiment.

"I appreciate that." She drank her coffee.

Madison took a sip of hers too while considering how to proceed. She'd come here to get something against Dameon Babcock and had inadvertently cleared Troy's name. The visit was already a success. Madison set down her cup again. "Was it a surprise that Richie hurt your friend?"

"Yes, though not really." She teetered her hand. "It's hard to say what was going on in his mind, and there was a lot of booze and weed going around that night."

"What was Dameon like with Richie and his friends?"

"I'm sure he hated them, especially Richie and Dylan because they would pick on him. Even as a senior, he hadn't come into his own yet. He had a rash of acne and, if I remember right, these beady little brown eyes."

He still has those, Madison thought. Could Babcock have been the awkward teen that Brooke had told her about? The one with braces they'd nicknamed Tinman? With Dameon Babcock coming into her purview, Madison had put all thoughts about this kid aside. "Did he wear braces? Have a nickname?"

"Oh, that reminds me." Melissa popped up and walked to a cabinet at the side of the room. "Brooke said you might want to see this." She returned with a yearbook. "It's from graduating year. I even took the liberty of bookmarking one page. She said you talked about Tinman."

"That's right, we did."

"Well, Billy Roth hated Dylan and Richie too, though he especially hated Richie. I don't remember why, or know if I ever knew, but they both picked on him something fierce."

Billy Roth... Something about the name sounded familiar. Madison chewed on that while she opened the book and hunted for his picture on the marked page. When she finally landed on the photo for Billy Roth, she nearly dropped the book.

CHAPTER 47

Madison hadn't been able to get out of Melissa Hatfield's house quick enough. Dameon Babcock was mentally and emotionally challenged, but he seemed innocent of any crimes. It was time to release him. She had a phone to an ear as she half ran to the car. Andrea answered on the second ring.

"I know who is behind the murders," Madison rushed out.

"Hold on. Talk *much* slower."

"Billy Roth."

"Okay, and who is he? Last I knew, you were questioning some Dameon Babcock and trying to see if you could connect him."

"We need to let Babcock go, but forget him for now. Roth works for Tiptop Movers." To think that she had a face-to-face conversation with him not long after Troy was first arrested sent shivers through her. She could have shaken herself, but how could she have known any connection existed between Troy's past and the mover? She should have asked Terry to pull his background, but she didn't have solid grounds. Besides, it's not like it would show where he went to high school.

"Just slow down and explain why you think Billy Roth is the killer. You said he works for the movers, and I'm suspecting that's how you figure he got a hold of Troy's gun."

"It can't be a coincidence. This Billy Roth was teased by Emily and her friends, also by Richie and Dylan. But I guess he especially hated Richie. Emily's friend couldn't remember why."

"So his motive is... getting revenge for childhood bullying? We're talking about twenty-four years ago. How does that manifest in two homicides and a frame job in the past week?"

That was where Madison lost the thread, but she had no doubt she was on the right path. "I don't have all the answers, but I bet that Roth does. We need to pick him up, Andrea, and question him. Troy deserves that much."

Nothing was said on Andrea's end, and Madison's hands were quaking as she put the call on speaker and set it on the dash. She brought up the database for the Department of Motor Vehicles on the onboard computer and searched Billy Roth. In this time, Andrea still hadn't said anything. Madison waited impatiently for the results to come back. "And he has a silver Hyundai Accent. This is our guy, Andrea. I feel it."

A few more beats of excruciating silence. "All right, I'll have Terry question him."

"He's gone home for the day. Let him be. I can handle this."

"No."

"What do you mean no?"

"Just that. You're far too close to handle this one."

"If it wasn't for me, we wouldn't be here." She was fuming at the thought of being cut out now.

"You're right. But we also want to make sure that how we handle this isn't called into question by some hotshot defense attorney down the road. We'll bring Terry back in for the interrogation."

Madison had a feeling more factored into her decision than what she'd said. "At least let me help bring him in."

"That's another thing that I'll make sure is taken care of. You go home, and stay put until I call you. Understood?"

She understood all right. She'd just been benched from the most important case of her life.

"I asked if you understood," Andrea prompted.

"I'll do as you ask." She wasn't in the mood to pacify her future sister-in-law, and she didn't agree with her decision.

"You do realize why you can't get involved? If Roth is the killer and things were to go sideways… Well, Troy would kill me if something were to happen to you. And I'd never forgive myself."

Madison didn't know whether to appreciate the concern or to recoil. "I can stand up for myself, but I'll back down this time," she relented, and Andrea was gone a second later with a promise to make sure Babcock was released.

Madison was left coming to terms with what had just happened. She wanted nothing more than to haul Roth in and start interrogating him. They needed to stitch this up sooner rather than later and get Troy out of jail. He'd already spent far too much time behind bars. The only aspect preying on her was Roth's motive. It was one thing if he didn't like Troy and his friends back in high school, but this was twenty-four years later. Sure, childhood bullying could have had Roth feeling less than. That sort of mental abuse and anguish could have long-lasting effects. But why wait all this time to seek revenge? Though crossing paths with Dameon Babcock taught her the past held power over some people for many years. Still, her gut told her there was a recent trigger. Had seeing Troy during their move served as the catalyst? Is that when he saw the gun and planned to murder Dylan Graham and set Troy up to take the fall?

What his motive was, Madison had no clue. Yet.

CHAPTER 48

Madison's head was spinning as she swapped the department car for her Mazda and headed home. She drove slowly, only reluctantly doing as Andrea had requested. It certainly wasn't easy for her to turn her back on this and hand over Roth's apprehension to someone else.

She pulled into her driveway and sat there for a few minutes, parked behind Troy's Ford Expedition. To think, not long ago their wedding was on the near horizon. Now all that excited expectation belonged to another lifetime. She could dismiss it as that, except for the fact it still stung. They should be on their honeymoon, basking in the sun or frolicking in their room.

She eventually left the car, trying to coach herself to think positively. Troy was going to get out, and they'd get back to their lives. After all their recent hardship, the thought felt more like fantasy. But with Roth in her sights, her confidence was returning. He was the one behind all of this. He had to be.

It did gnaw on her why Roth drew attention to Emily Kane though. He risked everything leading back to him. Was it pride? A taunting to the police? He must have figured he had done a solid job of framing Troy. To an extent, he was right. But things could have been different if the Braybury PD had worked harder from the beginning to root out the anomalies. Regardless, Roth had certainly taken a risk, and it was about to bite him in the ass.

She took her shoes and coat off in the entry, but there was no way she could get comfortable. She was living on the edge and obsessed with checking her phone. But there had been no missed calls. Her ringer was on and turned up.

Madison went to the kitchen and eyed the corked bottle of red on the counter. It was tempting to pour herself a glass, but she needed to keep a clear mind. She settled for a glass of water instead. As she was gulping it back, her blood ran cold, and her next breath locked in her chest.

The sound of a gun clicked behind her.

She reached for the gun in her holster.

"I wouldn't if I were you. I've got a clear shot. There's no way I can miss from here."

Billy Roth. She recognized the voice and put her arms in the air. "I'm just going to turn around." She did so slowly while thinking of a defense. There had to be some way to distract him and disarm him. Facing him, she said,

"What are you doing here?" She was shocked by how calm her voice was, given that her entire body was quaking. At least she had already informed Andrea about Roth. Officers would be out looking for him. If Roth killed her now, they'd know who had done it.

"Don't play all innocent with me," Roth hissed. "I know what you've done."

It would be best if she could keep him speaking, let him latch on to the illusion of control. "Tell me your story. I'm listening if you'd like to share." Playing this song and dance routine was taking all her willpower. But she wasn't left with much choice. He had the current advantage. He'd shoot her before she could draw her gun.

"Ah, you don't care. You only care about your precious Troy. Well, he's going away for life. The evidence is stacked against him."

Her stubborn nature urged her to protest and point out all the holes he hadn't plugged at Graham's murder scene. But antagonizing a madman with a gun wasn't a good idea. "You're right. You were brilliant."

"Don't patronize me." He waved the gun, ushering her to move around the end of the counter toward him.

"What do you want with me?"

"I want you to die, of course. It would be better if I could have Troy take the fall for it, but either way, he'll suffer. His beautiful fiancée shot to death in their new home. Tragic, yet glorious." Roth was smiling, the expression lighting his eyes.

Psycho! "Police are coming for you right now. They'll know it was you."

"Ah, well, they'll be too late. I'm going to kill you, and then I'm leaving town."

"You won't get away with this." Even as the threat fell from her lips, it felt so shallow.

"Guess we'll have to wait and see, won't we? Though you won't be around to find out." A snicker.

Her phone rang, and he flinched. Unfortunately, it wasn't enough to throw off his concentration. He still had a solid hold on the gun, and it was aimed firmly at her.

"I'll just reject the call." She cautiously retrieved her phone from her pocket. The caller ID told her it was Detective Snow. She accepted and flipped it face down on the counter. "There, Roth, I rejected the call," she lied, excusing this fib. "No need to keep holding that gun on me. Let's just talk."

His eyes jabbed to the phone, back up to meet her gaze. "You don't tell me what to do. You poke your nose around, and you expect to walk away unpunished?"

She listened while searching for an opportunity to make a move. The whole while she prayed Snow was catching every word. Then help would be on the way. "Why did you do this, Billy? What did Troy and the others do to you?"

"No, you don't get to question me." His voice cracked, and his arm faltered. The question she'd asked hit a sore spot.

"They were mean to you? Teased you? What Richie did to Emily must have made you mad. You had a big crush on Emily, didn't you?"

His face balled into a mask of contempt. "He deserved to die!" he spat. "He was the devil, but we don't need to think about him anymore. Your boyfriend, or should I say, *fiancé*, took care of that."

"We both know you did. You killed Richie, just like you killed Graham. But why not Troy? You obviously hate him too. Why leave him alive and frame him?"

"Troy was the worst of them all."

The accusation hit her as if it had been a spear thrust right into her heart, but she couldn't allow her personal feelings to intervene.

Roth sniffled and ran his left forearm under his nose, while still holding the gun on her. "I expected so much of him, but he… *he* took Richie's side."

"It was his testimony and that of the others that made you target them."

Roth didn't say a word, but he was heaving for breath like he'd run for a few blocks.

She went on, continuing her hypothetical. "You think the judge had leniency on Richie because of what they said."

"I don't think that. I am sure of it. Now get over here."

"Why? We're just talking." Madison tried not to eye the drawer right in front of her that housed a knife set. She'd have a better chance of drawing her gun and shooting him before he got her. Either way, the odds were not in her favor.

"You're going to come with me. No one will find your body… Yes, that's even better. Troy will never get closure. That will torture him even more." He smiled, as if the last bit was a conversation that he seemed to be having with himself. "Then I'll already be out of town, long in the clear." He reached out to grab her sweater, but she shrugged free of his grip on instinct.

"Shoot me if you want, but I'm not going anywhere with you."

"Huh." He grabbed her arm and pressed the gun muzzle to her cheek.

Regardless, she stomped the inside of his foot at the same time as she pivoted. She reached for his hand that held the gun.

Roth roared as he struggled against her. The two of them were in a tug-of-war for control of the gun. It was a dangerous match with potentially deadly consequences, but she saw it as her only chance of turning the status quo around.

They shimmied, and the gun went off. The round hit the ceiling, and plaster rained over them.

Another bullet fired. This time it struck a built-in sideboard.

Madison relinquished her hold on Roth, drew back, and punched him in the nose. Blood flew, and bile lurched up her throat, but the move had Roth relinquishing the hold on his gun and cradling his face.

She had his gun in hand and was getting ready to cuff him when he surprised her and thrust the back of his head into her forehead. An instant headache and flashes of white filled her vision. The gun fell from her hand.

"You will die now." He swept her legs out from beneath her with a swift kick before she had a chance to react.

The wind left her lungs as her tailbone smacked the floor. He was coming at her, like a man gone mad, nostrils flaring, saliva bubbling in the corners of his mouth. His gun was feet away, and he snatched it as he quickly closed the distance to her.

But she wasn't without a defense. She pulled her gun from her holster and squeezed off two shots. Both rounds struck the shoulder of his shooting arm.

Roth wailed and staggered back. His gun clattered to the floor.

Just then, the front door burst open and police officers with the Stiles PD stormed inside, announcing themselves.

"Madison?" Terry called out ahead of them.

She stood over Roth, her gun back in its holster, holding his gun on him to make sure he didn't get any other *bright* ideas. He was bleeding on her floor, and she wanted to turn away. She might work in Major Crimes, but blood really wasn't her thing. "In the kitchen."

Terry rushed into the room. "Are you okay?"

"Better than him. Just a jumbo headache and some touch-ups to take care of," she added in consideration of the wounded ceiling and sideboard. She handed off Roth's gun to Terry.

Roth was panting and bleeding. And laughing. Even with a handful of police around him, he still thought he had the upper hand. One *could* admire the spunk, but she detested the sight of him.

"Get him out of here before I do something I'll regret," she told Terry, and he nodded.

She watched Roth being taken away, grateful she was going to live another day to tell the tale. But she was also pissed. Not only had that man set Troy up for murder, but he'd shot her grandmother's house. Both were unforgiveable.

CHAPTER 49

Madison woke up the next morning facing Troy. Not a surprise, as she'd spent most of the night watching him sleep, afraid that if she closed her eyes, he'd somehow disappear. But he should be safe. The man behind all the heartache would be spending the rest of his life behind bars. The gunshot wounds to Roth's shoulder would only buy him a temporary reprieve. He was going to survive. Roth was handed over to Detective Snow, who thankfully had heard everything over the phone call. He'd then called it in to the Stiles PD.

The doorbell rang, and she hurried from bed, wanting to attend to whoever it was before they woke Troy. She grabbed a robe, put it on over her pajamas, and headed downstairs.

She got to the door and found Detective Snow on the front step. "Detective," she said, moving back to let him inside.

"What are you doing here? Am I having a nightmare?" Troy was on the staircase. His blond hair was tousled and his green eyes especially piercing. Madison wished to send the detective on his way and take her man upstairs.

"No nightmare, and I assure you, I come in peace." Snow smiled at them.

"Small mercies." Troy walked down the rest of the stairs and joined them in the entry.

"I'm getting the feeling that I woke you two up. Sorry if that's the case."

"Just tell us you're here with good news," Madison told him.

"I am."

"In that case, coffee?" she offered, but she was thinking more of Troy and herself than Snow.

"Sounds good."

She smiled at Troy and put a hand on his shoulder as she walked past him to the kitchen. There was no need to ask him if he wanted coffee. She looked over her shoulder and saw Troy was taking the detective to the living room.

As she made the coffee, she didn't hear them talking, but when she entered the room with a tray, three mugs of coffee, milk and sugar, and a few spoons, the air was relaxed. She didn't know what had changed Snow's take on Troy's culpability, but she was full of gratitude for the shift. As she'd briefly thought before, she might have rushed to judge the detective. Though she could hardly be blamed for taking an instant dislike to the man who arrested her fiancé in the middle of their wedding ceremony.

"Thanks." Snow raised his mug after fixing up his coffee and took a sip.

Madison had joined Troy on the couch, while Snow was in one of their chairs. They were both watching him. The clock was ticking away as they waited for him to share what he'd come to say.

"All right." Snow set his cup on the table and sat back. "I'm here because I feel for all you've been put through. I hope one day you can forgive me for stubbornly seeing things one way. You could say I was under some pressure to do so, though I take responsibility for my actions. Or inactions."

Madison gathered the *pressure* had come from his superiors. If she was right, she could relate to having a bossy and domineering superior herself. Though she'd never cave to pleasing her sergeant if her feelings ran in strong opposition to his.

"You question Roth?" Troy asked, not seeming to release any hard feelings easily. Madison couldn't blame him there, and just because Snow had redeemed himself, she wasn't eager to hand over forgiveness either. Though, if it hadn't been for Snow, she might be dead herself. Her perspective on the Braybury detective was certainly in flux.

"You bet, and forensics back up everything. Billy Roth will be going away for a long time. His prints were on the journal, articles found in Graham's desk drawer, and the silver cross found in Klein's motel room. That places him there. So too does tracking on his phone. It also puts him in Graham's neighborhood at the time of his death. Now, a lady from your lab, Cynthia Baxter, spoke to one of our lab techs and suggested a technique that can date fingerprints. Advanced technology does even better than that and allows layered prints to be pulled apart and analyzed individually."

"Science has come a long way." Madison was beaming from the mention of her best friend.

"That it has. Our lab was able to confirm Troy's prints were on the gun, as you know, but none were more recent than six months ago. Some of these were smudged, suggesting that another person handled it afterward. Presumably this was with gloves though, as no foreign prints were present."

"Did he say how he got my gun?" Troy took a drink of his coffee and cradled his mug in both hands.

"He took it during your move. He found the key for the box in a nightstand. I guess it was missed from being packed, and he admitted to helping himself to the gun box."

"This isn't on you." Troy took one of her hands and squeezed it.

He knew her too well to assume she'd take on that guilt. It was her nightstand under discussion, as he kept his key for the box on his keychain. "How long was he planning this, then? And why?"

"It was somewhat opportunistic. He saw Troy's name on the work order, and the past rushed back. But there is more to it." Snow took a deep breath. "Richie Klein raped a girl in ninth grade. Did you hear of that back then or remember this?" Snow leveled his gaze at Troy.

"I remember the rumor of it," he said, taking his hand back from Madison's.

"Well, apparently it was more than a rumor, and that girl was Roth's half sister. She was never the same. She got hooked on drugs, never graduated, and six months ago, her lifestyle caught up with her. She was found dead of an overdose."

"Because she never recovered from the rape in high school," Madison said.

"Doesn't seem so."

"That piece of shit." Troy's green eyes took on a dark intensity.

"Roth also told me that he saw Richie Klein rape and murder Emily Kane."

It made sense that Roth had made it to the beach party that night. After all, he was prone to following Emily around. But it didn't sound like Dylan was involved as Madison had briefly suspected. Otherwise, Snow would have said Roth saw him as well.

"But why not come forward or do anything long before now?" Troy asked.

"He was probably afraid for himself. He was bullied by Richie." She hadn't added this to make Troy feel worse, but his frown told her it had. "Which isn't on you," she said, showing him the support he had to her a moment ago.

"You're right, Detective Knight. Roth said he was afraid to act, but he also didn't want to come forward afterward because he was worried that it would upset his half sister. He didn't want to make her relive her nightmare."

"Though it seemed she was anyhow," Madison said, feeling for the young woman.

"And he let her go without justice," Troy said.

"A fact he has been especially haunted by for the last twenty-four years," Madison countered. Between his half sister's drug addiction and recent overdose, seeing Troy's name, and Richie's release from prison, there was the trigger she'd been searching for.

"Seems so," Snow agreed.

"All right, I see his issue with Richie, but why Dylan? Why frame me?"

"This might be hard for you to hear, Troy, but your friend Dylan wasn't of the straight and narrow either."

Troy stiffened. "What do you mean?"

"Guess he showed up not long after Klein had killed her and started scheming up a defense for him. He said he'd vouch for Klein, and he'd get you and Barry to do so too if it came to that. No irony lost on the fact the guy became a defense attorney."

And there it was. Dylan may not have been involved in the actual rape and murder, but he was responsible by proxy. "So Roth assumed that Troy was just as bad as Richie and Dylan."

Snow nodded. "Uh-huh. An opinion that wasn't helped when the three of you testified to Richie's character."

"Roth saw us as sharing Richie's guilt," Troy said slowly.

"He did. That's why he tried to point us to you for Emily's and Graham's murders and then Klein's. Which, by the way, he confessed to following you to the Sandman Motel and taking advantage of the situation there. He'd overheard your fight with Klein."

Troy sank against the back of the couch.

"Why even bring Emily into this at all?" Madison set her cup on the table next to her, not having taken a sip yet.

"Well, he couldn't have mentioned his sister, or his identity would have been too obvious. By bringing up Emily Kane, it gave him a way to frame Troy. He concocted a plausible motive and ran with it. In hindsight, it wasn't that well thought-out, but it was hatched by a desperate mind. He decided to frame Troy because he wanted to destroy his life and expose him for his *true* character, as he put it. Roth said he was most disappointed when Troy had stood up for

Richie. Guess you were nice to him on occasion, acknowledged his existence anyway."

Troy nodded and ran a hand through his hair. "What did he say about the suicide note at Dylan's crime scene? Why have that if he was trying to frame me?"

"Ah, I asked about that too."

Madison's respect for the Braybury detective was increasing with every passing minute.

"That was more to torture Graham. The note had said, 'I'm sorry for past sins but take these with me now. To the grave.' Roth dictated these words, so in a roundabout way, Graham would be confessing his contribution to what happened to Emily. Hence, the signs of distress that showed in his handwriting."

"Well, Dylan sounds like he was a horrible kid," Madison said, realizing it was a judgment but based on what she was hearing, it was well-founded. "One has to wonder what type of power Richie held over him."

Troy shook his head. "Richie put himself out there as the cool kid, and Dylan was a follower. If I had any idea that they..."

Madison took Troy's hand. "You didn't, and you were just a kid."

He peered into her eyes, and she wished she could suck the hurt and guilt from him.

"Well, that's about it for now." Snow stood to leave.

"Actually, I have one more question," Madison rushed out.

"Sure."

"You said that you contacted someone at the Stiles PD to notify them that you were coming to arrest Troy. Who was that?"

"I've already had this conversation with your police chief, so I feel comfortable telling you." His gaze dipped to Troy, back to Madison. "It was Sergeant Winston."

Madison dipped her head. It was all she could do. She had expected that answer, but hearing it was still shocking. Winston was someone she'd reported to for years. He was supposed to be one of the good guys. His remaining quiet was a professional and personal slight.

"Thanks, Detective," Troy said when Madison didn't respond, and he got up to show the man out.

She was frozen in place. How could she return to work and report to that man?

"Madison?" Troy's voice struck her from a great distance away, but she looked at him. "Andrea will take care of Winston. You can trust me on that."

She licked her lips. "I hope so. He deserves to be—" She snapped her mouth shut, too angry to speak.

Troy gently brushed her cheek with his fingertips. "Let's forget about Winston for now. I have an important question for you." He got down on his knees in front of her and took both of her hands in his. "When are you going to do me the honor of becoming my wife?"

CHAPTER 50

It took five minutes after Detective Snow left their house the day before for Madison and Troy to decide they would be getting married the next day. They still had the remainder of this week and next booked off from work. It was best they take advantage of that time. That and they couldn't wait to make their relationship legal. Since the whole big white wedding had gone horribly wrong, they opted for another approach and booked the first available slot at the courthouse. That turned out to be Thursday at five o'clock.

Troy had rebooked their honeymoon in Cancun, and their flight was set to leave at ten PM. It was cutting things a bit close, and they were putting a lot of faith in everything going according to plan. Considering the last several days, they were brave. But married or not, they were getting on that plane.

Madison was doing things her way this time. She was in a cream pantsuit, not the puffy concoction her mother and sister had guilt-tripped her into before. Besides, she had worn it and they had seen her in it. That would have to do.

They were in the hallway waiting to be called into the judge's chambers. Those closest to Madison and Troy were gathered. Her parents, sister, brother-in-law, nieces, Terry and his family, Cynthia and Lou, Troy's sister and brother-in-law, and a few from Troy's SWAT team were there, including his groomsmen, Marc and Nick.

Andrea touched Madison's arm and ushered her to the side. She then swept her into a big hug. "I'm so glad you're okay." She kissed each of Madison's cheeks in turn. "I also wanted to give you an early wedding gift."

Andrea wasn't holding anything, but Madison said, "That's not necessary." In fact, when they sent out the initial wedding invitations, she and Troy had included a note that gifts were not expected or necessary.

"This one you'll want. Trust me." Andrea's jovial bouncy energy left, to be replaced by a somber one. "I had a talk with Sergeant Winston, and he has agreed to take an early retirement package."

Madison's heart kicked up speed. "He… That easily? He just caved?" She had her suspicions the sergeant might be involved in shady business. The fact he took retirement so rapidly flagged for her, but at least he wouldn't be her problem anymore. No more talking through her every move and being scrutinized for them because she was a woman.

"I think he's wanted out for a long time, but I can't have people who I don't trust on my team."

"Does that mean that…" She looked over Andrea's shoulder to where Terry was standing with his wife and daughter.

Andrea glanced back, then at Madison. She shook her head. "Terry's an amazing detective, and he will make an excellent sergeant one day."

"One day." Madison grasped on to that. "I assume you've spoken with him?"

"I have. He helped you off the record, which *off* the record, I appreciate. But as someone who is going to be leading a division, that can't happen."

"So what you're saying is…?"

"Terry will remain at the rank of detective for the time being."

Madison wasn't sure how to feel, but she was conflicted. She was selfishly happy not to be losing her partner but sad for him. If he hadn't helped her track down Klein and Emily Kane's former friends, this conversation wouldn't even be taking place.

"He understands," Andrea added.

Madison nodded, but her heart was saddened regardless. "If Winston's gone, and Terry's not taking over, then who am I reporting to in the new year?"

"I have someone in mind."

"Please, I'm not in the guessing mood."

"Carson Snow."

"Snow? The detective who arrested your brother?"

"And who worked to clear him."

"Eventually."

"He showed himself as human, Madison. We've had a conversation too. He's not happy at Braybury PD and was considering an early retirement. But he loves the job. He just didn't like the people he was surrounded by."

"Okay, but he's detective rank. How does he go from that to being a sergeant?"

"Like Terry, he's already passed the sergeant exam. For him, it was several months ago. He'd expected to take over his department, but a young guy came in. For all intents and purposes, Snow is qualified to take over for Winston." Andrea raised her eyebrows as if to inquire what Madison thought of that.

"He came through when it mattered, though it would have been better if he'd put the work in up front before crashing our wedding."

"All down to a domineering sergeant and police chief. You don't need me to tell you what that's like."

"My police chief is great." Madison smiled at Andrea, but her expression faded quickly. "But I never let Winston manipulate me."

"No one ever could, but we're not all built like you, girl." With that, Andrea squeezed Madison's shoulder and kissed her cheek.

"The Matthews and Knight wedding." This from a clerk, who had stepped into the hall.

"Here goes," Madison said, mostly under her breath and to herself.

Troy was next to the door, and their guests filtered in ahead of them. He was holding out his hand to her. "Are you ready?"

"You bet."

They went inside, where they said their vows in front of family and loved ones. Madison wasn't sure how she kept herself together and didn't bawl like an embarrassing baby.

"You may now kiss your bride," the wedding officiant said at the end.

Troy pulled her in and kissed her hard, and she relished every second to the hoots and hollers of their loved ones. When she and Troy parted, their audience clapped.

"What do you know? They did it, and no one got arrested." This came from Lou, Cynthia's husband.

Cynthia playfully batted his arm. "Too soon—Ouch. Oooh. *Ouch!* Not false labor again."

Madison's mother swooped to Cynthia's side and put a reassuring arm around her. "Honey, this is the real deal." She pointed to the floor and said to everyone, "Her water broke."

CHAPTER 51

God must be rolling around in stitches up there, Madison thought as she paced the hospital waiting room. It was almost eight thirty. Still no word on Cynthia and the baby. She and Troy each had a wheeled suitcase and a carry-on bag with them. Their flight would leave at ten, and she preferred arriving early to running through an airport. But there was no way she'd leave until the baby arrived and Madison knew all was well. "We'll need to cancel again," she said to Troy, walking up to him.

"It will sort itself out."

She narrowed her eyes. "You're still saying that?"

"Hey, I'm a free man. It did get sorted."

"Touché. But where did you get that phrase? Your sister says it too." Madison hadn't even noticed it before this past week.

"Mom said it all the time."

She took his hand. "You haven't told me much about your parents."

"Something I'll fix, but we have the rest of our lives to talk about them."

"No sense putting it off—" She stopped talking when she saw Cynthia's sister run into the emergency room. Lou must have called her. It had been a long time since Madison had seen her. She went to Madison.

"Where is she? Is the baby here yet?"

"Not yet," Madison said, and Terry signaled her to come over to him. Everyone who was present for the wedding was here to see how this story ended.

"Yeah?" she said to Terry.

"I assume that Andrea told you about…?"

"She did. I'm sorry that you're not taking Winston's spot."

"No you're not." Terry smiled.

"Truth? I'm sorry for you, but not for me. I mean, you helped a lot this time around, but I can solve murders without you."

"I'm not sure what to take the most offense to. That I helped *this time around* or you're fine on your own."

She narrowed her eyes, sensing he really wasn't wounded either way. "You know what I meant, and besides, solving murder is more fun with you, even if we bicker and disagree almost constantly."

"Yes, and I just love how you pick on what I say sometimes."

"You bring that on yourself," she teased and laughed.

"Well, either way, I guess you're stuck with me for a bit longer."

"Not stuck. *Blessed*, buddy." Madison tapped a kiss on Terry's cheek. "You're the brother I never had."

Terry squirmed but grinned. "All right, let's not get too carried away."

Lou came through swinging doors, a doctor beside him. Lou was beaming as everyone clustered around him like metal shavings to a magnet.

"It's a boy!" Lou announced proudly.

"That was fast," Madison's mother said.

"Precipitous labor," the doctor said. "But mom and baby are doing well. Baby's eight pounds, two ounces."

"Oh, nice size," Madison's mother said, clamping a hand on her shoulder. Madison hoped that her mother wasn't getting any ideas. She had no idea that Madison had been pregnant with Troy's baby back in March and had lost it. That was for the best.

"So who's going to meet my son first?" Lou was looking around but met Madison's gaze pretty much right away. "Can we take three in at a time?" he asked the doctor, likely thinking about Cynthia's sister too.

"It's best to limit it to two," the doctor told him.

Lou turned to his sister-in-law and explained the situation. "Madison needs to catch a plane for her honeymoon in a few hours."

Less than a few... But Madison wasn't going to correct him.

"Honeymoon? Sure, go ahead, and congratulations," Cynthia's sister told Madison.

"Thanks." Madison didn't waste any time taking Troy's hand in hers and following the proud new father down the hall.

Cynthia was pale but smiling. She was holding her baby against her chest. Tears fell down her face when she saw Madison.

Madison moved in and was overcome with happiness. Tears beaded in her eyes. "Congratulations, Momma."

"Thank you."

"Oh, let me see the little guy." Madison worked to carefully tuck the blanket he was swaddled in from his face. He was awake, and his baby blues were wide and curious. "He's beautiful," she said.

"He looks just like Lou. He's got his nose. See?" Cynthia gently tapped the baby's nose.

Troy came up to Madison's back and rested a hand on her hip. "So what are we to call him?"

"Michael Glen, after our dads," Lou said.

"I love it," Madison said.

"Did you want to hold him?" Cynthia asked, and Madison found herself hesitating. He looked so tiny and fragile. What if she broke him?

"You can't break him, if that's what you're thinking," Lou said, as if reading her mind, "well, unless you drop him. Just don't do that, but I'm sure you'll be fine. Want my help getting a hold of him?"

"Sure."

He set his son in Madison's arms, and she was overcome. "Michael Glen, you are a handsome man and are going to be a heartbreaker."

"Don't go putting that in his little head," Cynthia said. "He's going to be a prince among men." She was grinning.

Madison smiled as tears splashed her cheeks. She put her fingers into his little palm, and he wrapped his hand around them. "I'm your aunt Madison."

For a few moments she sank into a bubble that was just her and little Michael.

Troy gently touched her shoulder. "We should go."

Madison swiped her cheeks. "I'm so happy for you both."

"Thank you."

"I don't want to leave them," she turned to Troy, but looking at him, she couldn't stay either. It was time to celebrate their marriage.

Madison handed Michael back to Lou and hugged Cynthia and then Lou. Troy followed up after her.

"Now get out of here, you two, or you're going to miss your flight," Cynthia jested, like she wanted them gone.

Madison gave the new family one final look before leaving the room to embark on her own adventure.

***

Was your heart racing when Madison faced off with the killer? If so, you'll be addicted to *Her Buried Past*, the next tense crime thriller in the series! Madison is called to investigate the murder of a therapist with a dark, secretive past. To get to the bottom of this mystery, she must navigate a web of lies and danger. But will she make it out alive?

Never miss the next Detective Madison Knight Mystery!

Sign up at the weblink listed below to be notified when new Madison Knight titles are available for pre-order:

CarolynArnold.net/MKUpdates

By joining this newsletter, you will also receive exclusive first looks at the following:

Updates pertaining to upcoming releases in the series, such as cover reveals, book descriptions, and firm release dates

Sneak peeks of teasers and special content

Behind-the-Tape™ insights that give you an inside look at Carolyn's research and creative process

There is no getting around it: reviews are important and so is word of mouth.

With all the books on the market today, readers need to know what's worth their time and what's not. This is where you come into play.

If you enjoyed *Murder at the Lake*, please help others find it by posting a brief, honest review on the retailer site where you purchased this book and recommend it to family and friends.

Also, Carolyn loves to hear from her readers, and you can reach her at Carolyn@CarolynArnold.net.

Upon receipt of your e-mail, you will be added to her newsletter mailing unless you express your desire otherwise.

Addictive reads. Twisty Plots.
Unforgettable characters.

Carolyn Arnold is a bestselling author of gripping crime fiction and psychological thrillers known for being fast-paced with chilling twists, and relentless suspense. Her novels often explore the darker corners of human nature, where secrets simmer beneath the surface and danger is never far away. Drawing inspiration from real-life crimes, investigative psychology, and her fascination with what drives people to cross the line, Carolyn crafts stories that keep readers turning pages late into the night.

Carolyn lives near London, Ontario, Canada with her husband and two beagles. When she isn't plotting her next (fictional) murder or unraveling a complex mystery, Carolyn enjoys reading, traveling, and spending time with friends and family. She loves connecting with readers who share her passion for heart-pounding thrillers and stories that linger long after the final page.

CONNECT ONLINE

CarolynArnold.net
Facebook.com/AuthorCarolynArnold
Instagram.com/AuthorCarolynArnold

And don't forget to sign up for her newsletter for up-to-date information on release and special offers at CarolynArnold.net/Newsletters.

www.ingramcontent.com/pod-product-compliance
Lightning Source LLC
Chambersburg PA
CBHW030333040826
49266CB00030B/216

9781998095018